#taken

#taken

TONY PARSONS

CENTURY

3 5 7 9 10 8 6 4 2

Century

20 Vauxhall Bridge Road

London SW1V 2SA

Century is part of the Penguin Random House group of companies whose
addresses can be found at global.penguinrandomhouse.com.

Penguin
Random House
UK

First published by Century in 2019

www.penguin.co.uk

A CIP catalogue record for this book is available from the British Library.

ISBN 9781780895963 (hardback)
ISBN 9781780895970 (trade paperback)

Typeset in 14/17.75 pts Fournier MT
by Integra Software Services Pvt. Ltd, Pondicherry

Printed and bound in Great Britain by Clays Ltd, Elcograf S.p.A.

Penguin Random House is committed to a sustainable future for
our business, our readers and our planet. This book is made
from Forest Stewardship Council® certified paper.

MIX
Paper from
responsible sources
FSC® C018179

For Nick Logan

PROLOGUE

As Personal as Hell

It was nothing personal.

She knew that the two men in the car behind her, driving far too close and grinning foolishly beyond the tinted windscreen, could have chosen any woman to bully.

She had been driving out of the West End, crossing the Marylebone Road and starting to pick up speed on Albany Street, the long stretch of straight road that skirts Regent's Park, and their big black four-by-four was suddenly there, filling her rear-view mirror, its diesel engine roaring and so close it was as if they wanted to drive straight through her.

And although it was nothing personal, their behaviour did not feel completely random. They wanted to teach her a lesson.

They wanted to show her. They wanted to show her good.

It was nothing personal, but there was a reason why they were driving that close. She had done something to push their touchy little buttons.

It could have been the car she was driving – the latest 7-series BMW, so new it still had that glorious showroom smell and sheen. And that would have been almost funny because it was not even her car – her battered little Fiat was in the garage, unable to squeeze past its MOT – but of course they did not know that.

And perhaps it wasn't the car. Perhaps she had pulled away too fast at the lights, anxious to be home, the hour late now, their insecure manhoods shrinking as she left them dawdling in exhaust fumes.

Or perhaps they had been offended by the jokey sign in her rear window, black words on a yellow background. *Baby, I'm Bored*, it said, a single girl's play on those *Baby on Board* signs you saw everywhere.

Not my sign, she thought. And not my life.

Or perhaps it was nothing to do with the brand-new car or the *Baby, I'm Bored* sign or the way she was driving. Perhaps they were just a pair of macho assholes. That was always a possibility.

As she skirted Regent's Park, all the beautiful Nash buildings to her right, like castles made of ice cream glowing in the night-time, and the park itself a sea of unbroken blackness to her left, the two vehicles were suddenly alone on that lonely stretch of road.

All that darkness to the left, all that moneyed elegance to the right.

And the car behind so close that if she braked it felt like they would crash into her.

And now she was scared.

Her foot gently brushed the brakes. Barely enough to slow her borrowed vehicle but enough to make its brake lights blaze red.

The driver behind slammed on his own brakes, rubber shrieking, and his face tightened with fury as their vehicle receded.

She put her foot down. She really needed to be home. She ached for home now.

She was watching them in the rear-view mirror, watching their car get smaller, watching them far too closely, because she almost missed the sharp left turn in the road, she almost kept going, which would have been very bad indeed, but at the last moment she looked forward and cursed and tugged down hard on the left side of the steering wheel.

She took a breath, held it, speeding past London Zoo, accelerating for the junction where she would turn right into St John's Wood and the road for home. She exhaled with relief, seeing the light was green.

'Imagine life is a highway and all the lights are green,' her father had once told her, and she smiled at the thought of him.

She turned right on her green light.

And they followed.

'Oh, what's your problem?' she muttered, already knowing the answer.

She was their problem.

St John's Wood now, the huge houses behind iron gates, and the streets empty.

And the black car filling her rear-view mirror.

The car edged closer, so close it must surely touch, so close she had stopped breathing.

And then suddenly they came to the big junction at Swiss Cottage and it was over.

They roared past her, and she glimpsed their faces as they tore away, not even looking at her, their simple minds bored with their vicious little game.

She exhaled. And she glanced over her shoulder to look at her six-month-old boy in the rearward-facing baby seat, feeling overwhelmed with relief and love.

'It's OK,' she said, though she knew he was sleeping.

Cars were the one guarantee of getting him to nod off.

And then there were the big roads that led to the small roads home.

The Finchley Road was clogged with traffic even at this time of night, but still no sign of the black car, and she turned right at the old church, up Frognal Lane, climbing all the while, heading for the rooftop of the city.

Now the big houses of Hampstead were on either side, and she was still climbing. She slowly turned on to a tree-lined back road that looked as though it were in the heart of the country.

There was a private security guard in his van across the street. He glanced up at her without expression as she turned on to the private road that led to her home.

And the way home was blocked by the big black car.

They were waiting for her.

She slowed and stopped, reaching for her phone, because this was so wrong, and it was against the law, and then it all happened very quickly.

The two men were out of the car, their faces covered with some kind of mask, those masks that look like skulls, designed to halt the heart with a stab of fear, and they were walking quickly towards her car.

As if it was all planned. All of it.

She fumbled with the central locking but her doors opened on both sides, and someone's hands were on her, gripping her by the arms just above the elbow, and the one who was on the passenger side walked round, his skull mask grinning in her headlights, to help drag her from the car.

She was screaming for help.

They lifted her from the ground as if she weighed nothing, the one holding her arms not changing his grip and the other one lifting her by the ankles. They carried her towards their car and she screamed and screamed and screamed.

And then the security guard was standing there.

One of the men said one word.

'Don't,' he said.

And the security guard didn't. He stood there, a boy in the presence of two men – unmanned, paralysed, just watching as they loaded her into their car.

And now she felt the violence in them. Not spite, or sadism, or wounded, woman-hating pride. But violence. Violence in the hands of deeply experienced professionals who did this sort of thing for a living.

She saw her baby son, and she called his name, and the child was still sleeping on the back seat, wet-lipped and head lolling under the *Baby, I'm Bored* sign, and she let out a howl like a wounded animal because she knew with total blinding clarity that she would never see him again in this life.

And that was when she understood.

This was personal.

This was as personal as hell.

1

It was the hour before dawn when I ducked under the *Do Not Cross* tape we had put up at the entrance to the private estate, early summer but bitterly cold, and I stood there for a moment, still waking up, watching the search team moving up the hill on their hands and knees like some slow and silent multi-backed beast.

Flanked by silver birches, the small road rose sharply and briefly to its summit, where a brand-new car was now a crime scene. A cluster of blazing spotlights lit it up, brighter than daylight. All the doors were thrown open and the white-suited CSIs moved through it and around it with their tweezers, cameras and plastic evidence bags, faces anonymous behind their blue nitrile masks. Above the trees, the night pulsed with the blue lights of our response vehicles.

Two women came out of the darkness, looking like a librarian and a supermodel, and on the frosty night air there was the vaguely metallic scent of vodka. Because the call comes in and you go, I thought. That's the job.

They don't ask you if you have been drinking. They don't ask you if you have taken a sleeping pill. They don't ask you if you have adequate childcare. They call in the middle of the night and tell you a woman has been taken from her car. And so you go.

The women were my boss DCI Pat Whitestone – slightly built, her eyes squinting sleepily behind John Lennon glasses, her fair hair streaked with grey at just forty – and TDC Joy Adams – young, black, extravagantly tall, her hair in tight cornrows. Joy was only a year out of Hendon police school and, I guessed, still up for a few shots of vodka on a work night.

'You see her picture?' Whitestone asked me. 'The woman they took? She's beautiful.'

I had looked at the photograph that had been sent to my phone when I got the call. It had been pulled from the driving licence of Jessica Lyle, twenty-two years old. Long, dark hair framed a pale face. Her expression was photo-booth serious but her eyes were smiling, almost blazing with life. And even in the sterile mugshot that was the only photo ID we had so far, I could see that Whitestone was right.

Jessica Lyle, the woman they had taken, was beautiful.

'Her parents have arrived,' DCI Whitestone told me. 'They're taking their grandson home with them as soon as the doctor has signed off on the kid. Have a word before they leave, Max.'

I nodded. An unwanted suitor was the most likely reason for this kind of abduction. Having a word with the next of kin of a kidnapped woman meant finding out if the parents were aware of any bitter ex-partners or lovesick stalkers hanging around their daughter who wouldn't take no for an answer and who could not tell the difference between loving someone and hurting them.

And the other reason for this kind of abduction was that it was like being struck by lightning, totally random, the worst bad luck in the world.

Whitestone shivered. It was June, but you would never guess it in this dead zone between night and day.

'The father was one of us,' Whitestone told me. 'Frank Lyle.'

'A cop?' I said. 'Still serving?'

'Retired after thirty years in the Met,' she said, her pale eyes weary behind her spectacles. 'That never makes this stuff any easier.'

Thirty years, I thought. How many enemies do you make in thirty years?

Across the street a private security guard was standing by his van, sucking hungrily on a cigarette. His military-style uniform was several sizes too big for him.

'What about Clint Eastwood?' I said.

'He claims he didn't see a thing,' Adams said. 'Missed it in his toilet break.'

'That's not good.'

'I haven't finished with him yet.'

Whitestone and I stood in silence, watching Joy approaching the security guard as she pulled out her notebook; not exactly the silence of old friends, but the silence of two professionals who had worked together for years.

Whitestone took off her glasses to clean them on her sleeve, giving her face a vulnerable, owlish look. You would never have guessed it from her bookish appearance, but Pat Whitestone was the most experienced detective in West End Central's Homicide and Serious Crime Command. She put her glasses back on, nodded briefly, and we started up the tree-lined road towards the car. It felt like it could be in the middle of the countryside. There was a sign by the side of the road:

EDEN HILL PARK
Private Estate
No thoroughfare
No dogs

Whitestone was carrying a small stack of transparent stepping plates so she could build an uncontaminated path to and from the crime scene. When we reached the top of the hill, she had me hold the stepping plates while she pulled blue plastic baggies over her shoes. The car was so new that it still had the showroom smell of new leather, polished chrome and fresh paint. It smelled like money. *Baby, I'm Bored* said a sign in the rear window. One of the CSIs was photographing the empty baby seat on the back seat.

Whitestone took the stepping plates from me and pressed her glasses to the bridge of her nose.

'And talk to Jessica's flatmate,' she said. 'Snezia Jones. This is her car.'

The road levelled out and as I walked towards the pulsing blue lights surrounded by silence I could sense that this was one of the highest points in London. The air was almost alpine-sweet up here. I inhaled deeply as the road opened up on to Eden Hill Park estate. It felt like a secret that had been hidden from the city. You would never guess it from the modest entrance, but the estate was large, consisting of a block of luxury apartments and a variety of houses that ranged from huge modern buildings with two-storey glass walls to a line of tiny ancient cottages that had somehow survived the wrecking ball of the property developers. All over Eden Hill Park the lights were on as the residents stared out at the convoy of police vehicles parked outside their homes. I took the lift to the top floor of the apartment block. Doors were open all along the corridor. The news had spread fast. There was a uniformed officer standing outside the apartment I was looking for. The doctor was leaving.

'The kid all right, doc?' I asked him.

'The baby is about the only one who is doing well. The parents are in a state of shock. So is the young lady. Miss Jones. The flatmate. Keep it as short as you can.'

Inside the apartment, two women were embracing on the sofa and a man was holding a sleeping baby. Jessica Lyle's parents and her flatmate. They all turned to look at me as I walked in.

Frank Lyle was a tough old ex-cop with cropped steel-grey hair, assessing me with cool, unimpressed eyes as he gently rocked his sleeping grandson.

Mrs Lyle was still stunning in her fifties, the image of her daughter three decades from now. If she survives, I thought, then pushed the thought away.

The flatmate, Snezia Jones, was perhaps thirty, tall and thin and almost albino-pale, her hair so blonde it was just this side of white.

Both the women had been crying. I told them my name and showed them my warrant card.

'I just have a few questions about Jessica,' I said.

But the parents had questions for me.

'Why would anyone take Jess?' Mrs Lyle said. 'Are they hurting her? What are they doing to her?'

'Stop it, Jen,' Mr Lyle quietly told his wife. 'Please stop.' He smiled gently at her then turned to me, lifting his chin, the smile fading away. 'Anything you find show up in IDENT1?'

IDENT1 is the police database containing the finger-prints of ten million people who have ever had contact with the law.

'We haven't got that far yet, sir. I just wanted to ask you—'

'But do you have any prints?' he said, flaring with impatience, and he rocked his grandson a bit harder as he turned his face away and coughed – the hawking cough of a lifelong smoker. The baby whimpered in his sleep. 'Fingers, shoes, tyres? Come on. There must be tyre prints, at least. I can't believe you're so incompetent that you can't even find tyre prints!'

I took a breath. Whitestone was right. Dealing with old cops never made our job easier.

'Our forensic people are still working on that,' I said. 'As you know, Mr Lyle, any tyre marks will have to be cross-checked against the cars of the residents. We assume the assailants were wearing gloves. Our search team has been out there all night and if they dumped gloves, we'll find them. We're going to find your daughter, sir.'

His mouth twisted with hard-earned wisdom. He knew as well as I did that every minute that passed without us finding his daughter, the less chance there was that we would find her alive.

13

'Spare me the slick PR spin, son. Just do your fucking job.'

'Frank,' his wife said.

'Has your daughter been threatened by anyone?' I said, looking from the mother to the father and back again. If Jessica Lyle confided in either of them, it would more likely be her mother. 'Any ex-boyfriend, or someone stalking her, or—'

'Everyone loves Jess,' the flatmate said.

Snezia Jones had an East European accent. Mrs Lyle squeezed her hand.

'Has she been dating—'

'Jess doesn't date,' Mr Lyle said. 'She had a fiancé, OK? Lawrence. And he died, OK? Sweet, sweet boy. An English teacher. Lawrence was killed in a hit-and-run accident six months ago. Some bastard knocked him off his bike. Never stopped. Never caught. You lot couldn't help us there. OK, Detective?'

I looked at the baby in his arms and I nodded.

'I can tell you now,' he said, 'my daughter doesn't have bitter ex-boyfriends or lovesick psychos hanging around.' For the first time, the old man's voice broke with emotion. 'Her life is her child. And her work. This makes no sense. This has been done by some stinking pervert—'

'It's just as Snezia told you,' Mrs Lyle said. 'Everyone loves Jess.' She stood up and indicated her grandson.

14

'We really have to get Michael home. I'm sure you can imagine what we're going through.'

They went off to another room to collect their grandson's clothes and I sat down on the sofa next to Snezia.

'How long have you and Jessica lived together?'

'Two years. We're both dancers. We met at an audition in the West End. Neither of us got the job but I saw her again in the shoe shop we all go to. Freed of London. You know it?'

I nodded. 'Covent Garden. Where they sell dance shoes to the pros.'

'That's it. We went for coffee. Her fiancé had just died. I think she was lonely. And I was lonely too.' She looked around the apartment. 'And it's hard to afford a place like this on your own.'

'We will need some recent photographs.'

For the first time, she smiled.

She reached for her phone. 'I have many lovely photographs of Jess.'

And Snezia did have a lot of photographs of the pair of them, together and apart. Snezia and Jessica looked like two young women enjoying life in London. At the gym and a dance studio. In restaurants and bars. In the park and on Hampstead Heath. And Jessica Lyle smiling her secret smile on quiet nights at home, curled up with a book and the baby.

'Everyone loves Jess,' Snezia said again, dreamy with exhaustion, stunned with shock.

And then there was a different kind of photograph. Snezia in a bikini and high heels, upside down on a silver pole.

'Oh, that's just me at work,' she said, scrolling quickly on.

'You said you're both dancers.'

'We're different kinds of dancers. Jess was a ballet dancer until she tore her cruciate ligament in her knee. Now she teaches – the little ones, you know. I'm more of an exotic dancer. Or is it erotic?'

I shrugged. It was probably both.

I could hear the parents in the next room. Their voices were raised in argument.

The mother was wrong. I could not imagine what they were enduring. I believed that I would tear my own skin off if someone took my daughter Scout.

But some things you can't truly imagine until they happen.

'Anyone threatening Jessica?' I asked Snezia. 'Harassing her? An ex-boyfriend who didn't want to move on? Just some guy in the neighbourhood who took a shine to her?'

'As Jess's mum told you, she had a fiancé. Michael's father. He died. And my friend – well, she is still in mourning.'

I handed back the phone.

'She borrowed your brand-new car? You must be very good friends.'

'Her car is in the garage. I lent her my car. That's nothing. We are more like sisters than flatmates.'

'Did she send you any message on her way home?'

She showed me.

Coming home. Please wait up xxx

'Why did she want you to wait up?' I said.

'Jess hated entering a quiet house.'

I stared at the message for a long moment, trying to find meaning in the five words and three kisses. But when nothing came I thumbed the button at the bottom, taking the screen to the home page.

And under the time and date at the top of the phone's screen, there was a photograph of Snezia with a man whose face I knew. A much older man. Perhaps sixty to her thirty. Arm in arm, as if pretending to dance. Grinning for the camera.

Harry Flowers.

What I knew about Harry Flowers was what everyone knew.

He was the Henry Ford of the drug industry, starting out in the Eighties, one of the first career criminals to see that recreational drugs were going to move away from middle-class bohemia – students, musicians, artists

– and enter the mainstream, and that the popularity of methylenedioxymethamphetamine – MDMA for short, commonly known as Ecstasy, or E – meant that every kid in every provincial club was going to be getting off their face on a regular basis.

'Is this you and your boyfriend?' I said. I could not keep the hardness out of my voice.

She nodded.

'Harry is a legitimate businessman,' she said, as if repeating a line that she had been taught, and with just a trace of defiance. 'Waste management. Recycling old cars.'

And maybe it was even true. Nobody deals drugs for forty years. They get done in or banged up long before then. Perhaps Harry Flowers had made his money and changed his ways. But I struggled to believe it.

The parents came out of the bedroom with bags of clothes and a sleeping baby.

'Do you have children, Detective?' Mrs Lyle said.

I stood up to face her.

'Yes, ma'am. Just the one.'

'Boy or girl?'

'I have a little girl, ma'am. Eight years old. Scout.'

'Like the girl in *To Kill a Mockingbird*?'

'That's where we got her name.'

'Then you understand how we feel.'

She gave me a hug.

'Find our daughter for us,' she whispered. 'Please.'

The old man looked at me as if I had done nothing yet that deserved a hug.

And as I was walking back to Whitestone I remembered the most famous story about Harry Flowers.

Back in eighties, height of the second summer of love, Harry Flowers had a business partner he fell out with. The friend became a rival. They both saw how big E was going to be, and how it was going to change the drug industry, and the kind of money there was to be made. Harry Flowers went to visit his rival with one man and a can of petrol. The rival was sitting down to Sunday lunch with his extended family. Harry Flowers and his man tied the rival to his chair at the head of the table and then they emptied the can of petrol over the rival's family.

All of them.

The wife. The grandparents. The four children.

Then Harry Flowers lit a match.

He didn't burn them. Because he did not have to.

And that was how Harry Flowers became the Henry Ford of the drugs industry.

Whitestone was waiting for me at the top of the hill. The brand-new car was being loaded on to the back of a lorry.

'Jessica Lyle's car is in the garage,' I said. 'So the flatmate, Snezia Jones, loaned her this one for the night. And Snezia, who is some kind of stripper, is dating Harry Flowers. If dating is the right word.'

She stared at me for a long moment. '*The* Harry Flowers?' she said.

'And it seems serious,' I said. 'She has Harry Flowers on her phone wallpaper.'

Whitestone's eyes were wide behind her spectacles. 'Let's hope Harry's wife doesn't find out how serious they are.'

'Who hates him?' I said.

'That would be a long list built up over many years,' Whitestone said.

I filled my lungs with that sweet Hampstead air.

And I smelled the vodka again and I understood that I had got it wrong. It was my boss who had been drinking vodka on a work night.

No dogs, said the sign at the entrance to the Eden Hill Park estate, but I could hear the dogs barking beyond the trees, our dogs, the K9 unit; they were out there now and all over the unbroken darkness, looking for a body.

'You know what happened here, don't you?' Whitestone said.

I nodded.

'Someone took the wrong girl,' I said.

2

In a quiet corner of the Black Museum of New Scotland Yard, an ancient 20-litre petrol can sits rusting inside a glass cabinet.

Thirty years ago, the can's metal would have been bright red, but passing time has turned it a dark, mottled brown. If you look closely, the words *Shell Motor Spirit* are still just about visible. Unlike most of the exhibits in the Crime Museum of the Metropolitan Police – to give the Black Museum its proper name – the old petrol can is exhibited without reference to a specific crime. It is displayed with only the briefest of notes.

Shell Petrol Can, recovered from the Kentish Town home of Patrick Mahone, July 1988.

'No victim, no offender and – officially at least – no crime,' said Sergeant John Caine, the curator of Room 101, where the Met remembers the capital's crimes of the last 150 years. 'No complaint was ever made and no charges were ever brought and no conviction was ever made.' He smiled at me in the museum's permanent twilight. 'It's like one of those T-shirts they flog to tourists,' he said. 'Harry Flowers invented the modern drug industry and all I got was this lousy petrol can.'

'Then the story they tell about Harry Flowers is true,' I said.

'It's a tale that has grown in the telling,' John said. 'There's no dispute that Harry Flowers and this Patrick Mahone were fighting for control of the Ecstasy market back in the Eighties. They were childhood friends and then they had a falling out. Harry took pride in his quality control, but his old mate was cutting the stuff with baby powder, rat poison, whatever dodgy white powder he could get his greasy paws on. Harry took exception to this deception of the great British drug-taking public. He sold the good stuff and Mahone was spoiling the market by flogging the fake, sub-standard stuff. And we know that Harry Flowers and one of his favourite thugs burst into Mahone's home one Sunday lunchtime carrying a 20-litre can of petrol. But I've heard that after dousing the Mahone family with petrol, Harry was strolling around with a lit cigarette – and I don't know if that's true. Whatever his little human flaws, Harry Flowers is not mad. And I've also heard that after emptying the can on Granny Mahone,

Mrs Mahone and all the little Mahones, Harry and his helper sat down at the table and enjoyed a traditional Sunday roast with Yorkshire pudding and all the trimmings. And I don't quite buy that.' John glanced at the old petrol can inside the glass case. 'As I say – a tale that has grown in the telling. But I do know that Harry Flowers built his fortune by threatening to burn a man's family alive.'

'I looked for Flowers on the PNC,' I said. The Police National Computer is the database used by law enforcement agencies across the country. 'But I couldn't find him there.'

'Flowers has never done time,' John said. 'And he doesn't have a criminal record. Flowers fed off the criminal class because he knew that villains can't go to the law. So you're never going to find Harry Flowers on the PNC. And beyond this old petrol can, you're not going to find much of him in here.'

I followed John to the exhibit on the old family firms who ran London half a century ago.

Eddie and Harry Richardson south of the river.

Paul and Danny Warboys in West London.

And Reggie and Ronnie Kray in the East End.

'Flowers was the first of the new breed,' John said. 'The first generation who didn't think the Krays were role models for growing gangsters. Flowers knew where all the Kray brothers had died – not just Reggie and

Ronnie, but their older brother Charlie, too – and they all died in jail. That wasn't for Harry Flowers.'

'But Reggie Kray didn't die in jail,' I said. 'Reggie died in the honeymoon suite of a hotel in Norwich. Some kind-hearted judge granted his last wish not to die inside.'

'You think Reggie Kray would have been allowed to put one foot outside that hotel in Norwich, Max?' John grinned. 'A honeymoon suite can be a jail too.'

'Snezia Jones called Harry Flowers a businessman,' I said. 'The flatmate of Jessica Lyle. The girl who calls Flowers her boyfriend.'

John chuckled. He was a sergeant with three decades of hard service on his face and not a gram of soft flesh on his body, one of those teak-tough old-timers who are the backbone of the Met.

'Every little scumbag I ever nicked thought he was some kind of businessman,' he said. 'Reggie and Ronnie Kray, Paul and Danny Warboys, Eddie and Harry Richardson – they all thought they would have done quite well at the London School of Economics. Given a little bit of social mobility, they all believed that they had the entrepreneurial spirit, even when they were nailing some poor bugger's earlobes to the carpet. So you think someone abducted the wrong woman? They meant to take this Snezia Jones?'

I nodded. 'I can't see it any other way. Jessica Lyle is a single mother who teaches dance. As far as I can tell, she is still grieving for her late fiancé. There's no reason to abduct her, beyond a random sexual assault. And of course, that's always a possibility. But it becomes a lot less likely when you learn that Snezia Jones is some old gangster's bit on the side. And that Jessica Lyle was driving her car.'

There were excited voices in the corridor. A group of young uniformed cadets down from Hendon were waiting for their tour of the Black Museum. As much as a repository of its own history, the Met uses Room 101 as a training facility for future police officers.

'What happened to Patrick Mahone?' I said.

'Mahone had a nervous breakdown after Harry Flowers paid him that visit. He tried to make a comeback ten years later – diversifying into cocaine – and got busted for trying to sell 10 grams to an undercover cop from Scotland Yard. He died of pancreatic cancer in a cell in Parkhurst.'

'So I'm not looking for Patrick Mahone.'

'You're looking for someone big and stupid enough to kidnap Harry Flowers' mistress,' John said. 'It's either an old grudge – and there are plenty of those where Harry is concerned – or it's a new rival. And there are always plenty of those, too.'

'I heard that Harry Flowers was into waste management these days,' I said, remembering what Snezia had told me. 'Recycling old cars.'

'Yes, he's very green, our Harry,' John chuckled. 'Concerned about the planet. Lays awake at night fretting about what plastic bags are doing to the dolphins. And it's true he's got some yard in Kentish Town where they mash up old cars and ship them off to a landfill in China.'

'You think he's still dealing?'

'No idea,' John said. 'But he is still a big name in the recreational drugs industry – even if he's retired. That kind of fame doesn't fade in the criminal class. So the kidnapping could be the work of some young firm who sees Harry Flowers as a dinosaur ready for extinction and fancies his name on their CV. Or it could be some foreign outfit trying to set up shop in London. You can't see why some aspiring young gunslinger would want to knock Harry off his perch. Flowers has a very nice life and he has enjoyed it for many years. He sits out there in his Essex mansion with his posh wife Charlotte and his two grown-up kids, and he comes into town to talk to his financial advisers, and to have lunch and to bounce on the bones of his mistress. And I am sure this Snezia Jones is a very attractive young lady. Harry Flowers' girlfriends always were. So a lot of villains want what he has. But there's somebody else who hates Harry Flowers...'

I waited. We could hear the excited voices of the young cadets waiting to be let in. The Black Museum is the most difficult room in London to enter. I knew senior detectives who had never been inside these cool, hushed, darkened rooms. And for the young cadets, their time was almost here.

'We do,' John said. 'The law. We hate Harry because he never did the time he has earned. And we hate him for an even better reason. We hate him because back in the day there were coppers in this very building who were willing to take Harry Flowers' shilling – and ended up going down for it. I don't know what happened to Jessica Lyle. I don't even know what side of the law butters Harry's bread these days. But if you have some reason to hate Harry Flowers, then you are standing in a very long queue.' He paused and rubbed his chin. 'This Jessica Lyle – is it true she's Frank Lyle's daughter?'

I nodded. 'Did you know him?'

'Our paths crossed a few times. We have had a few words. Frank Lyle always wants things done his way.'

'Yes, that's him. Would he have made the kind of enemies who would want to hurt his family?'

'Every cop alive makes the kind of enemies who would want to hurt their family. Do you think his daughter is already dead?'

'The kidnappers must know by now they took the wrong woman,' I said. 'From their point of view, it's probably too dangerous to let her go. They're in a state of panic. Their plan went wrong. And they want it to be over.'

'That poor girl,' John Caine said. 'And her poor kid.'

We stared in silence at the rusting petrol can. The voices in the corridor were getting more agitated. I glanced at my watch.

'I know you've got a ten o'clock, John,' I said. 'But can I just see her for a moment?'

He patted my shoulder. 'Of course, son. And you take all the time in the world.'

There is a large glass cabinet in those dimly lit rooms, a permanent and ever-changing exhibit that is being added to every year, a display case dedicated to the police officers of the Metropolitan Police who have died in the line of duty. OUR MURDERED COLLEAGUES, it says.

A century and a half of photographs, the oldest grey with age, all of the faces captured in official photographs, some of them smiling with the self-conscious shyness of the reluctant sitter, some of them deadly serious, a few grinning with amusement. All of them blissfully unaware that they would die in the line of duty, yet all of them aware of the risks. Some of them were not yet out of their teens, some of them were at the far end of their career, just one bad break away from retirement. They are all male officers for the first hundred years or so, but then more and more women officers start to appear in the middle of the last century. It is a simple and powerful memorial for the brightest and the best who gave their lives during the course of what they left home thinking was going to be a normal working day. There is not much on them, for their number is far too many. Just rank, name, age and cause of death. And she was there. And there was the smile that I had loved, and I still loved, and I will love for the rest of my days.

DC Edie Wren.
Age 26. Died of injuries.

I stood there for a long moment, because I could never get enough of that smile, that face, but then I was suddenly aware that the students were waiting and they would not be allowed in until I had gone.

'Thank you, John.'

'Any time,' he said, putting his arm around me. We walked towards his office, the voices in the corridor falling respectfully silent as we approached.

'Give Harry Flowers a tug,' John said. 'He'll tell you who hates him.'

'Will do.'

But I did not need to go looking for Harry Flowers. Because he came looking for me.

3

At the end of that first day I ate dinner in Smiths of Smithfield with Scout and Stan.

The dog dozed at our feet, stretched out in the classic Cavalier King Charles Spaniel resting pose, his front legs pushed out before him like a high diver about to take the long plunge, as I watched the meat market coming alive through the great glass windows of SOS and Scout read aloud to herself from her book. She was a good reader.

At eight, Scout's milk teeth had almost gone. She had lost four top front teeth and four bottom front teeth, and her words occasionally came out with a sound that was somewhere between a whistle and a lisp.

'*Taormina*,' she read, '*perched high on Monte Tauro, with Mount Etna ath a backdrop, lookth down on two grand, thweeping bays and is Thithily'th — Sicily'th!* — Sicily's! — *Sicily's best-known resort.*'

These last words punched out with considerable effort. Scout hated the speech impediment that came with the passing of her milk teeth and I tried not to let her catch me smiling. I glanced at the cover of her book. *The Rough Guide to Italy*. That's a strange book to choose for library club, I thought.

And then I saw the car.

A black Bentley Bentayga V8.

The meat porters stopped what they were doing to watch the luxury SUV make its stately progress down Charterhouse Street. The car stopped outside Smiths of Smithfield and a driver got out. A young man, probably of Indian or Pakistani descent, in a dark suit that was not quite a chauffeur's uniform but close. His head was shaven but his expression was too timid for him to look threatening. He looked more like a Tibetan monk than a skinhead.

He rang a buzzer on the door next to the restaurant. The building where we lived.

'*Sicily* considers itself a separate entity to the rest of Italy,' Scout said. She looked up from *The Rough Guide to Italy*. 'Are we going to have any dessert?'

'You order for us,' I said. 'I'm going to talk to the man.'

The driver looked up at me as I came through the glass door of SOS. The Bentley's big V8 engine rumbled with contentment.

'Mr Wolfe?' he said.

'Detective Wolfe,' I said. 'What do you want, pal?'

Although I had already guessed.

'Mr Harold Flowers is in the back of this car,' the driver said. 'He would like to offer his assistance in your current investigation.'

I looked at the blacked-out windows of the Bentley, feeling a spike of pure fury.

'And your boss thinks it is appropriate to come to my home?'

The driver looked apologetic.

'It's simply because Mr Flowers understands the urgency of the situation.'

'Does your boss have any new information about the abduction of Jessica Lyle?'

'Not new information as such, but Mr Flowers—'

'Listen,' I said. 'Tell him to come into West End Central tomorrow morning and make a statement.' I took a step closer to the driver. 'And don't ever come anywhere near my home again.'

The Bentley's back door began to open.

The driver hurried to hold it.

Harry Flowers got out and stood before me. He was a large man – a shade taller than my 6 feet, but twice as heavy – who looked like he had got that way not because of his genes but because of his appetites. His thinning hair was scraped back from his high forehead. Unapologetically balding.

He looked like he had been trouble for a lifetime, but when he spoke his voice was soft and polite, so soft that

I fought the urge to lean forward to listen more carefully, so polite that for a moment I didn't feel like kicking him all the way back to Essex.

'DC Wolfe? I'm sorry to disturb your evening and sorry for this intrusion.'

Harry Flowers' accent was unreconstructed London working class, but he had clearly been around people from more privileged backgrounds. Hadn't John Caine told me Flowers had a posh wife? She had smoothed out his Cockney vowels and his table manners.

'I want to help find Jessica,' he said, and shrugged. A businessman's shrug, the shrug of someone who understood the art of the deal. He was offering me something that I wanted too. He was making me an offer he didn't think I could refuse. 'That's all,' he said, the soft voice of reason. 'In any way I can.'

'Then come into West End Central tomorrow morning and make a statement.'

'I didn't want to wait.'

'I'm busy.'

'After your dinner.'

'After my dinner I'm busy walking my dog.'

He spread his hands. They were big hands. 'Then may I wait?'

And he did. I went back into Smiths of Smithfield, where Scout was wiping a blueberry pancake stain from the cover of *The Rough Guide to Italy* and Stan was awake, sniffing the air, alert and very aware that there were hot pancakes knocking about.

We finished our dessert. I got the bill, and when I came out Flowers and the driver were both back behind the tinted windows of the Bentley.

The engine was switched off now. They were waiting.

Let the bastard wait, I thought.

Scout and I took Stan down to West Smithfield Rotunda Garden. It was a peaceful little space, not big enough to be called a park, and you would never guess that this was once a place of public execution. William Wallace was hung, drawn and quartered here more than seven hundred years ago. Queen Mary burned 200 Protestants here five hundred years ago. You would never guess at that long history of violence, I thought, looking back at the meat market, just as you would never guess what the man in the back of that Bentley had once done to a business rival with a 20-litre can of petrol.

I didn't want this scum-sack anywhere near me, my daughter and our home.

I didn't want him near my dog.

But the Bentley was still parked outside Smiths of Smithfield when we got back, a couple of parking tickets fluttering under its windscreen wipers.

'You got your key?' I asked Scout. 'Put some water down for Stan and brush your teeth. Don't answer the door. I'll be up in five minutes.'

34

I let them into our building and watched Scout lead Stan into the lift. When the doors had closed I went back to the Bentley. The driver was standing on the pavement.

'He's got five minutes,' I said.

'Mr Flowers is waiting for you in there,' the driver said.

He was indicating Fred's gym.

I went inside.

At this time of night Fred's was almost empty.

James Brown was playing on the sound system, the volume turned up to ten, the lone treadmill runner seeming to move to that funky beat, while on a yoga mat a woman in her sixties with the body of someone forty years younger performed an immaculate surya namaskar, the sun salutation, her arms reaching up to the heavens and then down to her toes, bending and unfolding as she made the series of asanas look like some graceful pagan dance. Up on the giant TV screen, the first fight between Marco Antonio Barrera and Erik Morales was playing with the sound turned off, the two Mexicans refusing to retreat an inch. The yoga woman stared straight at them and did not seem to see them. You got all types in Fred's.

Harry Flowers was watching Fred sparring with a heavyweight who was perhaps twice his size. And Flowers was not alone.

35

The polite little driver had stayed on the street but there was a tall, good-looking black man standing by Flowers' side while an enormously fat white man in glasses lifted free weights with hands blurred by ancient tattoos.

The hired help, I thought. What kind of legitimate businessman brings his bodyguards to a gym?

The fat man lifting weights spoke as I passed him.

'How old is your kid?' he said.

I stopped and I stared at him. And I kept staring until he looked away. And when I saw that he was not going to open his mouth to me again, I walked to where Flowers was watching the boxing.

'The smaller man is faster,' he said thoughtfully, talking about Fred. 'But there's something else. He has no fear.'

Could I imagine Harry Flowers emptying a can of petrol on a terrified family? It was thirty years ago. It felt like somebody else, in some other lifetime. Maybe he had not done it after all. Maybe it was one of those myths that villains love. A tale that grew in the telling, John Caine had said, as if it was a story from Tolkien.

'What do you want, Flowers?'

He turned to look at me.

'What's happened to Jessica Lyle is a tragedy,' he said.

'Feeling guilty, are you? You should. Because it doesn't seem very likely that they were after Jessica Lyle, does it?'

The black man by his side stirred at the tone in my voice and I realised that I had seen him before. Long ago, in a professional boxing ring. He was good back then – big but fast, brought up on dreams of moving like Muhammad Ali.

'Where do I know you from?' I asked him.

'I'm Ruben Shavers,' he said, holding out a massive hand.

I ignored it. 'And who is the meathead on the free weights?'

Flowers chuckled. 'Meathead!' He liked that one.

'That's Derek Bumpus,' the black guy told me. 'Big Del.'

I turned my full attention to his master.

'We both know they didn't want Jessica Lyle,' I said to Flowers. 'They wanted your special friend. They wanted Snezia Jones. An innocent woman has been taken because someone wants to get back at you.'

'Is that your theory?' he said, calm and quiet.

'Or maybe you tried to get shot of Snezia Jones yourself.'

A cloud passed across his fleshy features.

'Why would I do that?' he said.

'All the usual reasons a man like you would press the eject button on his mistress. Because you're bored with her. Because you want her off the payroll. Because you found out she had her own bit on the side. Or any combination of the above.'

'I prefer your first theory. Someone wants to do me harm. If I was behind the abduction, I would not be very likely to seek out a detective in Homicide and Serious Crime, would I?'

He had me there. Or maybe not. Maybe coming to see me was a double bluff.

'Who do you think took Jessica Lyle?' I said. 'I can't believe you don't have a list of suspects.'

He shook his head.

'Whatever you have heard about me is ancient history,' he said. He gave me what looked like a business card but turned out to be one of those old-fashioned matchbox folders that advertised a business.

Auto Waste Solutions, it said on the cover.

'I don't know who took her, but I know what happens next,' he said. 'Whoever took Jessica, they are violent men, and they are stupid men, and by now they almost certainly understand they have made the biggest mistake of their lives. And that makes me fear for this young woman.'

It was exactly my take on the situation.

'Do you know Jessica Lyle?' I said.

He shrugged. 'She is the flatmate of ...' pausing to find the correct terminology, '... someone I am close to. We have been introduced and we say hello. I am not often at the apartment. Snezia and I usually meet at a hotel in town.'

I looked at the clock on the wall of Fred's. I thought of Scout alone in the big loft. This was taking too long. She had put down water for Stan and she had brushed her teeth, but what was she doing now? I looked at the fat man in glasses with the blurred tattoos on his hands.

'I need to get home to my daughter,' I said.

'I understand.'

But I had one more question.

'Who hates your guts, Flowers?'

For the first time, he bridled with impatience. It was no more than that. I sensed he was a man who kept his anger under lock and key.

'I'm into recycling solutions,' he said. 'It's not the Eighties any more. The people who made everything start with an E are either dead, doing time or – if they were smart – they moved on to other fields. And legitimate business.' He indicated the matchbox I was holding.

'Then who hates you enough to kidnap the woman they thought was your mistress?'

He lifted his chin and Ruben Shavers left us.

'Do you ever watch those David Attenborough documentaries? I love them. Sometimes a young lion tries to take the place of an older lion. And sometimes they succeed and the old lion has to crawl away to die. But not always. Sometimes the old lion still has more than the young lion can handle – too much strength, too much experience, and far too much to lose. And that's when the young lion gets his face ripped off.'

'And sometimes both of them get stuck in a zoo.'

Behind us, I could hear the sound of leather gloves hitting flesh and bone. The big man fighting Fred grunted with pain. I wanted to be home.

'I know you despise me, DC Wolfe,' Flowers said. 'But please don't let your personal feelings stop me from helping you find Jessica Lyle. Whatever you think of me, whatever you may have heard about me, it all dates, I am sure, from a very long time ago. But I still have resources. And I can help.'

Fred darted beyond the heavyweight's lowered guard and threw more punches than I could count, battering the far bigger man to his knees. The bell went and they embraced. It was time for me to go home. I could feel that sick anxious feeling rising in me – parental panic – but still I lingered for a few seconds more. Because for the first time I thought perhaps I could use Harry Flowers.

'It's possible they still believe they have the right woman,' I said. 'But I don't know if that is good or bad news for Jessica Lyle.'

'Then why don't they ask for a ransom?'

'I would be guessing.'

'Please have a guess, DC Wolfe.'

'Maybe they don't want your money, Harry,' I said. 'Maybe they just want to see you suffer.'

I ran home.

The lift took too long coming, no matter how many times I hit the call button, so I took the stairs, two at a time, all the way to the top floor. I burst into our loft sweaty with dread.

Scout was in her pyjamas, kneeling by the coffee table and holding her book in one hand while the fingers of her other hand stroked the sleeping head of our dog, who was snoring with contentment on the sofa.

Scout looked up from *The Rough Guide to Italy* and stared at me with her solemn brown eyes as I stood there with the panic receding, the last of the day's sunshine pouring through the big windows, knowing that I had never seen anything in this world more beautiful than my daughter.

'What?' she said.

4

Jessica Lyle's bedroom was large and full of light, a spacious room with views on two sides across Hampstead Heath. A good address in an expensive area. There was a cot at the end of the bed, and wardrobes stuffed full of clothes for a woman and a fast-growing baby boy. The bookcase was jammed with bestselling paperbacks for her and first books for baby Michael. Gillian Flynn, Liane Moriarty, Lisa Jewell and Audrey Niffenegger shared space with *The Noisy Farm Sound Book, The Wipe Clean Work Book, Cars! Cars! Cars!, I like Bugs* and *All the Things I Wish for You*.

And as I read the titles of the books, I felt her life surround me.

This is who we are, the room seemed to whisper.

The baby boy and his dancing mother.

Jessica Lyle was not a crime statistic in this room.

On the bedside table there was a single silver-framed photograph of a good-looking, rugby-fit young man with his arms wrapped tight around Jessica, grinning for the camera as if he was the happiest man who ever lived.

Lawrence, the dead fiancé, who got knocked off his bike and left for dead by someone who was never stopped and never caught. But this did not feel like the room of a woman who was still in mourning for the man she had planned to spend her life with.

Apart from the one bedside photograph, which looked as though it had been taken by the boating lake in Hyde Park, there was no other evidence of Jessica Lyle's dead fiancé in this room.

No clothes, no books, no reminders of that other life.

This room belonged exclusively to Jessica Lyle and her son.

There were dance trophies, books and electronic devices. Stuffed toys that looked faded with age, passed on from mother to child. I peered at a plastic pink-and-purple My First Laptop and recalled it from when Scout was a few years younger.

This felt like someone's home.

And it felt like the room of a woman who had been desperately, horrifically unlucky.

I went to the windows and stared down at Eden Hill Park. The security guard who had called the abduction in was making his rounds in his van.

DCI Pat Whitestone entered the room and came and stood beside me.

She stared down at the security guard. 'That useless piece of trash,' she said, shaking her head. 'A woman is dragged from her car and this guy – this plastic policeman – he doesn't lift a finger. He didn't even get a registration plate or ID.'

'Because they smeared the plates with mud,' I said. 'And because they wore masks.'

'And because he froze, Max. Because the worm didn't do his job.'

'Yes,' I said. 'That too.'

In an interview room at West End Central, the guard had broken down and confessed. The two men, those men with the skull faces, those men made of darkness, had told him not to get involved. And he followed their advice.

But in those moments, you do not choose, I thought. There's no time to choose. You don't think. There's no space for thinking. You act or you don't act. The security guard had not acted. In the terrifying moment, when there was no time to decide what was right or brave, he could not put himself in harm's way for a stranger. The decision was made for him.

'The job's not for everyone,' I said.

Whitestone laughed bitterly and again I smelled the vodka on her breath. It was early morning. The excuse for her that I had come up with last time – we had been called out in the middle of the night – didn't work today.

'Did you go to the Black Museum?' she said, still staring down at the security van patrolling the private estate.

'Yes.'

'And is Edie up there?'

'Yes,' I said. 'Edie's there.'

'Good,' Whitestone said, her voice thick with emotion. 'I'm glad they've got her name in there.'

We turned away from the window and the young man in the silver-framed photograph by the bed seemed to be smiling at us.

We all mourn in our own ways, I thought.

Snezia Jones was waiting for us in the living room.

'Any idea when I'll get my car back?' she said.

Whitestone settled herself in the sofa opposite, studying Snezia as she took her time to reply.

'You'll get your car back when the police have finished with it, sweetheart,' Whitestone said. 'Right now we're keeping it while our forensic people look for evidence.'

Snezia squirmed with embarrassment, as if we might think that her major concern was getting back her brand-new motor.

'I was just thinking that if you've finished with it...'

Whitestone shut her up with a lift of her chin.

'Would you like to tell us about someone who wants to hurt you, Snezia?'

She shook her head, and again I was struck by the paleness of her.

The hair just this side of snow white, the milky skin. She was undoubtedly beautiful, but it was the kind of beauty that looks like it has never been anywhere near sunshine.

'Snezia Jones,' I said. 'Where does the Jones come from?'

'My ex-husband,' she said. 'An English boy.' She examined her elaborately painted fingernails. 'We separated many years ago. Irreconcilable differences.'

'Does your ex-husband want to hurt you?' I asked.

She laughed at the thought. 'He is happily remarried. An English girl who keeps his house clean and doesn't ask questions about where he has been and cooks him bangers and chips.'

Whitestone and I exchanged a look.

'I've been looking for someone like that,' Whitestone said. 'Bangers and chips? Sounds good.'

'When was the last time you saw Harry Flowers?' I said.

I had remained standing. Snezia looked up at me and then back at Whitestone.

'Should I have a lawyer or something?' she said.

Whitestone smiled gently.

'You've done nothing wrong, Snezia,' she said. You are not under arrest. Of course not. So you don't need a lawyer.' The smile faded. 'But you are in a relationship that we believe is directly relevant to the abduction of Jessica Lyle. So you have to be completely honest with us. OK?'

'Harry came into my place of work three nights ago. I saw him then. We spoke briefly but he had business that night.'

'And where do you work?'

'The Western World.'

Whitestone glanced at me.

The Western World is a club in Mayfair. Table dancing, pole dancing, all kinds of dancing. A high-end strip joint for the black card set. A gentlemen's club for rich men on shore leave who are possibly not gentlemen.

'Did you have an argument with Mr Flowers?' Whitestone said.

'What? No!'

'Did you see anyone else have a falling out with him?' I said.

She shook her head.

On the coffee table between us, Snezia's phone began to play a melody from one of Abba's greatest hits. She picked it up and frowned at it, pulling at her plump lower lip.

'Turn that thing off,' Whitestone said, her voice flat and hard.

Snezia did as she was told.

I sat down next to Whitestone.

'Snezia,' I said. 'We believe that the men who abducted Jessica were planning to kidnap you. We think that they were planning to take you because in some way that we have yet to figure out, they wanted something from Harry Flowers. Even if it was just to hurt him. Do you understand?'

Snezia began to cry.

Real tears of shock and regret.

She picked up something from the corner of the sofa and clutched it to her chest. A pair of pink ballet shoes made of satin and leather, old and worn by a lot of serious dancing. Snezia Jones tapped the shoes against the pale skin of her forehead.

'I'm so sorry about Jess,' she sobbed. 'I want her to come home. And I can't sleep for thinking about her and what might be happening to her. But it's not my fault and it's not Harry's fault. It's *not*!'

'You know Flowers is married with two grown-up children, right?' Whitestone said.

'His childhood sweetheart,' Snezia sniffed, as if that explained everything and perhaps called his current marital status into question.

'This is an expensive apartment for two young single women,' I said, looking around. 'Does Flowers pay the rent?'

She wiped her eyes with the back of her hand. 'I make my own money,' she said. 'I was making my own money when I met Harry and I'm making my own money now.'

We waited.

'Harry doesn't pay the rent on this place,' she said. 'He owns it.'

There was a Rolex on her wrist and a chain from Tiffany around her neck. There must be a lot of money in recycling cars, I thought.

'I just think you're wrong,' she said, calmer now. 'I don't think Jess being taken is anything to do with Harry.'

'Then what do you think happened?' I said.

'These men saw Jess and they *wanted* her,' she said. 'They saw her and they wanted her and *so they took her*. Maybe they were drunk or stoned or just a pair of evil bastards who like hurting women. God knows there are enough of them around. But that's what I think happened.'

She inhaled deeply, gaining control of herself. For the first time, she looked at Whitestone with defiance.

'Some women are young and beautiful and hot,' she said.

Whitestone smiled and took off her spectacles for a quick clean. She peered owlishly at the smeared John Lennon lenses.

'And Jess – our beautiful Jess – was one of those women,' Snezia continued. 'If you saw her, you would understand.'

'Understand what?' Whitestone said, squinting blindly across the coffee table.

'Why everyone loves her,' Snezia said.

We were walking to my car.

'I think Snezia is exactly what she seems to be,' Whitestone said. 'A basic pleasure model. She met some old guy while she was doing the fandango upside down in a pair of pants like dental floss – except this old guy wasn't something big in the City or on the run from Russia. He was Harry Flowers. The only strange thing to my mind – why is she still working? She is the long-term mistress of Harry Flowers and yet she's still strutting her funky stuff in a tiny pair of pants at the Western World. Doesn't that strike you as odd?'

'Maybe she likes having a career,' I said.

Whitestone laughed.

'Shaking her tail feather in the face of drunken fat cats,' Whitestone said. 'Some vocation.' She paused. 'Give me a minute, Max.'

She veered off towards the security guard parked in his van at the entrance to Eden Hill Park estate. The police tape was gone. She tapped on the window and he buzzed it down.

'You sleep all right last night, chicken shit?' she said.

The guard was so young there was still a smattering of acne on his smooth cheeks.

He was a skinny white boy from the outer suburbs. This job – the toy soldier uniform, the car with its big-cock slogan *Spartan Security*, the responsibility of looking over all these rich folk – must have made him feel all grown up. Today he looked as though he wished he was back in school.

'What?' he said.

'Because I was just wondering how Jessica Lyle slept last night,' Whitestone said. 'And I wonder if she's dead in a ditch or chained to a radiator or locked in someone's cell.' She slammed her hands against the side of the van and the boy jumped. 'And I wonder how many men she has had to have sex with since they took her away. And I wonder if they beat her. And I wonder how scared she is and I wonder if anyone hears her screams.'

The security guard's face clouded with fear and shame.

Whitestone took a step back.

'Get out of your little van,' she said.

'Boss,' I said. 'Pat.'

This was not a good idea. Not with vodka in the mix.

The security guard looked to me for help.

Whitestone took another step back, giving him plenty of room.

'Come on,' she said, beckoning with the fingers of her left hand, the right hand balled as a fist by her side.

51

'Boss,' I repeated.

The security guard slowly got out of his car.

'What's your name?' Whitestone demanded.

'Modric,' he said. 'Ian Modric.'

Whitestone looked him up and down and smiled.

Then she gave him her card.

'You see those men again, you give me a call, day or night, you understand, Mr Modric?'

The young security guard stared dumbly at her card, as if he had never seen one before.

'Sure,' he said. 'But they were – you know – wearing masks.'

'So you said in your statement,' Whitestone said patiently. 'But sometimes a witness remembers something that they didn't even know they knew. The shape of a face. The way a man carries himself. Something comes back to them – something important, something valuable that a real policeman can use. And they spoke to you, didn't they?'

'They said, *Don't*,' Modric said.

'Don't,' she repeated, deadpan.

Whitestone and the security guard looked at each other.

My phone rang.

Joy Adams was calling from West End Central.

When I hung up I stepped between DCI Pat Whitestone and Modric. 'Someone sent us Jessica Lyle's clothes,' I said.

5

Jessica Lyle's parents were waiting for us in the lobby of West End Central.

They got up as we came through the door, steeled for the worst.

'What have you got?' Frank Lyle said.

'Please,' Whitestone said, ushering them through the security gate and into a lift. I hit the button for the first floor.

'A jiffy bag was left outside West End Central an hour ago,' I said. 'It contained items of clothing that we believe your daughter may have been wearing at the time of her abduction.'

'There's CCTV out there,' Frank Lyle said.

'Items? What items exactly?' said Jennifer Lyle.

Again I saw her daughter thirty years from now in the face of the mother. And again the thought – if Jessica Lyle lived that long.

'We are looking at the CCTV,' Whitestone said. 'But we suspect the bag may have been left beyond the reach of the cameras.'

The old man cursed. 'Typical! Bloody typical!'

'Three items of clothing,' I said, answering Mrs Lyle. 'But let's give you a chance to look at them.'

The lift stopped at the top floor.

Jessica Lyle's mother did not move.

'What items?' she repeated. 'I want to know.'

'A sweatshirt. Yoga trousers. And a pair of pants.'

She sank into her husband's arms. Whitestone and I held the lift door while they took a moment to recover. Then they followed us down the corridor to Major Incident Room One where Joy Adams was waiting with a young female CSI.

There were three transparent evidence bags on three separate workstations. Two big, one small. Each contained one of the items.

Black sweatshirt, black yoga trousers, black pants. The only splash of colour were words written in hot pink on the sweatshirt.

Last Chance to Dance

The parents stared at the evidence bags. They could not take their eyes from them. The mother nodded.

'It's her,' she said. 'That's the name of her company: Last Chance to Dance.'

'It was always a standing joke in our family,' Frank Lyle said, dazed now, as if talking to himself. 'I'm not

54

a dancer – never been a dancer; two left feet – and at family weddings, parties, Jess would always say to me, *Come on, Dad, this is your last chance to learn how to dance.*' He looked at his wife and he almost smiled. 'So that was what she called her dance studio, wasn't it?'

Mrs Lyle cried out like an animal that had been kicked, reaching for the evidence bags, clawing at them. Whitestone, Joy, the CSI and I all made a move to stop her.

But it was her husband who gently restrained her.

'We can't touch any of it,' he said. 'There could be evidence we can't even see, Jen. Some defence lawyer could get it thrown out of court if we go anywhere near it. OK? We can't give the bastards that chance. There could be all sorts of things on there, Jen. Fibre transfer. DNA.'

Whitestone glanced at me.

He had left out blood and semen.

His voice broke. 'It's ripped,' he said, indicating a tear in the seam of the sweatshirt. 'They ripped it.'

Whitestone nodded at Adams.

'Mr Lyle,' Joy said. 'Can you confirm that, to the best of your knowledge, these items of clothing belong to your daughter, Jessica Lyle?'

'Yes,' he said, his voice hoarse.

Then he took his wife in his arms as the CSI deftly gathered the three evidence bags and quickly left.

Whitestone nodded her thanks.

Frank Lyle's eyes drifted to the massive HDTV on the wall.

It contained a dozen mugshots of known MDMA dealers. Someone in the Met had told someone in the media that we were looking at convicted drug dealers in connection with Jessica's abduction. The men – and they were all men – were of every race and creed on the planet but they all stared at the camera with exactly the same dead-eyed defiance. The brotherhood of drug-dealing scumbags. Frank Lyle kept staring at them until I hit a key on my computer and the image disappeared.

He helped his wife into a chair. And then he turned to face us. Because the former cop had a theory of his own.

'Did you ever think that Harry Flowers is playing you?' he said.

He indicated the blank TV screen.

'I imagine your initial investigation is, inevitably, into any drug dealers who might possibly have business problems with Harry Flowers. But did you ever think that all this could be set up by Flowers himself? Think about it. An innocent young woman gets abducted and the full weight of the Met comes down hard and fast on all of Harry Flowers' rivals.'

His hard old face twisted into a savage grin.

'That would be convenient for him, wouldn't it?' he said.

'Yes,' Whitestone conceded. 'But we have absolutely no evidence that suggests that Harry Flowers was involved in the kidnapping of your daughter. We think that whoever did it was after Jessica's flatmate because of some grievance with Flowers – possibly from years back. We also believe that Flowers got out of the recreational drug market some time ago.' She indicated the blank TV screen. 'And those men on the screen? Yes – they are all known and convicted MDMA dealers. But we don't know if they are or have ever been Flowers' rivals. It would be remiss of us to not look at these guys. But it is a case of trace, interview and eliminate.'

'Were you aware that Snezia was involved with Harry Flowers?' I said.

Mrs Lyle raised her tear-streaked face.

But her husband answered.

'Do you honestly think we would have let our daughter share an apartment with her if we had known?' he said. 'Do you think we would have let our grandson anywhere near her? We thought Snezia was just some good-hearted girl from a poor country who was trying to earn an honest crust however she could. We knew she danced in some dodgy joint. Jess laughed about it.' He shook his head. 'But not *this*. We knew nothing about Harry

Flowers. And I want him arrested now. Do you understand me? I want him brought in and I want that bastard charged and I want it done *today*. The petrol-can man. Oh yeah, I know that story too.'

'We can't do that, sir,' I said. 'Harry Flowers is not a suspect. He claims to be a legitimate businessman. Waste disposal. He recycles old cars.'

Lyle's face twisted with contempt. 'And you believe all that crap, do you?'

'Until we get evidence to the contrary, we have to believe that's exactly what he is. And I will tell you why, sir – because we can't waste time and resources chasing Harry Flowers if he had nothing to do with Jessica's abduction.'

Lyle stood up and faced me.

'Then I'm taking over,' he said. 'I'm going to call a press conference. I—' he looked at his wife. '*We* are going to tell the world about our daughter and what's happened to her. We're going to get her story out into the world. I want the newspapers all over it, candlelit vigils, marches, social media saturation – the lot. I want the world watching.'

'Sir,' I said. 'We have Jessica's clothes. There is still a chance she's alive.'

'*Still a chance?*' Mrs Lyle said. '*Still a chance?*'

'We have to give our forensic people time to see if they can find anything.'

Then I tried speaking to Frank Lyle like a cop. Because talking to him like a father just wasn't working.

'You know how it works, sir,' I said. 'If you go public right now then every sick nutjob in the land is going to crawl out from under his stone and contact us. And that will make finding Jessica almost impossible.'

He took a step closer to me and for a moment I thought he was going to strike me.

'Yes, I know how it works,' he said. 'I know exactly how it works, son. I know that two hundred and seventy-five thousand people go missing every year in this country. And I know that a thousand unidentified bodies are found every year. And I know that the only missing the public give a flying fig about are *the beautiful ones*. Because they can't care about everyone who goes missing – there are too many. An army of missing people. The public only care about the special ones. That's right, isn't it? A beautiful missing woman, exactly like my daughter. A beautiful little child. People care about them and we have to exploit the fact that they care about the beautiful ones. Because my daughter, son, was the most beautiful of them all.'

I took a breath and held it. He was right. The missing have to be beautiful before the public gives a damn. But publicity could also explode in your face.

'Just give us a chance to do it our way for a little longer,' I pleaded. 'Before you go public.'

He shook his head. 'There's no time,' he said. He lowered his voice but I think his wife was beyond listening to him. 'Because I know that if we do not get her back quickly then we are not going to get her back at all,' he said. 'At least, not alive. She's my daughter and we're doing it my way. For you, she's just another job. But she's my flesh and blood. She's my life. And if we get a ransom demand, then we're paying it – whatever it is, understood? I don't care. I – we – will find the money. I – we – have got the money.'

'If you start talking like that in front of the cameras then we are going to have every scam artist in town calling,' Whitestone said, her voice cold and unsweetened.

'I don't care,' Lyle said, his eyes still drilling into me. 'And I don't give a monkey's how busy you get. *I just want Jess back.* That's the only thing in the world that I care about. And when I've got her home, and Jess is safe and sound, and she has her baby in her arms, then I am going to find the men who did this and I am going to kill them.'

6

I realised as I was driving to Auto Waste Solutions that I had been looking at it for years.

If you raise your eyes as you drive south past Camden Market, heading into town, then above the rooftops you will briefly see what looks like a mountain range made out of old metal and painted in primary colours. It is there only for a moment and feels as if you imagined it, or got caught by some trick of the light, for what you glimpse strongly resembles a child's drawing of a mountain range – soaring, brightly coloured peaks and plunging crevices all made out of pointy triangles, a Himalayan skyline made of scrap metal.

This was Auto Waste Solutions, and that mountain range was built by Harry Flowers on a light industrial estate below Camden and Kentish Town, and just above King's Cross. The area has been transformed in recent years but there are still pockets that have remained untouched for more than half a century, neighbourhoods that were bombed flat by the Luftwaffe but somehow escaped ever getting built over by the property developers.

Auto Waste Solutions was surrounded by businesses that all needed room to spread out in the middle of the city. A couple of car dealerships. A police car pound. The local council's recycling centre. There was lots of space for lots of cars: cars to be sold, cars that had been impounded by the law and – at the centre of that untouched, unchanging little nook of the city – cars that had come to die at Auto Waste Solutions.

The gates were open and I drove inside.

Within the boundary of climb-proof fencing and razor wire, the man-made peaks of scrap cars loomed all around, in some places piled as high as a four-storey house. I got out of the BMW and stared up at the view.

Most of the vehicles were dying of the passing of time, models that had not been produced for twenty or thirty years, but – shoved in among cars that had expired of old age – there were brand-new, store-fresh write-offs, cars that had been wrecked beyond repair, and now had ten, twenty, thirty or more vehicles stacked on top of them.

It was a big yard, half the size of a football field. Off to one side there was a wooden hut, like an office on a building site, and plenty of parking space for the half-a-dozen cars that were in front of it. Parked next to a yellow forklift that was big enough to pick up a family saloon, there was the Bentley Bentayga.

The two men who had been with Flowers at Fred's gym came out of the wooden hut.

The fat white man, Derek Bumpus, climbed into the yellow forklift and fired it up, frowning at me. The other one, the big black guy, Ruben Shavers, came over to me with a friendly smile on his handsome face.

I indicated the Bentley.

'Your boss around?'

He looked at the car. 'No, I'm borrowing it. Mo lets me sometimes.' He looked back at me. 'Mr Flowers is not here.' He smiled, and it was a charming smile, as if we were sharing a joke. 'You're welcome to look inside the office, if you don't believe me.'

'I believe you, Ruben.'

'Can I help you with anything?'

I raised my chin, taking it all in. 'I wanted to see this place for myself.'

His white teeth shone with amusement. 'Making sure it really exists?'

'Something like that,' I said. 'I saw you fight.'

'Then you must be older than you look.'

'You were a heavyweight, but one of those heavy-weights who can dance and move. Incredibly light on your feet, as I recall. And you had heavy hands. You knocked people out.'

'Long time ago.'

He raised his hand, gesturing for me to step back as Bumpus lumbered past us in the big yellow forklift.

We watched the yellow forklift select a washed-out Ford Cortina from the foothills of that metal mountain range of cars. Bumpus then turned the forklift round and headed for a machine that looked like a garage made of steel with one side missing. It was a car compactor, or car crusher, designed to pound three-dimensional, 2-ton cars made of steel, glass and rubber into flat-pack scrap metal.

The car compactor was built into the back of a large lorry and when Bumpus had carefully placed the Cortina inside, as though he had parked the old Ford in a garage with a missing wall, he proceeded to destroy it, reversing a few yards and then advancing forward, reversing a few yards and coming forward, using the twin metal spikes on the front of the forklift to pierce the doors, break the side windows and crumple the panelling.

'He looks like he's enjoying himself,' I said.

'He is,' Shavers said. 'But the compactor actually works better if the car being crushed has already been broken up.'

He saw me looking at his hands.

They were twice the size of my hands, the hands of a professional heavyweight boxer, and although I knew it was an occupational hazard for boxers to have what they called bad hands – hands that were easily injured, hands that were slow to heal, hands that hurt when you threw a punch – from what I recalled, Ruben Shavers had never shown any sign of his hands hurting in the ring.

He showed them to me now, lifting them up, palms down, and I saw that they were covered in white circles where someone had taken a hammer to them.

'Who did that to you?'

'It doesn't matter,' he said. 'Long time ago. Let's call him a jealous husband. Every fighter has his weak spot. Weak chin. Bad hands.' He smiled. 'My weak spot was that I liked the ladies and the ladies liked me. Even if they were married ladies.'

Derek Bumpus was out of the forklift. He hit a button at the side of the car compactor and the roof slowly came down with a long unbroken whine that covered the sound of the cracking steel and glass and rubber.

When the Ford Cortina was 6 inches high, Bumpus hit the button again and the car compactor slowly rose with that same unbroken white-noise whine as he climbed back into the forklift and trundled off to get another dead car.

'Mr Flowers took me in,' Shavers said. 'When my fighting days were done. After I got caught putting my hands where they shouldn't have been. Took me in, as he took in Big Del there when he was an abused kid from a care home working as a bouncer on the doors before his balls had dropped.'

I thought of the Mahone family having their Sunday lunch interrupted by a pair of men with a petrol can. But every big-name gangster who ever scared the living daylights out of someone had someone else who thought they were a plaster saint.

'Good old Harry Flowers,' I said. 'He's all heart.'

'Mr Flowers wants to help you,' Shavers said.

I started back to my BMW, thinking that one day it would end up in a car graveyard like this one. I nodded goodbye to Ruben Shavers, and I wondered if his boss knew that he sometimes borrowed his car.

'I enjoyed watching you fight, Ruben,' I told him. 'Drive carefully now.'

The old cop was right.

Most of the vast army of the missing are ignored by the public, their disappearance considered of no interest or importance beyond those who knew them.

But nobody was going to be allowed to forget Jessica Lyle.

She would never be one of the forgotten.

Because when her parents brought her baby son to the press conference a few hours later, they guaranteed that tomorrow morning her kidnapping would be at the top of every news cycle and on the front page of every newspaper and the big lead splash on every media website.

Frank and Jennifer followed Whitestone into the media room of West End Central, baby Michael sleeping in his grandmother's arms, only the top of his smooth bulging brow visible above his tartan blanket.

A room full of cameras flashed with excitement.

I was at home alone in the loft watching the news on my laptop and I shook my head in admiration. Frank Lyle had got exactly what he wanted. Now the whole world would know about his daughter.

The presence of the baby had a compelling effect on the press. In front of a blown-up photograph of Jessica Lyle's laughing face, Frank Lyle stared out at a room that was hushed with an almost reverential silence. In the corner of the image of Jessica's face, there were contact details for anyone with information. Below a telephone number and an email address at West End Central, there was a hashtag leaning up against one short cruel word.

#taken

'Everybody loves Jess,' Lyle began. 'My daughter – our daughter – is a kind, decent young woman. A wonderful mother. A loving daughter.' He looked up from his statement, his mouth set in a grim straight line, and the cameras flashed into life. 'Jessica is not *missing*. Jessica has been *taken*. We want her home. We want her home with her baby and we want it with all of our hearts.' For the first time, his voice faltered with emotion and the cameras flashed, as if in acknowledgement of the depth of feeling, the raw open wound of a father's grief. They're loving it, I thought. They're lapping it up. If it bleeds, it leads.

'We want our girl,' Frank Lyle said. 'Our grandson Michael wants – needs – his mother. My former colleagues in the Metropolitan Police are doing their best to find Jess. But as of this moment, only the men who have taken her have it in their power to bring her home. *We will give you whatever you want,*' he said, punching out every word, to an audible intake of breath. 'Money is no object. We are not negotiating. Name your price.'

Whitestone glanced sideways at Lyle, her face unreadable.

Lyle looked directly at the cameras.

'Please,' he said, and it was as if he was pleading to an uncaring world. 'Anyone with information can contact the police at the telephone number and the email address you see behind me.' He glanced back at the oversized picture of his daughter's smiling face and seemed to swoon with missing her. A tall man, it was as if he swayed in a wind that was only in his head. Then he recovered himself and turned back to the room. 'You can call us anonymously. You can contact us on social media using the hashtag you see behind you.' He paused again, a man who had happily lived his life without the presence of hashtags who now discovered that a hashtag might be his last chance to salvage his crumbling world. *'Hashtag taken,'* he said, and the words stuck in his throat like a tumour. 'We await your instructions,' he finished. 'Thank you all for coming.'

Whitestone and the Lyles turned away from a babble of questions.

'Frank, when you say you'll give them whatever they want—'

'Mrs Lyle – hold the baby up a bit, will you? Hold up Michael!'

'But how do you FEEL? How do you FEEL?'

'No questions,' Whitestone said.

I shook my head, this time in disbelief, as I looked at the hotline telephone number on the poster of Jessica Lyle. I pictured TDC Joy Adams in MIR-1, waiting at the other end of the line as every crank, sicko and keyboard fantasist in the land gave us a call.

Frank Lyle had ensured his daughter's disappearance would not be ignored.

But he might have made our job impossible.

I heard a car that I recognised pull up in the street below and I went to the giant windows of our loft.

Anne, my ex-wife, got out of the driver's seat.

Across the street, a pack of meat porters gearing up for the night shift at Smithfield turned to look at her. Anne did that to strangers. She turned their heads and kept them turned. She still looked like the model she had once been, but with ten years or so of disappointment behind her.

Scout clambered out of the back seat, clutching her book. And from the passenger side, a young man emerged. He was maybe in his early twenties, a decade or so younger than Anne, a real good-looking boy, fashionably unkempt.

As Scout was scrambling in the back seat to retrieve her rucksack, the young man placed a kiss on Anne's mouth.

I turned away from the window and looked at Stan, who stared back at me with his black, bulging, Manga-comic eyes.

'What now, Stan?' I asked him.

The dog didn't reply, but he headed towards the front door, his tail swishing with anticipation, sensing the return of Scout, smelling her scent, that Scout smell of shampoo and sugar, books and dog.

I knew there had been problems in Anne's marriage, her next stop after she had left our little family for a new life – new husband, new children – in a leafier part of town. And I knew her husband – Oliver – had lost his good job in finance. But I didn't realise that things had got to the point where handsome young men would be kissing her mouth in broad daylight in front of a bunch of leering meat porters.

I was at the open door waiting for them as Scout rushed into the loft, Stan jumping up beside her, wagging his tail off, delirious with joy as she threw herself on the sofa and opened her book.

Anne came in, the young man hovering sheepishly behind her, a fixed grin on his smooth face. He liked his smile, believed it was his secret weapon, but it wasn't working on me. Excited at the sight and scent of someone new, Stan veered off the sofa to make a huge fuss of him, ready to fall in love.

Oh, you little slut, Stan, I thought.

'Max, this is Roberto,' my ex-wife said, with a theatrical gesture of one hand.

He smiled and nodded.

I nodded and waited.

Married for years but divorced for a lifetime, I thought.

What now? I thought again.

'Roberto and I are going to Sicily,' Anne said. A delicate pause. 'And I want to take Scout.'

I looked across at Scout. The cover of her book displayed a sky-blue Vespa. *The Rough Guide to Italy*. And suddenly it all started to make sense. The book she had been carrying around was not from the school library.

It was from her mother.

'*Mud baths, the beach and spa treatments,*' Scout read aloud. '*Activities on Salina.*'

'When?' I said.

'Next week,' Anne said. 'For ten days. Leaving Monday.'

'No,' I said, not even needing to think about it. It was dead easy. 'I'm not taking Scout out of school for a holiday to Sicily or anywhere else. She has months off in the summer. It can wait until then. She needs to go to school.'

Anne flinched, as if my ignorance caused her real physical pain.

'But what's she going to miss?' she said. 'A bit of finger-painting and making things out of Lego?'

I took a deep breath and slowly let it go.

But it was still inside me, all of it, all the tension wound up tight, everything I felt about what had happened between the three of us over the last few years.

'She's not three years old – she's eight,' I said, as calm and quiet as I could make it. 'And it's not finger-painting and things made out of Lego any more. It hasn't been for a while. It's maths and English and *My Family and Other Animals.*' A beat. And I wanted to keep my mouth shut. I wanted to leave it there. But then I just could not resist it. The stuff about finger-painting and Lego pushed the wrong button. 'But then you wouldn't know that, would you?' I said.

Scout looked up from her book, her face falling.

'Are you having an argument?' she said. 'Please don't.'

'It's a discussion,' Anne and I said together, with the perfect harmony of a couple who had endured the assault course of a collapsed marriage.

I turned to smile at Scout. 'It's a school night,' I said. 'Why don't you say goodbye to your mother and get your kit ready for tomorrow?'

Anne and Scout exchanged a fierce and silent hug. Scout went off to her bedroom. Stan was still attempting to climb up Roberto's legs. The young man wasn't a dog person, you could tell.

Anne was studying me. There was mocking amusement in her eyes.

'Why don't you say it?' she said. 'What's really on your mind. Go on, Max. Knock yourself out. I know you want to.'

I nodded. She was right. She knew me so well, I'll give her that much.

'And I don't know you,' I told Roberto. 'No offence, pal, but who are you? I never met you. I never saw you before today. And I'm meant to let my daughter go on holiday with you?'

Stan lifted his huge round eyes.

Well, he seems like a really great guy to me.

Cheers, Stan.

But then our dog loved everyone – two legs, four legs, cats.

'I'll wait in the car,' Roberto said.

We let him go.

'Do you really think you have the power of veto over who I see?' Anne said. 'Or who I go to bed with?'

'No,' I said. 'And I don't care who you see. Or who you go to bed with. I did once. Not any more. But Scout can't go on holiday during term time because the school doesn't allow it.'

'Oh, fuck the school and its petty rules!'

'You must join me at the next parents' evening, because they would love you,' I said. 'And she can't go on holiday with some guy you just met in the gym. Because her father doesn't allow it.'

'Yoga class, actually. Not the gym. And Roberto does an awesome Downward Facing Dog.'

I could have made a cheap joke, but I rose above it.

We stared at each other without understanding or affection and I struggled to remember that there had once been a time when we had stayed awake all night long and felt so close to each other it was hard to tell where one of us ended and the other began. Or perhaps that had all been a dream in some other lifetime.

'What happened to your marriage?' I said. 'You seemed happy. Settled.'

'Everything ends, Max,' she said, heading for the door.

'Apart from being a parent,' I said. 'Can't you see it? That never ends.'

When I carried the poetry book into Scout's bedroom, Stan was once again stretched out on her duvet in the classic Cavalier pose, his paws stretched out ahead of him, like he was preparing to come off the high diving board. Scout was sitting up in bed with *The Rough Guide to Italy* on her lap.

'I've got a good poem for tonight,' I told her.

She didn't look up at me.

'It's about a dog,' I said.

A poem about a dog! How could she refuse?

Every night I read Scout what we called our bedtime poem. The poems about dogs always went down well. In fact, poems about dogs had been all I had read for quite a while. It was part of the routine that every family life is built upon. I knew I could rely on poems about dogs. But not tonight. Everything ends, as my ex-wife pointed out.

'I don't need a poem tonight,' she said. 'I'm going to read my book.'

I watched her for a while.

'It's my job to look after you the best I can, Scout. Taking you out of school to go to Sicily is not a great idea.'

She wasn't listening.

'*Getting around Sicily can be a protracted business*,' she read.

I kissed the top of her unresponsive head.

'I'm sorry,' I said. 'I don't want to spoil your fun.'

'But you already did,' she said.

And I realised that Scout's grown-up teeth must be coming through.

Because she wasn't lisping any more.

*

In the morning she was fine.

In the morning she was my Scout again, and we busied ourselves with breakfast, and feeding the dog, and getting ready for school, and working out who was picking her up.

Children are like dogs, I thought. Living totally in the moment.

But she never let her *Rough Guide to Italy* get far from her side, and there was a guarded look in her brown eyes that made me think that the children of divorced parents are different.

All of them are diplomats, every one of them, because they have to be, never letting slip what they really feel about the mess and chaos they must negotiate, adept at moving between different homes and adults who have decided that they don't love each other after all.

Scout was hefting her school bag when Pat Whitestone called.

'We got a ransom demand,' she said, her voice thick with something.

It could have been a bad night's sleep. It could have been a hangover.

'No shock after that press conference,' I said. 'How much do they want?'

'They don't want money,' she said. 'They want Harry Flowers.'

7

Later that morning TDC Joy Adams drove Harry Flowers in from Essex.

When they walked into MIR-1, Whitestone held out her hand for his phone.

'Thanks for coming in, Mr Flowers,' she said.

He gave the phone to her, his face impassive apart from a hint of amusement around the mouth.

'It's on WhatsApp,' he said.

'Which has end-to-end encryption,' Adams said. 'Meaning the message can be read at either end but by no one in between. I can get it checked by NCCU.' The National Cyber Crime Unit is part of the National Crime Agency. 'Some tech guys believe end-to-end encryption still leaves a forensic trace.'

'You can encrypt your end-to-end until the mad cows come home,' Flowers smiled. He flexed his massive neck, taking in his surroundings. 'The smart money says that message was sent with a burner that has since been chucked in a skip or dropped down a drain. Your computer boffins are not going to be much use if the message was sent on a one-use phone.'

'Is that how it works, Harry?' Whitestone said, reading the message.

His expression didn't change. 'That's exactly how it works.'

Whitestone read the message and then passed his phone to me. WhatsApp was open.

Come for your whore after dark, H.
Down Street station at midnight.
Are you free? Bring what you stole, H.
But bring the law then there is no more whore.
We are serious men, H. You know us.

'It looks like they still think they've got your special friend, Mr Flowers,' Whitestone said. 'That's bad news for Jessica Lyle. And bad news for everyone.'

Harry Flowers settled himself at a workstation, easing his bulk into a chair that seemed child-sized with him in it.

A man with big appetites, I thought again.

He looked around, taking his time, as if he had choices, and I guessed that this was not the first time he had been inside West End Central. But his previous visits had all been in an interview room or a holding cell.

'*Mr Flowers*,' he said to Whitestone. 'It's *Mr Flowers* now, is it? I like it. You need my help, so it's *Mr Flowers*.' If he had been a more boorish man he would have put his feet up on the desk, but he contented himself with a small smile, an almost delicate turning of the lips. 'Don't worry,' he said. 'I always like to assist the police with their enquiries.'

Whitestone stepped quickly to his side.

And the open palm of her right hand cracked hard across his face.

He blinked up at her, a red welt high on one cheekbone.

'You think this is *funny*?' Whitestone said, and I saw how much she loathed him. 'You find this *amusing*? There's a young woman who has been taken from her child because some cretins believe she's involved with you. And wherever she is as we speak, it's nowhere good. I don't know if we're going to get her back alive. And I don't know if she's dead already. So please don't find it funny, or so help me God I will bury you alive,' she said. '*Mr Flowers*.'

He placed his hands behind his neck, inhaled, and let it go slowly, like some kind of yoga man.

'I'm here, aren't I?' he said, the red mark growing on his face. 'And I'm trying to help.'

'Who calls you H?' Whitestone said.

'Nobody has called me H in years,' he said, flinching at this social faux pas. 'I don't care for it.'

I stared at the phone in my hand.

'But they know your number, Harry,' I said. 'How did they get your number?'

'How would I know? Perhaps I gave it to them – these people who call me H. Many moons ago.'

'Where's Down Street station?' Whitestone asked me. 'I've never heard of it.'

We looked at the giant map of London covering one wall of MIR-1 and I pointed to the bottom right-hand corner of Mayfair, bordered by Park Lane and Piccadilly.

'Down Street is a tube station in Mayfair that hasn't been used for nearly a hundred years,' I said. 'There have always been plenty of other stations nearby and the well-heeled locals in that neck of the woods were never big on public transport anyway. It closed between the wars and in the early days of the Second World War it was Churchill's deep-level shelter until the Cabinet War Rooms in Whitehall were completed.'

Whitestone held out her hand for the phone. She read the message again.

'You say you'll help us bring this young woman home, Mr Flowers,' she said. 'Are you prepared to put yourself in harm's way?'

He laughed. 'You think I'm scared of someone who would do this to a woman? I'll go down there for you. But I am going to take a couple of my people with me.'

I thought of the two hired hands I had seen him with in Fred's gym. The black guy who I remembered from some boxing ring of long ago and the fat white boy who had asked me Scout's age. Ruben Shavers and Big Dec. And I wondered again – why does a legitimate businessman need professional muscle on call?

'That's never going to happen,' Whitestone said. 'You will be accompanied by one of my officers.'

'No law,' Flowers reminded her. 'Do you want to get this girl killed?'

'That's exactly what I'm trying to avoid,' she said. 'We are going to need a signed statement from you, Mr Flowers. And a waiver. TDC Adams will take that from you.'

'A waiver,' Flowers sneered. 'Yes, you have to cover your butt in case it all goes wrong, don't you?' He stood up. 'I'll sign any bit of paper you put in front of me. But they're not getting any money from me.'

'The message is a little vague on that subject,' Whitestone said. 'But I don't think they want your money. Assuming this is not a hoax, I think they want to confront you. And I think that, quite possibly, they want to kill you.'

*

When Flowers and Adams had gone off to do the paper-work, Whitestone stared at me.

For the first time in a while, she seemed stone-cold sober.

'Are we really going to use this maggot as live bait?' she said.

'The maggot is the only bait we have,' I said. 'And he's not scared of what might be waiting for him down there, I'll give that to him.'

She stared at his phone in her fist, her knuckles white.

'But is it *real*?' she said. 'Have they really got Jessica Lyle?'

'They know him well enough to reach him.'

'But they don't know him well enough to know they took the wrong woman.'

'True,' I said. 'But Harry's WhatsApp message reminds me of a letter in the Black Museum that's meant to be from Jack the Ripper. It's a single sheet of paper, one hundred and fifty years old. It's brittle and rust-coloured. Looks like it was pulled from a fire, looks like it would fall to pieces if you touched it. It was sent to George Lusk, the head of the Whitechapel Vigilance Committee. There are a dozen lines, mocking Lusk. The letter arrived at Scotland Yard with a kidney. And there are words misspelt, and it was written fast, almost in a fever. *And it's real*. You can tell. You can feel it. It's from Jack the Ripper.' I nodded at the phone. 'And this feels real, too.'

'It reminds me of a different message,' Whitestone said. 'A cassette tape sent to a copper called George Oldfield in the Eighties. Ever heard of him? Assistant Chief Constable George Oldfield of West Yorkshire Police. He led the hunt for the Yorkshire Ripper. And Oldfield was sent a tape from someone with a Newcastle accent claiming to be the Ripper.'

'The *I'm Jack* tape.'

She nodded. 'The *I'm Jack* tape. And because the guy who sent it had a Newcastle accent, it had the law searching the north-east of England while the real Yorkshire Ripper was killing women in another part of the country. And everybody thought that seemed real, too.' She shrugged. 'You get a message like this and you are either Inspector Lusk, being taunted by the real thing, or you are Assistant Chief Constable Oldfield, being led up the Yellow Brick Road by some sick fantasist with nothing better to do.'

'They do have Harry's number.'

'That doesn't mean they have Jessica.'

'And they hate his guts.'

'Get in the queue.'

We went to the window and stared down at Savile Row, a winding canyon of a street through the heart of Mayfair.

'Did you tell Jessica's parents about the message to Flowers?' I said.

83

Whitestone shook her head.

'You saw that circus we had here? It's no good keeping the missing person in the public eye if you're endangering their life. I know old man Lyle loves his daughter but he's a dial-up copper in a digital world. I'll call Jessica Lyle's parents when I get their daughter back. One way or the other.'

She turned her back to the street and stared up at the wall map.

'If we do what they ask,' she said, 'and we send Flowers in there, how would you play it?'

I had already thought about it.

'I would have a minimal presence around Down Street station,' I said. 'The heavy mob can't be visible. One panic attack and Jessica Lyle is dead. And I would have surveillance officers at the three nearest tube stations backed up by teams of shots.' Shots are SFOs – Specialist Firearms Officers. 'Hyde Park Corner, Green Park, Knightsbridge and Piccadilly Circus are almost next door to Down Street. A bit further out there's Marble Arch, and Oxford Circus. If the Chief Super will sign off on it, I would have surveillance and shots there too.'

'Hold on – you seriously think the men holding Jessica are going to walk to Down Street from one of those stations?'

'I don't see how else they could do it. I think they've already planned their entry and exit.'

'And is that a plan that could work?'

'Oh, yes. If you know your way around down there — and anyone who ever worked for London Underground would know — then you could walk to and from Down Street station from any one of them. You're talking about two hundred and fifty miles of track on London's tube network, with two hundred and seventy working stations and forty ghost stations.' I tapped the map. 'The entrance is on Down Street Mews. But whoever sent that message is not going to be coming through the front door. If he comes at all.'

Whitestone stared hard at the message.

I saw that her hands were shaking.

'Look how much he hates Harry Flowers,' she said. 'He'll come.'

8

'Harry Flowers has bottled it,' Whitestone said, her voice larded with contempt and vodka. 'Some tough guy he turned out to be.'

It was knocking on for midnight and we were at the window of an unfurnished studio apartment across the road from what had once been Down Street underground station.

The entrance to the abandoned station is a grey service door, unmarked apart from a warning that this door is alarmed, private and entry strictly forbidden. It sits under three wide semi-circular windows just to the left of the Mayfair Mini Mart in a façade of glazed red terracotta blocks, the signature architecture of London Underground in the early twentieth century. Apart from the entrance door, Down Street is unchanged in the century or so since the station closed to the public, but the grey door is now used for engineering access and as an emergency exit from the London Underground.

And we had just watched Harry Flowers walk straight past it. He kept going down the street, and he could have been a tourist giddy with jet lag, out for a late-night stroll.

'What did we expect?' Whitestone said, slipping something out of her shoulder bag. A silver hip flask. She unscrewed the top, took a quick hit and then put it away. 'There's nothing in it for him,' she said. 'Why should he give a toss if Jessica Lyle lives or dies?'

But then Flowers stopped at the end of the street.

And he turned back.

And moving awkwardly, his large body bulked up even more by the stab-proof vest he wore under his designer flying jacket, he came back to the entrance and went quickly through the unlocked, unmarked door.

Had he simply missed the door, or was it last-minute nerves?

It did not matter now.

'All calls,' Whitestone said into the radio attached to her lapel. 'He's in.'

There were surveillance teams at the exits of the three nearest tube stations. Hyde Park, Green Park and Knightsbridge. They were all backed up with Tactical Support Teams of shots in their unmarked vehicles. And there were ambulances and paramedics in case it all went wrong.

But Harry Flowers would not be alone down there. Because I was going down there with him.

Whitestone glanced at her watch.

'Let him have five minutes on you,' she said, and nodded at Adams.

Joy Adams had a map spread out on the floor but the light from the street was not enough to see it clearly. Whitestone found the stump of an old candle from the flat's tiny kitchen and I realised that I still had the folder of matches that Flowers had given me. I handed them to Whitestone and she lit the stump of candle. She looked at the cover of the matchbox folder.

'Auto Waste Solutions,' she read, slipping the matchbox into her pocket, and we crouched beside Joy as her finger traced the Piccadilly line.

'Last train westbound is at eleven forty-five and the last train eastbound is five minutes later,' she said.

'I thought the last train was in 1932,' I said.

'Funny,' she said. 'But the Piccadilly line still runs through Down Street. It just hasn't stopped for a hundred years. Trains travelling east and west between Green Park and Hyde Park Corner still pass through Down Street.' She checked her watch. 'And you should hear both those trains on the way down.'

'Got those times, Max?' Whitestone said.

'Eleven forty-five westbound, eleven fifty eastbound,' I said.

'Apart from the live tracks, there is a siding tunnel in use for servicing and reversing westbound trains,' Adams said.

'And we suspect that's the entry point for our unknown suspect,' Whitestone said. 'If someone's down there, then the route they took to get there was almost certainly the service track.' She nodded towards the entrance. 'Nobody has gone through that door all day apart from Flowers.'

'I walked your route down this afternoon,' Joy told me. 'Access to the platforms is by the emergency stairwell. It's pitch-dark in there but the stairs are kept clear because they are still used as an escape route from the Piccadilly line to the surface. Stick close to the wall and you will be OK. There are two lift shafts. Neither operational. Both removed to allow better ventilation for the engineers who work down there. There is also a two-man lift that hasn't been used since the war. Officially declared unsafe. They reckon you can still smell Churchill's cigars. Best skip the lift.'

'How far to the bottom?'

'I had a count of one hundred and three steps on the emergency stairwell. Then there's a corridor followed by nineteen steps that lead to the platform. You are going to have to count them down, unfortunately. Platforms are located 22.2 metres below street level – and it's filthy down there, a century's worth of muck and grime, and the only light comes from passing trains.' She looked at Whitestone. 'Really, Max could do with a torch.'

Whitestone shook her head.

'The lights have to stay out until the action starts,' she said, looking at her watch. 'That's your five minutes, Max.'

I stood up and faced her.

'Just remember your training and you'll be fine,' she said.

I nodded.

A formal arrest will always be accompanied by physically taking control.

'Subdue and control anyone who's down there,' she said. 'And then give us a shout.'

I adjusted the weight of the Kevlar stab-proof vest I was wearing, but it still felt uncomfortable. Although not quite as uncomfortable as being stabbed. I remembered that as being really uncomfortable.

Adams was folding her maps.

'What do you think Flowers will do if someone's waiting for him down there?' she said.

'I think he will try to kill them before they kill him,' I said, feeling a trickle of nervous sweat run down my spine.

And then I followed Harry Flowers underground.

Beyond the unmarked door there were lights on the top level and I quickly left them behind me as I went down the emergency stairwell and into the darkness, counting every step.

103, 102, 101...

There were red and white tiles on the walls, coated
with a century of filth, as Adams had promised, but they
quickly faded to black as I went down the unlit spiral
staircase. And soon there was only the darkness and the
countdown inside my head.

89, 88, 87...

The wind seemed to rise up to meet me as I heard the
first of the trains, roaring far below.

I looked at my wrist but it was too dark to see.

The 11.45 westbound, I thought.

Flowers could not have been far ahead of me.

But I felt totally alone, as if the city had swallowed
all trace of him.

36, 35, 34...

And then the train was gone, and there was only
silence below me, and I could hear my breath and feel
the blood pumping in my veins.

10, 9, 8...

I paused to listen for Flowers. Nothing.

3, 2, 1...

I stopped. Controlled my breathing. I could see nothing but the unbroken darkness, yet I knew I was standing
at the start of the corridor that led to the platforms.
There was a noise in the distance, getting louder. I
walked slowly towards it.

And as I reached the end of the corridor that had once
taken long-dead commuters to and from the platforms,

a train roared through Down Street station without slowing down, close enough to take my breath away, throwing out a dazzling light, the faces of the passengers all a ghostly blur. In the sudden flare of light I saw a modern sign that was there to orientate the engineers. *Piccadilly Line – Westbound,* it said. *Earls Court – Hammersmith – Heathrow – Uxbridge.* As the light faded with the disappearing train, I saw the entrances to both eastbound and westbound platforms were boarded up with walls that had massive ventilation grilles.

But one of the grilles had been torn away at the bottom corner.

As if someone had recently gone through it.

I listened, heard nothing, then pulled the grille back and scrambled through it and on to the platform. There was a long moment of total silence.

And then soft footsteps approached me in the darkness.

A torch shone in my eyes, blinding me.

'Harry?' I said.

But it was not Flowers.

It was a woman in an orange hi-viz jacket with a Transport for London logo. She was perhaps sixty. A short, stumpy woman in thick glasses. She had to be one of the engineers that Adams had told me about. She hobbled towards me with the painful gait of the arthritis sufferer.

'You can't be down here, ma'am,' I said.

She smiled brightly. 'Why's that then?'

'There's a police operation in progress. I need you to take the emergency stairwell to the surface. Please do it now.'

She nodded, and I had half-turned my head to look for Harry Flowers when I saw the aerosol can in her hand.

She lifted it.

And sprayed it in my face.

And then all I felt was the burning in my eyes.

Acid, I thought. *Please help me God.*

My skin did not begin to melt from my face and so I knew that it was not acid, but my eyes were on fire, the lids closed of their own will, slammed shut as if they would never open again, and I could feel it in the membranes of my nose, mouth and lungs all beginning to seize up.

Phenacyl chloride or chemical mace or pepper spray, I thought, fighting the panic.

I doubled up in shock and pain, my heart pounding with fear because I could no longer breathe. My airways shut down and I sank to the ground, coughing, choking, sick to my stomach.

Drool slid from my mouth, my body no longer my own.

And I howled in pain and terror.

Pepper spray is forty-five minutes in hell, they say.

But that is if you stand stock-still and give them a free shot while they spray you. My head had been half-turned so one eye was not as bad as the other. That was the good news. The bad news was that I was on my knees, retching my guts up, and knowing it was pepper spray because it was too strong to be anything else. Chemical mace is like tear gas – an irritant designed to take the wind out of a riot, designed to make you feel like stopping protesting for the day and going home for your tea.

But pepper spray is designed to immediately incapacitate an assailant.

And that was what had been sprayed in my face.

And then I heard a man's voice.

I looked up. One eye was still glued shut but I could half-open the other one, although it was red raw and streaming with tears. And it was open enough for me to see the young man who also wore an orange hi-viz jacket with a Transport for London badge. He was small and stocky like the woman, but perhaps thirty years younger.

'Who is it, Mum?' he said, and a torch played over me.

'Just some dumb pig,' the woman said, shining her own torch in my face.

She had sprayed me from about twelve feet. Maximum effectiveness for any kind of self-defence canister is less than ten feet. These things are designed to spray in the eyes of someone who is right on top of you and attempting to rape or murder you, or both.

So although one eye was gone, the other was working well enough for me to see through my blurred and streaming vision that Harry Flowers had been flattened.

He lay on his back, motionless in the piercing white beams of their torches, and I believed he must be dead.

'Just the one pig, Mum?' the young man said.

'You all alone, little piggy?' the woman said conversationally and kicked me in the ribs. 'He's alone. The rest of them will be waiting up top, skulking around, as is their wont.'

Then Flowers groaned, clawing at his eyes, and I saw that they had sprayed him with the same pepper spray they had used on me.

The young man pulled out a butcher's knife. 'Remember me, Harry? It's been a while.'

Flowers made a whimpering noise and attempted to get up on one elbow.

The young man placed the sole of his boot on Flowers' arm and casually shoved him back down. Flowers was coughing and choking and puking. He must have been a lot closer than me when he took the spray in his eyes.

'Is Harry tooled up?' the woman said.

'I'll ask him,' the young man said, leaning over Flowers. 'You tooled up, H? Let me have a look.'

They spoke to him with a horrible familiarity, as if they were the oldest of friends or the deadliest of enemies. The young man searched Flowers and pulled something from his flying jacket.

'Knuckle dusters, Mum.'

'Brass, dear?'

'No, that modern lightweight stuff. Like grey plastic. Polymer?'

He tried them on for size.

'Mum?' the young man said. 'Should we do the pig or Harry first?'

She did not have to think about it for very long. 'Let's do the pig quick, and then we can take our time with Harry,' she said. 'Nobody's going to bother us down here for a while. They're all waiting upstairs. So let's put the pig out of his misery and then have some fun with Harry. Chop all sorts of bits off him. Stick the bits in his mouth. And up his Wembley Way.'

They had a good chortle at that.

'Where's your whore tonight then, Harry?' the woman said.

'You're not going to find her down here, H,' the young man said. 'We haven't got your whore.'

They laughed even louder.

They were enjoying themselves.

They had waited a long time for this moment. A lifetime.

Then the young man came towards me with the knife, suddenly all business.

He began making pig noises, a throaty snorting that died in his throat as Harry Flowers lashed a foot out and the young man stumbled over it, falling towards me and then regaining his balance and steadying himself. He had dropped his torch. As he stooped to pick it up, I drove the sole of my shoe into his knee.

If you are going to kick someone with plans to kill you, then kick them in the knee. A smashed knee makes everyone change their plans.

He screamed and fell, clutching the smashed ligaments in agony.

And then Harry Flowers was screaming too, and getting to his feet, his eyes closed and streaming, as the woman fell on me to finish what the young man had started.

I smelled roll-up cigarettes and Chanel No. 5 as she dragged her fingernails down my face, trying to take my eyes out. I threw her off me and she grunted as she hit the wall.

Harry Flowers blinked furiously, cursed and cried out as he scanned the ground.

'I can't see! I can't see! I can't see!'

But he blindly reached down and when he stood up I saw that he had the knife in his hand.

And for the first time I saw the violence in him.

He slashed out at the young man as he tried to stand up with his ruined knee and then he went for the woman. She threw herself at him and the knife skittered away into the darkness.

The young man was hopping around on his one good leg.

Flowers picked up the can of pepper spray and emptied it into his face.

Then the three of them were locked in a brutal, tumbling, half-crippled embrace, all of them yelling in the darkness, the torches dropped and lost and forgotten.

I was shouting into the radio on my collar.

'*Grade A response! Grade A response! Jesus Christ, get down here, Whitestone!*'

But there was only the white noise of dead air on the other end.

Harry Flowers grunted as the woman lifted one of her short legs into his groin and it doubled him up and she tore at his face as he bent over, her fingernails in his eyes, but when he got back up he had the knife in his hand and began to blindly slash out, screaming a promise of murder.

'Mum!' the young man cried, and there was real fear in his voice, because they had not killed us when they had the chance and now his body was broken and the chance had gone.

The woman turned at the sound of her son's terror and she went to his side and then they fled, the young man holding his mother for support, the fight suddenly all out of them. I went after them but I stopped, my way blocked by Flowers and his swinging knife sightlessly stabbing at thin air.

'Kill them – not me, you bloody fool!' I told him.

He let the knife fall to his side, his eyes staring at me without seeing as I heard a metallic *clang-clang-clang* of the mother and her son attempting to get through the hole they had made in the ventilation grille.

They wanted to reach the other platform.

They wanted to get to the other tracks.

Because that was the route they had taken to get here, I realised.

And that was how they had planned to leave.

Down the westbound tracks, I thought. From Hyde Park Corner.

That's where they came in, I thought. Not far at all. Almost next door. One stop.

And it had been a good plan. Until it all went wrong.

Their exit strategy wasn't going to work because the young man's injury prevented him from climbing through the ventilation grille and he was far too big for his mother to lift, carry or push through it. They were trapped down here. And suddenly they knew it.

They abandoned the torn ventilation grille and stumbled off down the platform, heading for the darkness of the tunnel.

They glanced back and saw me coming after them, although I felt like I moved in pain-racked slow motion, the agony in my damaged eye blotting out all thought and my legs not working as they should.

There were some service steps at the end of the platform and, arm in arm, they hobbled down them. I called a warning and they looked quickly back before disappearing into the tunnel. I held my breath as the first dazzling light of the approaching train broke the darkness, illuminating two silhouettes on the curve of the tunnel's wall.

They did not have time to scream.

Flowers was sitting with his back to the red-tiled wall.

I had turned on my torch. I shone it on the ID that I had found on what remained of the two bodies. A woman's pension book. A man's driving licence. Both torn and bent, both smeared with blood and dirt.

I brushed it off to read the names.

'Janet Mahone,' I said, looking at the pension book. I shone the light on the driving licence. 'And Peter Mahone. Ever met anyone by the name of Mahone, Harry? Ring any bells?'

He did not respond.

He was swabbing at his burning eyes.

'I'm guessing Janet was married to the late Patrick Mahone,' I said. 'Your old business associate. And

I reckon that Peter was one of their children. The eldest?' I could just about read the date of birth. 'Peter Mahone must have been a very young child on that day back in the Eighties when someone came to their house as they were sitting down for Sunday lunch and soaked the entire family in petrol. And then lit a match.'

I kicked his leg.

'Are you listening to me?'

'I'm listening.'

'This was thirty years ago. Janet Mahone was a young wife and mother. And Peter Mahone – that young man on the tracks down there – was a little kid. But they never forgot what happened that day, Harry.'

'I never saw them before in my life,' he said.

That's the worst thing about my job.

People lie to you. They lie to you all the time.

And they lie to you even when they know that you know they are lying.

I stood up, wiped my eyes with the back of my hand and looked down at Flowers.

'Better get up,' I told him. 'It's a long walk to the top.'

He got slowly to his feet.

He stared into the darkness.

'What happened in there?' he said.

'That last train was a bit late,' I said.

9

The sun was coming up when I drove Flowers home.

He had come off far worse than me. His eyes were still half-shut and bloodshot, the surrounding skin as raw as sunburn and slick with the vegetable oil that had been used to soothe his burns.

He watched his ancestral homeland of the East End pass by as if it was a foreign country. It was still early, so I drove quickly through the light traffic. The only people on the streets were the men and women who cleaned the shining glass towers of Docklands, and they all used public transport.

Whitestone had conducted the hot debrief – the interview that takes place in the immediate aftermath of any serious incident – as Flowers and I lay on adjacent beds in St Bart's and the nurses cleaned our eyes with hand soap, because hand soap can remove the oil in pepper spray like nothing else can. It hurts like hell, but works quite well. There wasn't much to tell her but we told it time and time and time again as the nurses flushed the poison from our eyes.

And as the night wore on, Whitestone had things to tell us.

Peter Mahone, the eldest son of Flowers' former business partner, Patrick Mahone, had worked briefly on the London Underground ten years ago, until a drink problem forced him to retreat to the south coast and the small caravan where his mother Janet Mahone lived. When word spread that the mistress of Harry Flowers had been kidnapped, Peter Mahone knew enough to get himself and his mother into Down Street tube station.

But not quite enough to get them out.

The search teams were still pulling apart the caravan where mother and son had lived.

But nobody was expecting to find a trace of Jessica Lyle.

Whoever had taken her, it wasn't the alcoholic Peter Mahone and his arthritic mother Janet.

'You didn't have to drive me back,' Harry Flowers said as the city's eastern suburbs slipped into the flat Essex countryside. 'My man could have picked me up.'

This was true. And I was sick of the sight of Harry Flowers. And I was in pain, one eye still burning, although the other one, the eye I was driving with, was almost as good as new. And I would have preferred not to have to ask Mrs Murphy to stay at our loft overnight, and not to have to ask her to walk Scout to school and feed and walk Stan. I would much rather have done all that myself. But I was reluctant to let Flowers go because I could not believe he had no idea about who would hate him enough to snatch his mistress, even if they were dumb enough to take the wrong woman.

'Maybe some foreign mob tried to kidnap your friend,' I suggested.

Harry Flowers shook his head.

'The influence of what you call foreign mobs has been vastly overstated,' he said. 'Foreign mobs don't run London. Are you interested in history, DC Wolfe? Then you know this country has not been invaded for one thousand years. Think about that for a moment. That *means* something. The idea that the British are going to roll over and surrender for a bunch of Russians – or Kurds, Albanians, Turks, or whatever they might be – is fanciful. And this kind of abduction is not their style. Too subtle. Our foreign friends just go in with all guns blazing and slaughter everyone in sight. Like the Russians did in Berlin in 1945. Foreign mobs? No. This feels personal.'

London was behind us now and there was nothing ahead but the open road and the green fields of Essex in summer.

I put my foot down.

'You must have a theory about who wants to hurt you,' I said. 'About who tried to snatch Snezia. That operation to take her – although a royal cock-up – was meticulously planned. Peter and Janet Mahone might not have been up to it, but somebody was, and I can't believe you don't have a short list of suspects.'

Flowers said nothing.

'The kidnapping has been all over the news, thanks to Frank Lyle,' I said. 'But your link to it is not public knowledge. So how did the Mahones know about it?'

'Are you kidding me? Because *the police talk*,' he said. 'You lot talk for money, and you talk to even up scores, and you talk because you're like a bunch of old fishwives gossiping over the garden gate.'

Flowers snorted with contempt.

'If you want to get something into the public domain, just tell a secret to a policeman,' he said. 'Some old copper with a grudge slipped the word to the Mahones – that's my best bet – and they crawled out from under their stone, howling for my blood. Maybe it was your boss. Maybe it was DCI Patricia Whitestone.' He touched his face where she had slapped him. 'Did she always like a drink or ten?'

No, I thought. That's a new thing.

'That's the way it works, isn't it?' Flowers said. 'The law always lets somebody else get their hands dirty. Present company excepted. You got your hands quite dirty last night.'

I felt a surge of anger.

'You poured petrol over the Mahone family when they were having their roast beef and Yorkshire pudding,' I said. *'Allegedly.* You can see why they might bear a grudge.'

'That never happened,' he said, not for the first time. 'Not the way you think. Not the way it gets talked about.' He rubbed at his eyes. 'And what's your story? How did your legs get messed up?' He smiled at my face. 'What – you don't think you walk right, do you?' His grin broadened. 'And you don't think you hide it, do you? You walk like a sailor on shore leave, son! What's all that about?'

'Accident at work,' I said.

'No,' he said, suddenly not smiling. 'I heard about that terrorist who detonated a couple of old Croatian grenades she had stuffed down her burka. Around the Angel, right? Killed one detective – a woman. A young woman. And injured another detective. A man. And that was you, Wolfe, wasn't it? And that's shrapnel in your legs, isn't it?' He nodded at the rolling countryside. Harry Flowers was almost home.

'You should take the next exit,' he said.

The Flowers' home stood in a wealthy commuter belt, an area of golf courses and gardener's vans, the residents outnumbered by the daily workers who came in to clean, prune, cook, walk the dogs and drive the children.

A lot of green, expensively managed, and curving gravel driveways with multiple vehicles out front.

It was a neighbourhood for the men and women who caught the early trains into Liverpool Street and Fenchurch Street, and pushed money around on computer screens. Many of them were from families who, like Flowers, had headed east in the decades following the Second World War to a different world of private schools and orthodontists, riding lessons and ski trips. It was just a thirty-minute fast train to the City, although you would never guess it from the leafy, tree-lined streets we were driving through.

Harry Flowers lived in the biggest house of them all.

The Bentley Bentayga V8 was out front. The driver I had seen in Smithfield, the young Asian with the shaven head, was polishing the chrome and glass and gleaming steel.

I parked my filthy old BMW X5 next to it.

Ruben Shavers and Derek Bumpus came out of the house and stood either side of the open doorway.

Welcoming their master, waiting for orders.

'I know your man,' I said.

'Ah,' he said. 'Yes, you probably would. Derek Bumpus. Big Del. I found him working on the doors when he was fourteen. Hardest bouncer in London. Can you imagine that? Working the doors at fourteen?'

He thought I was talking about the fat white man who favoured the Michelin Man.

'The other one,' I said. 'The black guy. Ruben Shavers. He was a boxer. Heavyweight. It must have been ten, fifteen years ago.'

'More like twenty.'

I remembered that slick, fast, good-looking heavyweight and a string of first-round knockouts. And I remembered when I went to Auto Waste Solutions and I saw the hands with the ugly white circles where a hammer had come down.

'What really happened to him?'

Flowers smiled with affection.

'Ruben liked the ladies,' he said, getting out of the car. 'One of them was married to a close personal friend of a big boxing promoter.'

I followed him as he approached his driver.

'Mo,' Flowers said, 'where's Junior?'

'Not back yet, boss.'

Flowers looked at his watch, then his eyes drifted to the roof. Two men had climbed a ladder and were attempting to attach something to the roof of his house. Cables flapped behind them.

'How are your cousins doing, Mo?'

'Nearly finished, boss.'

And I saw that Mo's cousins were fitting CCTV cameras.

'Beefing up security around here, Harry?' I said.

He turned to look at me.

'You need to use the bathroom before you head back?'

'I need to ask you one more question.'

He waited.

'It's about Snezia Jones,' I said.

He glanced towards the beautiful house with his blood-shot eyes.

'Not out here,' he said.

We stepped inside.

The atrium was two storeys high. At the top of the staircase to the first floor there was a huge painting. At the centre of it there was a young Harry Flowers in minimalist swimming shorts holding a surfboard like a shield, his six-pack glistening in the sunshine. There was a grinning blonde bombshell spilling out of a string bikini hanging on to his arm, an inch or two taller than her man. Two small children, twins, a smiling cherub of a girl and a frowning little boy, frolicked in the sand at their feet, building castles of sand.

Flowers saw me staring at it.

'Do you like art?' he said. 'I had that done for me. That's Charlotte, my wife, and our kids. Meadow and Junior.' He got a wistful look in his sore eyes. 'When the children were babies,' he said.

'Boss?' Mo said behind us. 'Delivery for Meadow.'

A FedEx delivery van was parked outside. A courier and some men who looked like more of Mo's cousins – how many did he have? – carried tottering piles of white boxes into the house. The boxes were of every size and shape imaginable – from tiny cubic things to massive rectangular packages that it took two men to carry – but they were all wrapped exactly the same way. Pure white boxes delicately tied with a cream-coloured ribbon. The FedEx man and the cousins gently placed the packages on the ground and went back to the van for more.

'It's here!'

There was a young woman in a T-shirt and jeans at the top of the stairs. She was clearly the girl in Harry's family painting, his daughter, all grown up. She came down the stairs, placing a quick kiss on Harry's cheeks before she began to tear open the boxes. A white veil appeared. And then a long tailored white underskirt. And some elaborate little tangle of costume jewellery, which I knew was a headpiece for the bride's hair, because I had got married once. And there were two pairs of white shoes – barefoot sandals and high heels, one for the wedding itself and one for the reception – and Meadow Flowers gasped with wonder at all of it, and she kept opening the boxes to reveal their snow-white treasure until only one package remained.

Then she held her breath as a circle of men watched in reverential silence and she opened the biggest white box of them all.

It took both hands for Meadow Flowers to lift out her wedding dress, and it unfurled from its rustling nest of paper like a great white sail, and Harry Flowers stared as his daughter clutched it to her chest and closed her eyes.

'What do you think, Daddy?' she asked.

'Bad luck for a bride to be seen in her gown before the day,' he said. And then I saw something soften inside him. 'I think you will be the most beautiful bride in the history of the world,' he told his daughter.

'What on earth happened to you?' said a voice from the top of the stairs.

Charlotte Flowers was dressed for the tennis court.

And she was not what I was expecting.

There was a Grace Kelly cool about her, the kind of good looks that seem subtly chilled to encourage the world to keep its distance, a beauty that feels as though you are always looking at it from behind glass.

Gangsters usually marry a girl from the old neighbourhood.

Harry Flowers had gone upmarket.

She was in her middle fifties, in the kind of great shape that you can only get from both gym and genes. All those summer days on the tennis court had left her skin a little too tanned and her hair, already fair, streaked lighter by the sun. Her accent was too cut-glass for the wife of Harry Flowers. She should have been married to an art dealer, not a drug dealer. As she descended the stairs, I recognised the way she walked. That lazy poise. It is how off-duty models walk.

'Harry,' she said. 'Your poor eyes.'

'Bumped into the Mahones,' he said.

'The Mahones?' she said, flinching. A blast from the past, clearly.

'Peter and Janet. The wife and one of the kids. It's all done now. Don't worry about it.'

She shook her head. 'But the *Mahones*?'

'It's all sorted, Charlotte.'

She smiled indulgently at her daughter examining her wedding-day delivery and then she turned her gaze on me, still smiling. If she knew I was a policeman, she gave no sign. Perhaps she had other things on her mind. Perhaps she didn't care. The gilded class have this wonderful gift of not caring. You have to admire that about them. When she smiled at me I felt like the only person in the room.

'This is Max Wolfe,' Flowers said. 'He gave me a lift home.'

She nodded politely and then turned back to her husband, the smile finally fading.

'That journalist keeps calling on the landline,' she said. 'How did she get the number?'

Harry looked shifty. 'What about?'

'How would I know? She wants to talk to you. But she says she doesn't mind talking to me.'

Flowers visibly stiffened. He gestured to me to follow him.

'You know what to say to journalists,' he told his wife.

'But even when I say no comment, she keeps calling back for a comment, doesn't she?'

'Then don't answer the phone!' he shouted.

I followed Flowers to his office and he closed the door behind us. It was a good room. A man cave built with a limitless budget. Harry was free to indulge his passions in here. And his passions included West Ham United and what looked like bespoke shelves full of 12-inch vinyl. There was a lot of heavy hard wood, and a lot of claret and blue. A black-and-white photograph hung above Harry's desk. Bobby Moore, Geoff Hurst and Martin Peters, the West Ham team that won the World Cup in 1966.

He turned to look at me.

'She doesn't know, does she?' I said. 'Your wife. Charlotte. She doesn't know about the kidnapping. And she doesn't know about Snezia Jones.'

'She knows something has happened,' he said. 'She knows someone has tried to hurt me. But she doesn't know the details. Why would she? And who's going to tell her – you?' He nodded impatiently. 'So what's your question?'

'Snezia,' I said. 'Do you love her?'

He laughed with something like embarrassment.

'That's a funny question.'

'Because it doesn't make sense unless you love her,' I said. 'Getting at you through Snezia doesn't make any sense if she is just a girl you keep on the side. I imagine – just guessing here – that Snezia is not the first girl you have had on your payroll. And the only way kidnapping her makes any sense is if she is *special* to you. The only thing that makes sense is if you love her.'

'I love my wife,' Harry Flowers said. 'Did you see her?'

'Yes.'

'But did you look at her? That's the kind of woman you fall in love with. I've been married for twenty-five years. I intend to be married for another twenty-five years. And it's the kind of love that comes from going through things together. Having children. Watching your parents die. The ups and downs of any career. With Snezia – I love her the way I love my Bentley Bentayga. How could I not love it?' He was smiling now. 'Twin-turbocharged, 4.0 litre, and it does nought to naughty in 4.4 seconds.'

'But if that's the way you care about her – the same way you care about your car – then why is she still dancing in the Western World?'

He looked shocked.

'You can't stand in the way of a woman and her career,' he said. 'Don't you know anything about women?'

As I came out of the house, a car roared up the drive.

I had to stop to avoid being hit by it. A green Porsche 911.

Two young men got out of the car.

The little boy in the beach painting was grown up too. Junior Flowers. His shoulders were wide with lifting weights, and he walked with a self-conscious swagger, a man displaying the strength of a manual labourer who would never have to do any manual labour. His friend got out of the passenger side and they stared at me with a default aggression, a pair of Essex boys who had been up all night.

'Boo,' I said.

They looked at each other and laughed.

'What are you?' Junior asked. 'Some kind of tough guy?'

'That's me,' I confirmed. 'Some kind of tough guy. Catch you later, kids.'

I heard them laughing behind me.

'Look at the gimp go,' Junior Flowers chuckled.

The men from the roof were on the ground now, the cousins of the driver, Mo Patel. I wasn't sure if they were real cousins, although they were so like him that they could have been. They turned away from admiring the new CCTV cameras they had just fitted to stare at me. So did the two bodyguards, the enormous white man, Derek Bumpus, and the taller, leaner black man, Ruben Shavers, both considering me with a professional interest as I made my way to the old BMW.

Harry Flowers was right.

I walked funny these days.

Then a shirt fluttered at my feet like some dying bird. A white shirt, the same shade of impossible virginal white as the wedding dress of Meadow Flowers. And then two more shirts. *Emmett, Jermyn Street, London, Slim Fit*, it said on the collar. And then a Loeb shoe. *Hand-made in England*. Impressive. And then another, its identical twin. Then the jacket from a Savile Row suit. *Alexandra Wood, Savile Row*. And then the trousers.

All Harry's stuff. All of Harry's beautiful stuff. I remembered a book from school. Jay Gatsby throwing his beautiful stuff at the feet of the woman he loved, trying to hold her heart.

But this was something else. This was stuff being thrown by a woman.

I lifted my eyes just as Charlotte Flowers began to scream.

'You *bastard … you fucking bastard … you cheating whore-monger lying bastard …*'

The lovely face of his wife was at the open second-floor window, her yellow hair unkempt and her over-tanned face twisted with tearful fury. She still sounded quite posh. The hired help fluttered around the drive, picking up the shirts and suits and shoes. Mo the driver. The enormous white man. The taller, leaner black man. The cousins. All of them stooping like frightened housekeepers to pick up Harry's possessions.

'Leave it!' Charlotte Flowers screamed at them. *'Leave it all!'*

And they did as they were told.

They left it.

Meadow Flowers came out of the house and stared up at the window. She was still in her T-shirt and jeans combo but she was wearing a wedding veil over her face, completely ignoring her dear old dad's advice about bridal superstitions. She looked up at her mother. And now there was a crowd of us looking up at Charlotte Flowers throwing things from the window. Junior and his friend. Mo and the cousins. Big Del who worked the doors when he was just a lad and Ruben Shavers who could have been a contender if he hadn't liked the ladies quite so much. Meadow and me. And we were all watching the woman in the window furiously hurling her husband's possessions on to that curving gravel driveway.

'Bastard ... whore-loving bastard ...'

I got into the BMW. My wheels crunched on gravel as I pulled away and it was the sound of serious money. In my rear-view mirror, I watched some more of Harry Flowers' favourite things flutter from that first-floor window. Cashmere sweaters. Silk ties. Vinyl records like big black frisbees.

Well, I thought.

Looks like his wife finally found out about his mistress.

10

By the time I got home, Mrs Murphy had taken Scout to school and Stan was watered, walked and fed. The dog snuggled on the sofa and stared at me with his enormous wet eyes. Mrs Murphy was carrying a stack of freshly ironed daisy-yellow school shirts to Scout's bedroom.

I felt weariness and gratitude wash over me.

'Thank you,' I said.

She smiled and shrugged off my thanks.

'No work today?'

'Day off.'

'Good,' she said. 'You deserve a day off.'

'Is Scout OK?'

Now there was a touch of sadness in the smile.

'You know. She was hoping to go on holiday with her mum.'

I nodded.

'But I'm not going to be one of those parents who takes their kid out of school so they can sit on some beach staring at their phone. And Scout's not going to be one of those kids.'

'Our Scout will never be one of those kids. She's just ...'

She looked for the words.

'I was going to say she wants to know her mum, but it's something else. It has been a while since she left. Your ex-wife. Anne. Scout's mum. Years. Scout was how old?'

'Four,' I said, and the absurdly low number stuck in my throat.

'And I think Scout is trying hard to remember what it was like,' Mrs Murphy said. 'So she wants to know her mum. Of course she does. But she wants to *remember* her mum, too. Because I think it's slipping away, that time they had together.'

Mrs Murphy smiled brightly, as if all these things could be worked out with some goodwill and common sense, and I opened up the laptop that I left on the kitchen table while she went off to finish some last tasks before going home. Making sure we – Scout, Stan and me – were all fine before she left us for her own family.

I always left her money in one of those old-fashioned airmail envelopes, the ones with the red, white and blue borders, because both Mrs Murphy and I felt shy and embarrassed about money. I knew she would have looked after our little family for nothing.

She took her airmail envelope and nodded her thanks. Then she paused when she saw what I was looking at on my laptop.

Best hotels in Sicily

The best hotels in Sicily, chosen by our expert. Including luxury hotels, boutique hotels, budget hotels and Sicily hotel deals. Read the reviews and book.

Belmond Villa Sant' Andrea. Hotel Borgo Pantano. Capofaro Malvasia and Resort.

'You poor man,' Mrs Murphy said, and I felt her hand lightly touch my shoulder as she turned away. 'Sicily has got nothing to do with it.'

The newly dead do not go far.

Edie Wren came back as I slept the long summer day away, fresh pain creeping into old dreams, and although she did not speak, and she did not reveal herself, I felt her presence in my room, Stan snoring by my side, she was right there as I rose from the deepest part of sleep to that shallow state where it is only your dreams that let you know you are not awake.

She was there, because the newly dead are always there, watching on, before they fade, or go, or whatever the secret of that mystery is.

I can't explain it, because I hold out no great hope for any kind of afterlife. But I know with total certainty that the recently dead do not leave us immediately. They stay close by, held by the unimaginable sadness of leaving, and the human bonds that were made in this world.

Edie Wren watched me as I healed from that hard night, as I slept the summer day away in the bedroom we had briefly shared. And she was so real, so tangible, so undeniably present but just out of reach, and my throat choked with the knowledge that she would be just out of reach forever. But the newly dead are always with us. And I longed to wake and look and find her there, but of course I was also scared to open my eyes and see her there, those green eyes measuring what we had lost.

Do not be afraid, she seemed to whisper, and the sun moved across the sky while I was sleeping.

This is not a spirit. And this is not a ghost. This is nothing for you to fear.

Sleep now, sleep now, sleep now.

This is an echo of love.

11

The alarm went off at three in the afternoon.

Everything hurt. My eyes, my ribs, the shrapnel in my legs.

Stan sighed, stretched, yawned, scratched and began to clean his paws. He padded after me as I went into the great open area of our loft and it was filled with a heavenly light.

But I was alone. I lived with that thought for a while.

Then Stan and I went to pick up Scout from school.

I had feared that Scout would resent me for denying her Sicily. But when the going-home bell rang, she raced to my arms, then knelt to greet her dog, his tail going like a mad windscreen wiper, ecstatic with love for her.

Perhaps one day she would bear a grudge, I thought. One day – how many years from now? – she would decide that her father didn't know much, and certainly didn't know best, and quite possibly knew nothing at all.

But not today.

Today she was eight years old, and Scout put her hand in mine.

'Do you want to read your book?'

As Scout settled down for the night, *The Rough Guide to Italy* sat on her bedside table like an invitation to another life. She raised her chin, indicating the book in my hands.

What you got?

'It's a poem about a dog,' I offered. 'By one of your old favourites – anonymous.'

'Yes,' she said, poker-faced. 'Anonymous has written some good stuff.'

And then we grinned.

Stan hopped on to the bed and settled down right at the bottom, as if nobody would even notice him if he kept very still.

Scout closed her eyes and I thought she was ready for sleep. But then I saw how tightly her eyes were squeezed shut. And then I heard the bells.

We lived with the bells of St Paul's Cathedral. They were a constant backdrop to our life, and like a family living under a flight path to the airport, we didn't even notice them. Until now.

'Scout?'

'The bells,' she said. 'Mia said that if you make a wish when you hear the bells, then it has to come true.'

'And what do you wish for?' I said, although I already knew.

She wished for what all the children of all the divorced husbands and wives wish for, at least the very young children, the ones who have not been around long enough to understand how easy it is for a family to fall apart and never, never be put back together again.

She opened her brown eyes and smiled.

'I wished that things would be the way they were before,' she said, very softly, as if wishes should be spoken of in hushed tones.

'But, angel, you understand that's not going to happen, don't you?'

I tried to make my voice as soft as hers, but of course it was impossible, and something in my face wiped away her smile.

'Yes, I know,' she said.

'Sometimes we want things to be the way they were before and it's just not possible,' I said, aware of how pathetically trite this must sound to an eight-year-old who still missed the family that she spent the first four years of her life with, the family that was slipping even from her memory now.

'I know,' she repeated, her voice flat in this rotten world where wishes don't come true even if you shut your eyes when you hear the sound of the bells.

I sat down on the side of the bed and I began to read.

'Yes, I went to see the bow-wows and I looked at every
  one,
Proud dogs of each breed and strain that's underneath the
  sun.
But not one could compare with — you may hear it with
  surprise —
A little yellow dog I know that never took a prize.'

Our dog was already snoring.
  Scout closed her eyes, her lids suddenly heavy.

'Suppose he wasn't trained to hunt and never killed a rat,
And isn't much on tricks or looks or birth — well what of
  that?
That might be said of lots of folks whom men call great
  and wise,
As well as of that yellow dog that never took a prize.'

'Hmm,' said Scout thoughtfully, leaning back into the
pillow and slipping into sleep. I finished our poem.

'It isn't what a dog can do — or what a dog may be.
That hits a man — it's simply this:
Does he believe in me?'

I kissed her on top of the head and crept from the room,
scooping up the sleeping Stan and taking him with me.

125

Mrs Murphy was watching the news. They had finally put it all together and Jessica Lyle's face filled the screen.

'Police sources say that the kidnapping of Jessica Lyle was a case of mistaken identity and the abductors meant to take an associate of this *man.'*

And then there was Harry Flowers.

Not a mugshot, for Harry Flowers had never been arrested for a thing in his life.

He was smiling at the camera, Charlotte Flowers by his side, towering above him in her heels, each of them holding a champagne flute for the camera. It looked like some charity bash, or possibly Royal Ascot. Charlotte Flowers looked like a woman who would feel at home at both.

'Harold Flowers – alleged former gangland figure.'

'Where is the poor girl's baby?' Mrs Murphy said.

'With its grandparents,' I said.

'The baby was with her when she was taken?'

'Yes,' I said. 'But the baby's fine. Baby Michael is fine.'

She hesitated.

She did not like to ask me about my work. But the smiling face of Jessica Lyle was on the news.

'And do you think you are going to find her?'

'Yes,' I said. I hesitated. 'If we find her soon.'

We left it at that.

The summer night crept in.

I checked that Scout was sleeping.

And then I went to work.

I sat outside the Western World watching the dancers arrive.

Some of them walked briskly through the streets in trainers, others tottered on their massive spike heels. Bouncers lifted a red velvet rope to let them pass, a surprisingly delicate gesture for such large men.

There was no sign of Snezia Jones.

Whitestone and Adams turned into the street in an unmarked squad car. They stopped further down the road, the parking spaces scarce in that corner of Covent Garden. Whitestone slipped into the passenger seat of the BMW X5 beside me and Adams got in the back.

'The Mahones didn't take Jessica Lyle,' Whitestone said. She took off her glasses, breathed on the lenses and began to polish them. 'The search team are still at the seaside taking apart Janet Mahone's caravan. We have already been all over the site, but we have no expectation of finding any traces of Jessica there, dead or alive. The Mahones were lifetime losers, Max. They saw the opportunity to even the score with Harry Flowers. And they tried to take it.'

She put on her glasses and nodded at Adams.

'The Mahones have a history of violence,' Joy said. 'Violence inflicted and violence endured. Everything fell apart for their family after that Sunday lunch when Flowers turned up with his petrol can. Both parents became full-blown alcoholics. The kids were all taken into care. Two of them, Peter's siblings, committed suicide. There's just the one survivor now, Liam Mahone, the baby of the family. But Liam Mahone is in Broadmoor.'

Broadmoor Hospital is a high-security psychiatric hospital in Berkshire. It holds just over two hundred men diagnosed with severe mental disorders who either committed serious crimes or who have been declared unfit to stand trial for serious crimes. Back in the nineteenth century, a less caring age, it was known as the Broadmoor Criminal Lunatic Asylum.

'What did Liam Mahone do to get a room in Broadmoor?' I said.

'Nothing he has ever been convicted for,' Joy said. 'He was arrested for killing a man in a bar fight but was diagnosed with paranoid schizophrenia before he came to trial.'

'What did the guy he killed do to him?'

'Apparently he just looked at him.' She paused. 'Liam Mahone would have been four years old when Flowers and his goon came knocking with their petrol can.'

'Can we talk to Liam?'

'No,' Joy said. 'He's catatonic.'

'What do we know about his brother, Peter Mahone?'

'Peter Mahone had a job on the London Underground but lost it for head-butting an unhappy commuter who was even more unhappy after Peter Mahone head-butted him. Peter inherited his drink problem from his parents. Janet Mahone has been away – she did two years in Holloway for assault after attacking a woman at the school gates. Beat her up quite badly before bystanders could get her off.' Adams' dark eyes glistened. 'The woman she attacked was Charlotte Flowers.'

Harry's wife.

I saw her again at the window, her face twisted with rage at the discovery of her husband's mistress, Harry's beloved stuff flying through the air.

'I met Charlotte Flowers earlier today,' I said. 'Just before she found out about Snezia Jones. Some journalist shared the information.'

'The wife is always the last to know,' Whitestone said. 'What does Harry say about Snezia? Are they going to build a love nest? Was that the plan?'

'Unlikely. He told me he loves her the way he loves his car. Which I guess means that he finds a new model every few years.'

'Who said romance is dead?' Whitestone said.

More dancers were starting to arrive.

And finally, Snezia Jones was among them.

She was flanked by the two minders.

Derek Bumpus and Ruben Shavers.

'Flowers must be quite keen on her if he has his body-guards watching her back,' I said. 'But I still find it strange that she has never stopped working here. All through the affair, she was still at the Western World.'

'Maybe Harry is not the jealous kind,' Whitestone said. 'Or maybe he thought it kept her occupied. That's the married man's big problem when he has a mistress. Most nights, he's not there. Most nights, he's with his family.' A rueful smile. 'That was the problem for my husband and his mistress. That's why he ended up marrying her.'

We watched the dancers arriving in silence.

'Maybe someone just took her,' Joy said. 'Jessica Lyle. Maybe some men saw her and they wanted her and so they just took her. The motive wasn't that they thought they were taking Flowers' mistress. The motive was that they saw a woman they wanted.'

I knew it could happen. Men could see a woman and take her. And I knew too that the missing are all different. Some run away and some are taken away, and never stop longing for their home. Some are found and some come home and some are never seen again and some don't want to be found or seen again. Some are glimpsed, years later, on a passing train or a crowded street and some are seen only in dreams. Some die in a ditch or a drain or a skip or are found stuffed into three separate suitcases.

And some suffer a fate far worse than death.

And it was usually the ones who looked like Jessica Lyle.

'Or Harry Flowers did it himself,' Whitestone said, as if she was reflecting on my thoughts. 'But his heavy mob got the wrong girl.'

'You think Harry tried to kidnap his own mistress?' I said.

'I think it's as likely as a couple of random passing predators,' she said. 'Maybe he got tired of her. Maybe she was being a little too demanding and he wanted her off the payroll. Sometimes – often – a mistress can overplay her hand. Ask for too much, too soon.' She exhaled, the kind of sigh you let go at the end of a long day, and I smelled the acrid tang of vodka. 'Maybe she was threatening to go to Harry's wife with all the gory details. They do that, you know. Sometimes they just threaten it and sometimes they actually do it. But if you're a mistress, that's always the nuclear option.'

On the neon hoardings across the way the smiling faces of the women advertising the Western World lit up the dingy street.

I opened the car door. 'What do you want in there?' I said.

'I want a motive for Harry Flowers to have planned this abduction,' Whitestone said. 'Find out if the sex had worn off.'

Snezia danced.

She wrapped her long limbs around the fireman's pole in the centre of the podium and slid slowly down it. And she did it in heels, a string bikini and upside down. I had not seen her in her work clothes before and for the first time I understood why Harry Flowers had gone to all that trouble.

The minders, Shavers and Bumpus, sat at the far end of the bar, watching me at my ringside table. Now that I had a chance to observe them, it was obvious they were not young men. Shavers, the former boxer, still looked as though he spent more hours in the gym than he did in places like this, but his hair was flecked with grey and his face was weathered by the years.

Bumpus, the child prodigy of nightclub bouncers, was almost spectacularly out of shape, with a beer gut proudly hanging over his elastic-waisted tracksuit bottoms like a prize marrow.

They occasionally eyed Snezia with a cool professional detachment, no trace of lust in their eyes.

Snezia danced with a pink floaty shawl thrown over her shoulders, an item of clothing so insubstantial that it was hardly there at all, but she wrapped it around her neck as she came to join me at my table, as if protecting herself from the air conditioning.

'You have to buy me a drink,' she said.

A waitress materialised. She wore a tailored dinner jacket with a ruffled white shirt and bow-tie but nothing below the waist apart from high-denier black tights and precarious shoes. It was as though Hugh Hefner had never died. I let Snezia do the ordering and then I nodded at Bumpus and Shavers.

'What are the goon squad doing here?' I said.

'In case they come again,' she said, rubbing the palms of her hands on her thighs. 'The men who took Jessica.'

Her hands were shaking.

Behind the polished smile, I saw she was terrified.

It could have been her in that car. It should have been her.

'What does Harry tell you about what happened?' I said. 'What does he say about that night?'

'We haven't spoken for a while,' she said. 'It's difficult for him. Someone tried to hurt him last night. Some people who pretended they had Jess.'

'Yes, I heard about that,' I said. 'But Harry's got a lot of enemies. And what about you? You got any enemies, Snezia? Anyone hassling you? A jealous ex-boyfriend?'

I indicated the Western World. The near-naked women wrapping their young flesh around those fireman poles and the men who were not as young or as firm and who sipped their drinks without taking their eyes from the women.

'You ever get any customers in here who can't take no for an answer, Snezia?'

133

'Drunks who think money can buy anything. The bouncers can take care of them.'

'Never tempted? You must have got a bit lonely when Flowers was out in the suburbs playing happy families.'

'I've been true to Harry,' she said.

Flowers had made their relationship sound like a cold commercial transaction.

But Snezia made it sound more like a love story.

'What was the long-term plan?' I said. 'If none of this had happened with Jessica. What was going to happen next with Harry? Did he tell you he was going to leave his wife? What were you hoping for, Snezia? And what were you expecting?'

She was silent while the waitress brought a bottle of something sparkly and two glasses.

'There was no long-term plan,' she said, brushing away an invisible tear, as if to be polite. 'I knew it was coming to an end. I knew it could never be. Not forever. Not with a married man. I was already thinking about moving out of the apartment.'

Beyond what seemed like a genuine sadness, there was a clear-eyed pragmatism about her as she took a sip of her Prosecco.

'Harry is not a young man,' she said. 'And an older man – he needs stimulation. The kind of stimulation that calls for variety. Someone once said – *why would a man go out for hamburger when he has steak at home?* And that's easy – because a man gets tired of the same diet. Harry was seeing me less and less. When he came to the flat, he never stayed the night. Not for months. And when he was there, he seemed keen to get away. We were heading towards a conscious uncoupling – you know, like Gwyneth Paltrow and Chris Martin.' She paused. 'I am glad you are looking for Jess,' she said. 'Because I know that not everyone is so lucky. There was a girl here – Minky – and she just stopped coming to work.'

'Missing?'

'Gone. Is that the same as missing?'

'When was the last time you saw Minky?'

'Not so long ago. I don't know. Maybe around the time that Jess was taken? It must have been around then.'

'And was Minky's disappearance ever reported?'

'I think it was reported. It must have been. I know some policemen came to ask questions. But just once. They were more interested in the girls. And I am sure she is fine. Gone home to Prague, or maybe it was Budapest. Or Belgrade. No – Riga.'

'Minky was Latvian?'

'Or maybe she found a rich man,' Snezia said, brightening at the prospect. 'She was a very popular girl. Big Del liked her. They went out.'

I glanced down the bar at Derek Bumpus. He was staring up at a dancer with a faint smirk on his fleshy face.

'Lots of men liked Minky. I am sure she found someone who would take care of her. A sponsor. But Minky disappeared too. And my point is – nobody is looking very hard for her, are they? It doesn't seem fair.'

'You're right,' I said. 'It's not fair. Sometimes we turn the world upside down to find the missing. And sometimes we don't try as hard as we should.'

Then the waitress was back, lifting her head towards the empty podium.

Snezia nodded.

'I must dance,' she said, bolting down the rest of her glass.

The goon squad were still watching me. I remembered that an unidentified male had accompanied Harry Flowers to that Sunday lunch at the Mahones all those years ago. And I wondered if it was one of them. They would have had to have been very young.

And as I was thinking about how old Ruben Shavers and Derek Bumpus would have been on the day of that petrol-soaked Sunday lunch, the hen party arrived. There were around a dozen women, all dressed in a parody of school uniform, white shorts and stripy ties and skirts hitched up. One of them, drunker than the rest, carried an inflatable pink phallus, a giant penis balloon, that she waved above her head as if it was their battle flag.

And I saw it was Meadow Flowers.

The hen party took their places at the bar, half of them seated and the other half ordering drinks and dancing to the music. It was no coincidence that they had walked into this bar. They were here for Snezia.

Meadow Flowers began slapping at the dancer with her inflatable penis. Light and jokey at first, almost an invitation to play.

And then harder, nastier, with real spite. Snezia backed away, twirled to the far side of her fireman's pole.

And kept dancing.

The hen party roared with laughter. Then bouncers were suddenly there, ushering the women dressed as schoolgirls away from the stage and back to one of the stand-alone tables.

I watched as they began throwing peanuts at Snezia, cheering when one of them bounced off her butt. I saw Bumpus and Shavers in heated discussion, unsure where their loyalties lay between their master's mistress and their master's daughter. And then the chanting began, low at first but growing louder.

'*Whore … whore … whore …*'

Snezia snatched up a wine glass from the bar and hurled it at them. It shattered at their feet and Meadow Flowers flew at her, tears of rage streaming down her face. She did not seem drunk now.

'You lousy rotten hooker!' she screamed.

'I'm an erotic dancer, you spoilt little rich bitch!' Snezia screamed back.

There were men between them, the Western World bouncers, Shavers and Bumpus, and they all wore the look of men who knew that they were the only thing that stood between the two women and real emergency-ward violence.

'You think they just *dance* at this club?' Meadow Flowers shouted at nobody in particular. 'He cheats on my mother with some whore who will bang anyone for a few quid and a bucket of chicken nuggets! They all do in here!'

And I saw that she meant it. She was not accusing Snezia of having an affair with her father.

It was more than that.

The bouncers were leading Snezia away, Bumpus and Shavers trailing behind them, unsure how to play it as Meadow Flowers kept shouting.

'This slag is all about the money! A hooker. A whore. A prostitute. That's what she *was* – that's what she *is* – that's what my dad brought into our home! Into his marriage! Into our lives!'

I looked at Snezia. She looked like she was done for the night. She looked as though she might be done for-ever. She picked up her pink silk shawl and wrapped it around her shoulders.

'I know all about her!' Meadow was explaining to one of the bouncers, tears of rage and grief streaming down her face. 'She has caused so much suffering. To me. To my mother.'

The hen party were chanting louder now.

'*Whore! Whore! Whore!*'

They turned off the music and I heard the hiss of escaped air. In the ruckus with the bouncers, the giant inflatable phallus had sprung a leak and it began to crumple, the big pink plastic prick folding in on itself.

Snezia was leaving the stage with as much dignity as she could muster. In the strange silence of a club with no music, someone threw a bottle at her. It missed, shattering against the fireman's pole, leaving a splash of beer on one of her long legs that looked somehow obscene.

Snezia held her head high and took her time, but she avoided all eye contact and under the lights her pale face was burning with something that might have been shame, as if she had suddenly realised that she was almost naked, and the entire world was looking at her.

Joy Adams was curled up and sleeping on the back seat of the BMW but Pat Whitestone was wide awake and clear-eyed, watching me as I crossed from the Western World to the car.

'You were right,' I said. 'Harry Flowers did have a motive to want his mistress gone. The sex had worn off.'

12

One hour before dawn we went in hard.

Four vehicles. The lead was a white transit van with *Avant Gardens — let us be your green fingers* emblazoned on the side in fading green letters, in reality a Tactical Support Unit beefed up with reinforced steel beams and shatterproof glass.

The thing was a tank and it went through the big electric gates of Harry Flowers' mansion as if they were made of wet cardboard.

I followed in the BMW X5, Whitestone beside me and Adams in the back, all of us operating on a few hours of snatched sleep, all of us wide-eyed with adrenaline, bumping over the smashed gates as the Specialist Firearms Officers in their grey body armour began emerging from the back of the *Avant Gardens* van and heading towards the front door, their Sig Sauer MCX assault rifles swinging to their shoulders. Behind me came two big marked vans loaded with uniformed officers in riot gear.

The little gentle skinhead driver – Mo – was already up and on the driveway and cleaning the Bentley. He paused in mid-polish, staring at us in wonder. There was another car parked in front of the house. A Range Rover with Ruben Shavers at the wheel and Derek Bumpus in the passenger seat. They were both sleeping. It must have been a late night at the Western World, I thought.

The shots lined up either side of the front door, like a guard of honour, their assault rifles swinging back to the 45-degree angle they liked to adopt when they were waiting for something to happen, which was most of the time. One of the uniforms walked purposefully forward carrying a heavily scarred bright red battering ram that weighs 16 kilos and is variously known as the bosher, the big red key and the Nigel.

The Flowers' front door was reinforced with a London Bar, a solid steel bar designed to fit over the door frame and lock, which would have prevented an army of intruders from kicking it down, but the big red key popped it on the first try.

A burglar alarm began to ring.

The uniformed officer stepped aside with a flourish and the shots poured inside, their assault rifles coming back to their shoulders, screaming a warning to embolden themselves and subdue whatever was waiting.

Harry Flowers came down the stairs in his pyjamas.

In each hand he carried a thin dark stick.

I recognised them as the fighting sticks of Eskrima, the Filipino martial art, 28 inches long, made of hardwood that could crack a skull open without the user breaking sweat. And if the user could claim a legitimate interest in the noble fighting art of Eskrima, then no judge in the land would consider them offensive weapons. It was a clever thing to have by your bedside to confront a trespasser and Harry Flowers was reluctant to put them down.

'*Drop the weapon!*'

'*Do it now!*'

'*Show us your hands!*'

There were ten assault rifles aimed at his chest. He smiled at Whitestone as if he had been expecting her and let the Eskrima sticks drop when he reached the bottom of the stairs. She stepped forward and turned him around, marching him to the nearest wall. She was clear-eyed in the early morning and I saw the pattern emerging. The drinking took over as the day wore on. At dawn my boss was her old self, supremely confident, vastly experienced and, despite her modest frame and weak eyesight, quite capable of taking physical control of any man alive.

'Harry Flowers, I am arresting you on suspicion of the Kidnap and False Imprisonment of Jessica Lyle.' Whitestone banged his head against the wall, as if for punctuation. 'You do not have to say anything.' She banged his head again, a bit harder this time, and Flowers gasped with shock and pain. 'But it may harm your defence if you do not mention when questioned something which you later rely on in court.'

Bang.

'Anything you do say may be given in evidence.' She spun him around. A thin dribble of blood ran down his large forehead. 'Let's go.'

The goon squad were awake and rubbing the sleep from their eyes when we went outside.

Ruben Shavers took one look at our mob and wisely wanted none of it. But that old-school machismo learned bouncing on the doors obliged Big Del Bumpus to show some dissent. He did not have it in him to let us just walk away. He made a move towards Whitestone and I was on him, kicking his legs from beneath him and getting him face down in all that expensive gravel.

He half-turned his head to talk to me.

'All this fuss for some dumb slut who's probably already dead,' he said.

'That's not very nice,' I said.

'Stupid slag,' he said. 'Little whore.'

I jerked the wrist of his right hand towards me as I pushed the elbow away from me as hard as I could. There was one sharp crack, and then another, so close together that the double crack almost sounded like one sound. But there are two long bones in the lower arm, the radius and the ulna, and I had broken both of them.

He screamed. And he kept on screaming.

I got to my feet and left him down there.

'If you're going to call a woman names,' I said, 'best not do it when I've got you in an arm lock.'

And now the house was wide awake.

In the smashed front doorway, Junior appeared, still in his clothes from the night before, and then his sister Meadow, in her pyjamas, pushing past her brother and running out of the house, the tears rolling down her face as Joy Adams gently guided Flowers into the back seat of the BMW.

'Daddy! Daddy! Daddy!' Meadow Flowers cried, tears streaming, but Harry Flowers had already slipped into the zone, the stone-faced, blank-eyed passivity of a man who knew the form. He was conserving his energy and, whatever his thoughts, he was keeping them to himself.

And then his wife was at exactly the same window where I had seen her throw away his things.

Charlotte Flowers leaned from the window, wearing some floaty, gossamer-thin nightdress, like a princess in a fairy story who had never been rescued as promised.

She shook her head.

And then, almost delicately, she spat.

That old cop hatred, I thought. Some of these people carry it around for a lifetime.

It was only when we were on the road back to the city that I realised she had been spitting at her husband.

One hour later, Harry Flowers sat in an interview room of West End Central with the Zen-like calm of the career criminal.

'I'll tell you what I think,' Whitestone said. 'It had gone smooth with Snezia in the past. The bit on the side you had set up in the apartment. The basic pleasure model on the payroll. It worked out well for both of you. You got exclusive access to a beautiful young woman. Snezia got free accommodation in a great postcode – and the benefit of your charming personality, Harry. And you'd got away with it before. How many times, Harry? How many women on the side over the years? But this time it went wrong. Snezia was going to tell your wife. Or she wanted to get married. One or the other. Maybe both. Or you got bored but she wanted an extension of the lease. And then she became quite strident about it.' Whitestone snapped her fingers. 'Oh. Or was she pregnant? Is *that* what happened? She wanted to keep the baby and you were not so keen?' She exhaled. 'It all comes down to the same thing, doesn't it?'

He shrugged. 'Does it?'

Whitestone nodded.

'*She wanted more than you were willing to give.* And you decided to remove the problem. It's not such a big step.

Not for the man who poured petrol over the Mahone family. How many children were at that table, Harry?'

His lawyer leaned forward. 'No charges were ever—'

Harry Flowers silenced him with a look.

'One flaw in your theory?' Flowers said. 'The bored-sponsor theory?'

'I'm all ears,' Whitestone said.

'Snezia was not kidnapped, was she?' he said.

'Because villains are stupid,' Whitestone said. 'Because professional criminals all have an IQ lower than their shoe size. If they weren't stupid, they would get a real job. They saw the car, checked the reg, and they thought they had the right woman. They took Jessica Lyle when they were meant to take Snezia Jones. And you, Harry, were the man who sent them.'

'And I'll tell you what I think,' Flowers said. 'You're drowning, DCI Whitestone. You're floundering around, coming up with nothing, and you need an arrest. Because all of this is very big news thanks to that old cop with the very big mouth.' He meant Jessica Lyle's father. He meant Frank Lyle.

Then Flowers turned to look at me and for the first time he let some anger tighten his mouth.

'*And you are wasting time when you could be looking for that missing girl,*' he said.

'Sex wear off, did it, Harry?' Whitestone said. 'Need a bit of extra stimulation at your age?'

The lawyer leaned forward again. 'Really, you don't have to—'

'Shut up,' Harry said, not even looking at him. 'The truth is that Snezia is a sweet girl. But she was acting like she owned the place.'

'She moved in a flatmate,' Whitestone said. 'Jessica Lyle. For all the nights when you were with the wife out in Essex. Another dancer.'

'Two different kinds of dancer,' he said. 'But yes – two dancers.'

'You've owned that apartment up on Eden Hill Park for twenty years, Harry,' I said. 'Snezia has been there for less than three. So is that your official love nest?'

'It's the best investment in the world,' he said.

'Strippers?'

'London property.'

'Do you have the next girl lined up and ready to install?'

He shook his head. 'No, because that flat is going to be my wedding present to my daughter Meadow and her young man. Her new husband. Don't you know how hard it is for a young couple to find a decent place in London these days? So, yes, I wanted Snezia out – but it's crazy to suggest that I wanted her hurt.' He folded his thick arms across his chest. 'And I had nothing to do with the kidnapping. You want my advice? Look at everybody who cooks.' He wasn't talking about Jamie

147

Oliver. 'Look at every little home brewer in the city,' he said. 'Look at everyone who makes illegal substances in their backroom. They all want my scalp. Even though that all ended for me years ago. Young gunslingers like to take out an old gunslinger. It looks good on the CV.'

'How did Snezia feel about moving out?' I said.

'She knew she would be well reimbursed. Truth is, a lot of my special friends are glad when it ends. They want to meet a man they can have a life with. It's only natural.'

'Snezia was really that understanding?'

He nodded.

'Snezia understands,' he said. 'Everything ends.'

We held him for twenty-four hours.

With a charge as serious as Kidnap and False Impris-onment, Whitestone could have applied to hold him for thirty-six or ninety-six hours without charging him. But by the following morning the certainty and strength seemed to have gone out of her. She seemed tired and preoccupied.

'Let him go,' she told me in MIR-1.

I went down to the basement and signed Harry Flow-ers out with the Custody Sergeant.

'She really thinks I had something to do with it,' he said. '*Everything* to do with it. Do you all think that?'

'No,' I said.

I walked him to the lift.

'My young colleague, TDC Adams, reckons it was random. That Jessica was taken and is being held against her will somewhere unknown.'

A cloud passed across his face.

'Why?' he said.

'Because that's what some men like,' I said. 'And they are willing to pay for it.'

The lift came and we stepped inside. I hit the button for the ground floor.

'What about you?' he said. 'What's your theory, Detective Wolfe?'

'I think someone hates you, Harry. I think they hate you more than you know. I don't know if it is someone from the old days of dealing MDMA in Ibiza clubs, or if the beef is more recent. But I think it is someone who lies awake at night thinking about how much harm they would love to do to you. And they got the wrong woman because – like my boss told you – villains are stupid.'

It was still early and the Bentley was parked right outside 27 Savile Row, the engine idling, Mo at the wheel.

He hurried out to open the door for his boss.

I had been expecting the goon squad to show their faces, but perhaps they had disgraced themselves during the arrest. Or maybe Big Del was still getting his broken arm put in plaster.

But Junior was there.

Harry Flowers smiled with genuine pleasure and his son grinned bashfully. Harry began walking towards his Bentley.

I felt I saw him breathe out.

The good life was calling him home.

An hour on the soft leather seats of the Bentley bonding with his son, as the city slowly slipped away behind tinted windows, then safe and sound in his big suburban mansion, somehow making it all up with his poised, privately educated wife.

A free man.

And then Frank Lyle stepped around the corner with a hammer in his hand.

13

The son froze.

At the sight of the big man coming towards his father with a hammer in his hand, Junior Flowers was paralysed, overwhelmed by an anaesthetising combination of shock, fear and inexperience.

All those hours spent pumping the free weights in Essex gyms. All the nights spent swaggering around the pubs, bars and clubs between Bond Street and Basildon. All those moments spent punching and kicking things that would never hit him back.

And he could not react.

The fight or flight reaction is beyond rational thought, I realised, as I felt myself move. You are all at once fighting for your life or you are suddenly running for your life without having the time to weigh the pros and cons of your action.

You fight or you run.

The only other option is what was happening to Junior Flowers. He stood there with his mouth half-open as

Frank Lyle brushed past him and struck Harry Flowers in the face with the hammer.

Harry went down and curled up in the foetus position, covering his face and his balls, like a man who knew how to take a good hiding.

I jumped off the steps outside West End Central and was on my way to the man on the ground and the man with the hammer. Then Frank Lyle raised the hammer again and my heart lurched because I saw that the plan was not to punish Harry Flowers but to kill him, to beat his brains out right there on the Mayfair pavement, to mete out punishment for bringing his daughter into another world.

I was shouting a warning, a threat, a war cry to buck myself up as Junior still stood there, shivering with shock at the eruption of sudden, unfettered violence.

Then suddenly Mo the driver was there before me, screaming something I didn't quite catch and bravely attempting to wrap his thin arms around the old cop. Frank Lyle shook him off easily, sending him flying with little more than an angry shrug.

Junior's chin trembled and he began to cry as the hammer came down again on his father's flesh and bone.

Harry Flowers grunted with the pain and Frank Lyle was screaming, screaming, screaming as he raised the hammer for the third time, for the killer blow.

But by then I was on him.

He was the bigger and stronger man and I would not have fancied my chances against him twenty years ago. But he was older now and rusty and made no attempt to defend himself when he saw me coming and so I hit him at the run, the full weight of my body slamming into him, my shoulder connecting with his chest, banging him backwards, the open door of the Bentley the only thing that kept him on his feet.

He had dropped the hammer.

Mo gently picked it up and stared at it, as if it was someone's lost glove and should be returned to its rightful owner as soon as possible.

And the fight was all out of Frank Lyle as I bent his right arm, his hammer arm, halfway up his spine and sank my right knee into the back of his legs, folding them up like a closed umbrella and slowly sinking him to the ground.

Uniformed cops were coming out of West End Central. One of them helped Harry Flowers to his feet and I saw that his mouth was bloody mush and he had a lump on his forehead the size of a small Easter egg. As I watched, it grew to a medium-sized Easter egg.

Flowers spat out half a broken tooth and pushed off the cop who had helped him up, staring at Frank Lyle where I had him pinned to the pavement.

'I'm sorry,' Flowers said, his voice hoarse. 'But I never hurt your daughter.'

'I'll … kill …' Lyle said, but the words stuck in his throat.

Then Lyle turned his face to look at me and I saw his eyes were shining with tears, the bitter tears that flow when it all comes at once and overwhelms you – anger and loss and a grief that rips out your heart.

'What would *you* do?' he said, quietly enough for only me to hear. 'If it was your girl – and someone did this – what would *you* do?'

'Stop talking,' I said.

And we stared at each other and we said nothing more.

Because we both knew what I would do.

Harry Flowers declined to press charges.

So Frank Lyle did not go to the holding cells. Instead, I drove him home.

He sat in silence in the passenger seat of the BMW X5, gingerly touching his face where it had been pressed into the pavement and covering his mouth politely while he coughed. That old smoker's cough that sounds as though it comes from the bottom of the lungs.

'Who does it help?' I said, because I had to say something. 'If you kill Harry Flowers, or put him in a hospital bed, does that bring back your daughter? Does it help your wife or your grandson? And do you know what they do to ex-cops in jail, Frank?'

'Probably better than you,' he said, and began coughing, louder now, less controlled.

I shook my head and let the old man cough in peace.

As his home came in sight, a small white house in an Islington terrace, he took out a crumpled tissue and hawked up a chunk of thick blood.

I was surprised at the blood.

Because I knew I had not hit him that hard.

His wife heard the key in the door.

Jennifer Lyle came down the corridor with baby Michael in her arms.

I remembered Scout at that age. I remembered exactly that short neat haircut, carefully brushed to one side for both boys and girls, because they are so new that their hair has not had time to grow. And very soon, I thought, they are no longer babies but not quite toddlers. Six months is a great age. Frank Lyle gently touched his grandson but did not look at his wife.

'What happened, Frank? Your face.'

She was staring at the raw mark high up on one cheekbone where I had pushed his face into the street.

'Nothing, Jen,' he said, walking past her. 'Man-bags at ten paces. Don't make a fuss. God, woman!'

He went into the small back garden. There were high fences on both sides, the garden of a man who liked his privacy, or disliked his neighbours. There was an old,

weather-worn Wendy house out there. I had always
wanted one of those for Scout. I guess it's too late now.
Yes, eight is too late for a Wendy house. Frank Lyle sat
down on the worn wooden porch of the Wendy house
and pulled out a packet of cigarettes.

There was a boy in the garden, a big boy with wild,
unkempt black hair that looked like it had never met a
comb, and he was booting a plastic football up against
the side of the Wendy house. He kept kicking it as Frank
Lyle sucked hungrily on his cigarette. Man and boy did
not speak to each other, but the boy was watching him
as he kicked that football, he never took his eyes off
Frank, and the ball eventually careered off into a bed of
roses.

Expertly cradling her grandson in one arm, Jennifer
Lyle put her head around the door to the garden.

'Tommy?' she called. 'Watch the roses with that ball,
darling.'

The boy turned to look at her and I saw he was not
a boy at all, but a man in his twenties, maybe older. He
carried himself with the loose-limbed gait of a kid but
his face was stubbled with the beginnings of a dark
beard, as untouched by grooming as his hair.

'That's Tommy,' Jennifer Lyle told me, closing the
door again. 'Our son.'

Tommy stared back at the house with blank, uncom-
prehending eyes. Then he returned to his game, watching

his father smoke, the old man making no acknowledgement that he was there.

'Tommy is special,' Jennifer Lyle explained. 'They've been doing tests on him all his life, but they still can't tell us what's wrong. He has difficulty learning. Retaining information.' She looked from her son to me. 'Some wayward chromosome in some unlucky cell.'

'That sounds like Down's syndrome,' I said. 'But Tommy doesn't have Down's syndrome.'

'No,' she said. 'And do you know what those doctors would have told us in the past? They would have said – your son is simple. And we would have all proceeded from that point. But they can't say that any more. So we subject Tommy to all these tests that will never change anything and can't even explain anything.'

I watched the father and son standing metres apart in the back garden.

The father smoking his cigarette, the son kicking his plastic football against the Wendy house. They could have been in different countries.

'Is my husband in trouble?' Jennifer Lyle asked me.

'He went for Harry Flowers outside West End Central. With a hammer. Flowers is not pressing charges. I don't know how your husband knew he was up there.'

She stared at her husband.

'Frank still has a lot of friends in the job. Someone must have called him and told him you were holding

Harry Flowers. They would have thought they were doing him a favour.'

'Your husband's friends are not doing him any favours by letting him loose on Flowers. If he does it again, we can't give him a pass.'

She watched her husband sitting on the porch of the Wendy house where their daughter had once played.

'Frank blames Flowers,' she said. 'Frank blames him for everything.'

'Mrs Lyle, I don't think Harry Flowers had anything to do with the abduction of Jessica.'

'Not for taking Jess. But for letting his world touch her world. For ruining her.'

We watched him smoking. Coughing. Smoking. Covering his mouth with the back of his hand and then examining the contents.

'And how sick is your husband?' I asked.

She gave me a look.

'I've seen lung cancer before,' I said.

'The doctors give him nine months,' she said, no emotion, a bitter truth that she had learned to accommodate. 'The tumour in his lungs has spread. When people ask him what kind of cancer he has, he says, *The end-of-the-road kind*. Stopping smoking now would not make a lot of difference. He just wants a chance to say goodbye to his daughter. He wants Jess home before he goes.'

'You seem a lot calmer than your husband.'

Michael was sleeping in her arms. She held him close.

'Because I know you will find my daughter,' she said.

I didn't know what to tell her. I didn't want to spin her a line. She knew as well as me that we had to find Jessica soon or we were never going to find her at all.

'We can't give up hope,' I said, and it was the best I could do. 'There's a possibility that it was a random abduction, that there was no connection to Harry Flowers.'

'Is that what you think?'

What I thought was that Harry Flowers had accumulated too many enemies. What I thought was that Jessica Lyle had got caught in the crossfire of some dirty war of half a lifetime ago.

'It doesn't matter what I think,' I said. 'Your husband was in the job for a long time. You know how it works. We get it wrong. We change our minds. We test new theories. We explore all possible leads. We wait for new leads. But we're going to find her. I'm going to find her.'

It felt like worse than cold comfort, the possibility that her daughter had been taken by random men for profit and pleasure.

It felt like no comfort at all. But Jennifer Lyle smiled at me.

'Thank you,' she said. 'For all your efforts. I have felt from that first night that we will see Jess again. I have never doubted it.'

Michael stirred in his grandmother's arms and she lovingly smoothed his nearly brand-new hair with the palm of her hand.

'I sometimes feel as if Jess is beside me but out of sight. In the next room, almost. Or as if she just passed through a door. As if she is gone, but not gone very far.' She smiled. 'I sound like a mad old woman, but I am not imagining it. Do you think I'm imagining it?'

I shook my head. 'No, ma'am.'

The newly dead do not go far, I thought, and pushed the thought away.

'Did you ever have that feeling, Detective?' she said. 'As if someone you love is very close but just out of reach?'

I nodded. 'Yes, ma'am.'

Then she smothered Michael's sleeping face with kisses and a love so fierce that it might rip out her heart.

And I knew that feeling too.

14

I was lying on the sofa with Stan and the new issue of *Your Dog,* feeling myself slipping into the sweet deep sleep of exhaustion.

And then the doorbell rang.

It was just after midnight. As always, our neighbourhood was coming awake. Lights were blazing at the meat market on the other side of Charterhouse Street and the dancing kids in their glad rags were heading for the clubs that line our street.

But my doorbell ringing at this hour meant trouble.

There was a little monitor that showed the street.

DCI Pat Whitestone was standing outside the front door.

I buzzed her up.

She stood in the doorway, running a hand across her mouth.

I saw she was shaking. Not just her hands. All of her. The smell of vodka was very strong.

'I didn't know where else to go,' she said. 'Sorry.'

'What happened?'

'I hit someone, Max.'

I thought she meant that she had lost her rag and given someone a beating. I thought of the yellow security guard at Eden Hill Park and how angry his cowardice had made her. I knew she had it in her to fly at anyone if her blood was up. I remembered her slapping Flowers in West End Central.

But it was too much to hope for.

This was worse, I saw as she came into the loft.

Much worse.

She had not hit someone with her fists.

'I was in my car,' she said. 'And he came out of nowhere.' Behind her glasses, her eyes were wide with shock. 'And I didn't see him, Max. Not until it was already over.'

Stan stirred himself at the happy sight of an unexpected visitor.

Whitestone sank to the sofa and absent-mindedly ran her hands through his fur.

I went to one of the huge loft windows and stared down at the street.

Her Prius was parked right outside and even from four floors up I could see that the headlamp on the driver's side had been caved in and was now a crumpled mess of broken glass and smashed metal.

The car was parked right under a streetlamp. That was not good.

'*What happened?*' I repeated.

She had her head in her hands.

I stood before her.

'Pat,' I said. 'Come on. What have you done?'

She looked up at me and nodded, composing herself, ready for a hot debrief.

'I was driving home,' she said. 'Round the back of King's Cross. The area that didn't get developed. Where it still feels like – I don't know – a wasteland. Like the surface of the moon.'

She looked up at me and bit her lip. There were tears in her eyes. I felt my heart falling. Whatever had happened tonight was something that she was going to live with for the rest of her life.

'A kid on a scooter came out of the petrol station down there,' she said. 'Do you know the one I mean?'

'Yes.'

'He came out really fast. No indicator. No warning. No chance to miss him. It sounds like I'm making excuses, doesn't it?'

'What did you do?'

'I kept going.'

A pause.

'Did you kill him?'

Silence.

'Did you kill him, Pat?'

'I don't know! There was that moment where I could have stopped and I let the moment pass. And then it was gone forever. And nobody saw. And nobody came. And the kid – he looked like one of those delivery kids, Max, on a scooter – he was just lying there. And his scooter was at the side of the road and it had L-plates on, Max. He was just some kid on a scooter who still had his bloody learner plates.'

I grabbed my keys and my coat and headed for the door.

'What are you going to do?' she said.

'Listen out for Scout,' I told her. 'She's not going to wake up. But listen out for her anyway.'

I left the Prius where it was under the streetlamp outside my home and I drove to King's Cross.

The area above the station that had somehow missed out on development covered a bleak, sprawling expanse of the city.

But there was only one petrol station up there.

I slowed the BMW as I drove past it. And I didn't see anyone in the street. I didn't see anyone at all. Whitestone was right. It looked like the surface of some uninhabited planet. Even the streetwalkers who used to patrol the area before the developers arrived further south in King's Cross had moved on.

I breathed out.

And this is what I hoped.

That someone had spotted the kid in the street and called for an ambulance. Or the kid himself had only been stunned and had got up by himself. And that, impossibly, everything had turned out all right.

At the end of the street I did a U-turn and came slowly back.

And that was when I saw the phones in the middle of the road. Dozens of them. Maybe hundreds, scattered across that empty street. It took me a while to realise that they had been stolen, snatched from the hands of the owner by a scooter that mounted the pavement and was driven away at speed by a rider who knew the police were not going to follow him because they would get into trouble if he got hurt during a pursuit. Which was ironic.

I pulled over and got out.

A trail of stolen smartphones led towards the lights of the garage.

And then I saw the scooter.

It was on its side in the darkness of the old automatic car wash. Nobody used the car wash any more. *People are cheaper*, some garage owner in some other place had once told me.

I walked towards the scooter.

And now I was not hoping.

Now I was praying.

Praying that someone had found him. Praying that he was at this moment being treated in some emergency ward.

But his body lay not far from his scooter, hidden in the darkness of that old car wash. I bent over him, doing deals with God.

But there were no deals to be done on that lonely road, and his lifeless eyes stared up at the orange glow of an empty sky.

The smell of coffee filled the loft.

Whitestone looked at my face and she knew what she had done.

She reached for her phone and started dialling 999.

'Pat,' I said.

'*Which service do you require?*'

I took the phone from her and turned it off.

'I have to tell them what I've done,' she said.

'Too late,' I said. 'You had to do that when it happened or you can't do it at all.'

She shook her head. 'No!'

'Listen to me – hitting him was not your fault.'

'I was on the Grey Goose! Of course it's my bloody fault! I'm in the wrong, Max. And I'm sick to the stomach with it.'

I smelled the vodka on her breath and in my home.

'Then maybe hitting him was your fault,' I said. 'I don't know. And nobody is ever going to know. Certainly leaving the scene is on you, Pat, and it will always be on you. But this is the cruel truth – *confession doesn't help anyone now.* Not that dead boy. Not you. Not your son. And not Jessica Lyle. If we lose you, then we are all finished. If you go down for this – and you *will* go down if you tell them what you did – then it's all over. I need you, Pat. And your boy Justin needs you. And Jessica Lyle needs you.'

She was not convinced.

Her every instinct was to tell the truth about what she had done. Her every instinct was to face the punishment for her crime. She was a decent woman. I did not tell her that the boy she had killed probably didn't have a decent bone in his body.

Because Pat Whitestone would not have cared.

'What if someone saw me? What if they ask you what I did, Max?'

'I'm never going to lie for you,' I said. 'But I will never rat you out.'

She shuddered with the horror of it.

'This is what is going to happen,' I said. 'You are going to go home to Justin. And in the morning, you are going to take your car into the garage and get it fixed. And you are never going to talk about this to anyone. Not even me.'

'But it's *wrong*,' she said. 'Isn't it just *wrong*, Max?'

'Not if we find Jessica Lyle,' I said.

15

Stan was on dog time.

I had never bought the notion that one dog year equals seven human years, but as we walked into the café and Stan looked around with the calm, peaceful air of the seasoned café goer, I saw the truth – my dog was already on the cusp of middle age. How quickly their lives go, I thought. How heartbreaking that a dog's life rushes by so fast. Stan looked around the café with his huge, melancholy eyes, as if contemplating the mystery of where the time goes. And then I realised he had merely caught a whiff of someone's cheese-and-ham toastie.

My ex-wife was waiting at a corner table. Anne looked good. Tall, lean and suntanned after ten days in the jewel of the Mediterranean. But something was subtly different. She was looking older, suddenly older, after the collapse of her second marriage. Divorce takes it out of you.

'I don't think it's allowed in here,' she said.

Stan and I exchanged a look.

It? Who's it? She's not really talking about me, is she?

'Are you kidding?' I said. 'All the kids who work in these places have got dogs back in Rome or Budapest or Warsaw or wherever it is they come from. London baristas love dogs.'

Stan took a few tentative steps backwards.

'What's it doing?' Anne frowned.

Stan only engaged his reverse gear for one reason. He was about to scratch his bottom. Stan's unshakeable belief was that by taking a few steps backwards, he put himself closer to his bottom, and so would find it far easier to scratch. I saw no need to explain this to my ex-wife. Scout and I thought it was an adorable habit, but to Anne it would have just seemed dumb.

'How's Fernando?' I said, changing the subject.

She sighed. How many sighs in our marriage? And how many more sighs since the divorce? A land of exasperated sighs. A planet of slowly exhaled irritation.

'You *know* it's Roberto, Max. Why do you insist on calling him Fernando? Is it a ham-fisted attempt at humour, or are you just being gratuitously rude?'

'I knew it was an Abba song.'

'Did Abba do a song called "Roberto"? I don't think so, Max.'

We considered each other. And I saw now that her sun-kissed skin – and she glowed in the cool twilight of that café – was not merely the result of ten days in Sicily. Anne's tan had been topped up closer to home.

'How's Scout?' she said.

I stared at her. *You are missing so much,* I thought. *She changes every day and it is so fast that I find it hard to keep up. Such a smart, kind, curious little girl. How can you live a life that is separate from her? How can you stand it?*

'Good,' I said.

'I want to see her. This weekend. Pick-up at ten.'

'Fine.'

'Is it fine, Max? Is it really? Oh, good. Because I get the impression you want to use our daughter as a stick to beat me with.'

I shook my head. I had thought about this a lot.

'I want her to have some kind of normal relationship with you,' I said. 'Not because it will be good for you. But because I know it will be bad for her if she doesn't. If we – you and me, Anne – are too stupid or too angry to work that out.'

'I'm glad you include yourself in the equation.'

'But I'm not going to let you hurt her,' I said, and I had thought about this a lot too. 'If this was a nice normal divorce – if you and I were like everyone else – or how I imagine everyone else to be – then none of this would be difficult. But you come and you go, Anne. That's the truth. You do your thing. You start a new family and then that's over and Fernando is flying off to Sicily with you and Scout is expected to just try to keep up with the changes and understand that you'll fit

170

her in when you can. And maybe I'm too hard on you and me – perhaps the world is full of divorced idiots just like us who allow all this other crap to be put ahead of their children. But that doesn't work for Scout.'

She smiled with what looked like real amusement.

'You don't get it yet, do you? *You can't control my life!*'

'I'm not trying to control your life. I don't care about your life. If you're with the husband or the new boyfriend – I don't give a damn, Anne. But I have a duty of care to Scout. And I just want ...'

My voice trailed away, and I looked down at Stan sleeping at my feet. What did I want for my daughter? What did I want?

'I want her to have a happy life,' I said. 'I want her to grow up knowing she's loved, and with something resembling normality. Routine. Stability. And if that disrupts any plans you have with Fernando, that's too bad.'

'Scout's fine,' she said, the useless soundbite of the absent parent.

'But she's not fine,' I said. 'Sports day is coming up ...'

Anne stared at me with disbelief.

'Sports day? What – the egg-and-spoon race and hours spent lolling about on the grass before they start handing out the sausage rolls? You're telling me that sports day is a problem?'

'Sports day is hard for some kids,' I said. 'It's hard for a girl who was born in the summer and just made the

cut for her year. A girl who always – and I mean always
– tries her best and runs her heart out but always comes
last against older, bigger, faster kids.'

'And Scout is prettier than all of them,' Anne said.
'And she is smarter. And she is nicer. Let them get their
medals for the stupid sack race. Fat lot of good it will
do them in the real world.'

'You don't get medals on sports day. You get *stickers*.
Gold, silver and bronze stickers. And they give them
out even in the heats, Anne. So all the kids who are no
good at sports – the fat kids, the slow kids, the nerdy
kids – all go home with something. But not Scout,
because she has always come last, even in the heats. And
she doesn't complain, and she doesn't cry, because she's
a brave little girl, and she shrugs it off as something she
has to get through. But it is tough for her. And it hurts
her. I know it does. And you don't because you are never
there, are you?'

'I'll come to bloody sports day, OK, Max? I'll be there
this year. I'll cheer her on. And maybe she will even get
a sticker. How about that?'

'See you there,' I said.

Anne stood up.

She was sick of looking at me.

'Ten. Saturday. Have her ready for me.'

'OK.'

But there was one last thing on her mind.

'As far as I can make out, Max, your closest relationship in the world is with that flea-bitten mutt,' she said. 'You spend all your spare time in that stinky boxing gym, hitting things as hard as you can. There was a girl you liked but now she's gone and you don't have the heart or the balls or the will to find another one.'

'Fair comment,' I said.

'Then why the hell am I the unhealthy one?' she said.

The most exclusive prostitution ring in London is run from a small office above a Peking duck restaurant on Gerrard Street, Chinatown. You go up a short flight of stairs, your mouth watering at the scent of the roasting duck below, and there is a white door with a simple sign.

SAMPAGUITA
Social Introduction Agency

Named after the national flower of the Philippines, Sampaguita is the former home of Ginger Gonzalez, founder and sole proprietor of the business. It has no online presence.

The way Sampaguita worked, Ginger made contact with men of a certain income bracket in the bars of high-end hotels – the American Bar at the Savoy, the Rivoli at the Ritz, the Coburg at the Connaught, the Fumoir at Claridge's, the Artesian at the Langham – and then she put them in touch with her ever-changing stable of girls.

She grinned as Stan and I came into her office, throwing open her arms, revealing the tattoos that run down her lower inner arms.

Never for money, said one.

Always for love, said the other.

'To what do I owe—'

Her smile faded when DCI Pat Whitestone walked in behind me with TDC Joy Adams.

'We're looking for a girl, Ginger,' I said.

Ginger Gonzalez was my friend. She had helped me when we were breaking open a ring of child abusers in one of those old abandoned mansions on The Bishops Avenue. I had helped her when a couple of Kray twin obsessives were shaking her down for protection money.

I liked her.

But this wasn't a social call.

'This is about that woman on the news,' Ginger said, her eyes watching Whitestone as she wandered over to the window and stared down at Chinatown. 'The one they took by mistake.'

'No,' Whitestone said. 'This is about the woman they meant to take. Show her, Joy.'

Adams placed a blown-up passport photograph of Snezia Jones on Ginger's desk.

Ginger studied it and looked up at Whitestone.

'Did this woman ever work for you?' Whitestone said.

'She's a dancer,' Ginger said. 'East European. From Montenegro, I think. Tallest people in Europe.'

'You get many dancers up here?'

'We get all the glamour professions,' Ginger said. 'Dancers. Models. Actresses. A lot of actresses. Any job where it's either feast or famine. Mostly famine. Romantic novelists. Poets. Bloggers.'

Whitestone indicated the photo of Snezia Jones, who was one of the few people I had ever seen who looked good in their passport photograph.

'So she did a bit of whoring for you, did she?'

Ginger pushed the photo away. 'I didn't say that, did I? And this is a Social Introduction Agency—'

Whitestone raised her hand for silence.

'You can call it a lonely-hearts club if you want to, sweetheart,' she said. 'I know that Max here is fond of you, but to me you are just another pimp. You might be a female pimp. And you might get your johns in bars where they charge £30 a time for a glass of sparkling wine.' Whitestone took off her glasses, rubbed a spot of grime from one lens, and put them back on. 'But to me you're still a pimp.'

'This woman has never worked for me,' Ginger said. 'We were only in preliminary talks.'

'Christ,' Whitestone said. 'Preliminary talks? Who do you think you are? Microsoft?'

'I heard she had found a gig at the Western World,' Ginger said. 'And then I heard she had found a sponsor.' She looked at me. 'So they meant to kidnap her, did they?'

'We don't know for sure,' I said. 'Maybe Jessica Lyle was just taken for no reason beyond the fact that some men liked the way she looked. And so they took her.'

'But if Jessica Lyle was raped and murdered after her abduction, then we would almost certainly have found her body by now,' Whitestone said.

'We think Jessica is alive,' I said. 'Alive and locked up somewhere. And that's why we're here.'

Silence in the small white room.

'We're not asking you if any of your johns are into a bit of slap and tickle,' Whitestone said. 'We're not interested in sado-masochism, bondage and discipline. Nanny smacking very naughty boys on the bottom? We don't care. This is the hard stuff. This is a woman being held against her will for the gratification of whatever sick bastard is holding her. And – of course – his special friends and possibly paying customers.'

'Ginger,' I said. 'Have you come across any men who are into that kind of thing?'

She hesitated, her tongue touching her lips, and Whitestone saw it.

'Who is he?' she said.

Ginger Gonzalez shook her head, anxious to backtrack.

'Some men want to make their own pornography,' she said. 'They fantasise about going into some cell with a woman who can't say no. A woman who is not pretending – who is not playing some BDSM game – but who really has no choice. *But that's not what we do here.*'

Whitestone put her notebook on Ginger Gonzalez's desk.

Then she slapped it as hard as she could.

'Names,' Whitestone said. 'Just give me the names of these men who want to make their own pornography. I *know* you have someone in mind, sweetheart. Just give me the names – give me one name – and we will leave you to your social introductions.'

Ginger Gonzalez stared at the notebook.

Then she shook her head.

'It's a *fantasy*,' she said. 'And that's all it is. None of the women who work for me have ever been subjected to force. None of them are ever held against their will. They all want to make money until their career picks up or until they meet someone special. All of them are adults and my clients are all men who trust me. If I thought for one second that any of these men were hurting women, then I would tell you.' She looked at Whitestone with defiance. 'I'm not going to ruin their lives so that you can make an arrest,' she said.

Whitestone nodded. 'OK,' she said. And then to Adams. 'Shut her down.'

And as the red and gold lights of Chinatown spilled into the white room, TDC Adams formally arrested Ginger Gonzalez for inciting prostitution for gain.

'These men who come to me,' Ginger said as we took her down to the holding cells of West End Central. 'They are all someone's husband, someone's father. You have to understand – they all have a family back home.'

'And so does Jessica Lyle,' Whitestone said.

When I got back home someone was waiting for me in the shadows of Smithfield meat market, the tip of his cigarette glowing in the darkness. Thin and beaky with a jet-black, spiky hairdo, he had spent a large part of his half-century on earth trying to look like the young Keith Richards but actually looked more like an elderly and unwell crow.

He was a criminal informant called Nils. My favourite CI.

He threw his cigarette away when he saw me coming because he knew I didn't like it.

'You still looking for that chick?' he said.

16

Nils scanned the crowded pub.

We were the only men who were not in the white coats of Smithfield meat market. And there were only men in here.

'I don't want any trouble,' he said.

'This makes your trouble go away,' I said. 'Have a drink. You need a drink.'

His hands were trembling.

He took a nervous gulp of his beer. And then he began to talk.

'I was making a delivery,' he said. 'Alprazolam.'

I felt my stomach fall away.

'It calms you down,' he said. 'It calms you right down. Sometimes it calms you down so far that you might never get up again.'

'I know what it does, Nils.'

'No need to snap at me, Max.'

If you wanted to keep someone quiet and pliant then you would feed them Alprazolam, available under the trade name Xanax, among others. Alprazolam belongs to a class of medications called benzodiazepines which produce an intensely calming effect on the central nervous system without inducing any feeling of euphoria. No real high, but it knocks you right out, working on the brain and nerves to melt away feelings of anxiety and panic disorders.

No matter what is being done to you.

It is highly addictive.

'So you're dealing now, Nils?'

'I wish,' he said. 'I'm just a delivery boy.'

'So who are you delivering for, Nils?

'Somalian drug dealers from Dagenham who will break both my legs if I give them up to the law. But do you want some low-level dealers or this woman who was taken?'

We both knew the answer.

'Where?'

'Belgravia,' he said. 'Eaton Square.'

I pictured the beautiful white stucco-fronted houses of London's most exclusive square.

'One of those big gaffs that are left unoccupied for years by some rich thieving bastard who robbed his own people back in the old country,' Nils said.

I must have looked sceptical.

'They're not using all of the house,' he said. 'Just the basement. The rest of the place is locked up. From the street, it looks like one more oligarch's holiday home. I made the delivery at the tradesmen's entrance. You know those big houses in Belgravia have still got tradesmen's entrances, some of them? As though we were living in ye olde Victorian days where the workers come around flogging their strawberries and fish every morning. Sharpening your knives and so on.'

'Get on with it, Nils.'

'You've been very short with me lately. The tradesmen's entrance is at the side of the building. You can't see it from the street. The order was for five hundred two-milligram pills at a tenner a time, delivered in an Amazon package. Guy I've never seen before gave me five grand in new fifties in an unsealed, unmarked brown envelope. I did the count, sealed the envelope and went away.'

'And what are they doing in there?'

He looked around the pub. 'What do you call it? Fantasy enactment. That's my guess, Max. Fantasy enactment – where you get to live the dream. Whatever the dream might be. Now, *my* problem,' he said, moving on to what I could do for him, 'is that I have this uniform at New Scotland Yard who has taken a real dislike to me. If you could have a word, get him to take a step back, tell him that I am your highly valued CI ...'

I stood up and took his beer from his hand.

'Where we going, Max?'

'Belgravia,' I said. 'Take me to this place.'

*

We drove across town and then slowly cruised the vast expanse of Eaton Square. Nils squinted uncertainly at the pristine rows of white five-storey buildings. Many of the houses appeared to be shuttered for the summer or for longer. The only sign of life was the odd uniformed doorman.

'I know it was *definitely* Eaton Square,' Nils said. 'And it had the – you know – the tradesmen's entrance down the side of the building ...'

'You weren't given the address?'

'I was driven. Did a few deliveries around town. And I remembered Eaton Square because – well – look at it. It's Eaton Square.'

Nils was right. Eaton Square was beautiful, like somewhere fancy in one of those old musicals where London is full of singing street traders asking who will buy this beautiful morning?

But Eaton Square is huge, far more like a highly exclusive neighbourhood than anything resembling a square. The residential gardens that occupy its leafy centre are so large that they are crossed by two side streets and have the King's Road running right through the middle. And although we circled so many times the uniformed doormen were noting my registration plate, Eaton Square kept its secrets.

'Were you stoned when you came here, Nils?'

'Absolutely not,' he said. He hesitated. 'Although I might have had a Xanax just to calm my nerves.'

'And who were they? This crew you saw?'

'They looked like Albanians.'

'How do you know they were Albanians?'

'I know what Albanians look like, don't I? They're just – you know – Albanian-looking.'

'You go inside?'

'No.'

'How many of them in there?'

'I don't know.'

'Are they armed?'

'I don't know.'

'You don't know very much, do you, Nils?'

He shrugged.

I stared around the vast expanse of Eaton Square. Then I looked at Nils' beaky, drug-ravaged face in the half-light of my car.

And I believed him.

'This place you went to,' I said. 'What makes you think they have Jessica Lyle in there?'

'Because I could hear a woman screaming,' he said.

17

It was so early that I was still on my first triple espresso when Whitestone and I walked into the interview room at West End Central where Ginger Gonzalez was waiting for her lawyer to show.

'We don't need you any more,' Whitestone told her, not bothering to sit down.

Ginger looked at me through eyes that were sticky with lack of sleep and I saw something like hope pass across her face. Whitestone crushed it like a Ford Cortina getting flattened inside the car compactor at Auto Waste Solutions.

'When our day staff show up in a couple of hours, you will be formally charged with owning, managing and running a brothel,' Whitestone said. 'Good luck with convincing the judge that you front a dating agency. If the prosecution can establish coercion, then you are looking at two to five years. If they can't establish coercion, then you will do anything between six months and two years. Either way – you're shut down and you're going down.'

Ginger was still looking at me.

Whitestone answered her unspoken question.

'One of DC Wolfe's criminal informants has pointed us in the right direction,' Whitestone said. 'Which is good news for that CI and bad news for you. You see how this works? If someone helps us, we help them. Maybe give them a pass. Maybe give them a slap on the wrist instead of something stronger. Get one of our colleagues to take a step back. And if they don't help us, if they choose not to – like you – then we leave them to their fate.'

I saw the fight going out of Ginger. She stretched out her bare arms on the table. Weary, pleading. The end of a very long night and the start of what could be the hardest day of her life.

Never for money. Always for love.

'If I had any way of helping you, then I would,' she said quietly.

'So you've never heard of this place?' I said, wanting her to help us and save herself. 'Some kind of dungeon in Eaton Square? A private members' club for perverts? That doesn't ring any bells? Come on, Ginger!'

She took a deep breath and let it go. 'I did hear a rumour that there was somewhere in Belgravia,' she said. 'In one of those big houses that are always left empty.'

Whitestone shook her head with disbelief.

'I can't believe it. We finally jogged her memory, Max!'

185

'I didn't know it was in Eaton Square! And there are all kinds of rumours about all kinds of places. All the worst fantasies – the very worst – are normalised online, made to seem OK, made to seem like some mainstream taste. These men sitting in front of their screens with a credit card in their hands and something else in the other. One click and they can make their dream come true. Any dream. Any fantasy. Everything you can think of and plenty you can't. You heard about those sex dolls that put up a fight? Why do they *make* dolls like that? *Because some men like it.* Because there's a *market.* There's a market for everything these days.'

'And sometimes these men – the men that want to make their sick dreams real – sometimes they come to someone like you,' Whitestone said, more gently now.

I watched Ginger making the calculation. From the moment we walked out of this room, it was all over for her.

'Ginger,' I pleaded. 'You need to tell us who came to you.'

'That's right,' Whitestone said. 'Last chance. Don't worry about client confidentiality. That's a doctor. Not a pimp.'

'But I sent him away,' Ginger said weakly.

'It doesn't matter,' Whitestone said.

'And I don't know if he ever actually *did* anything,' she protested. 'I don't know if he ever tried to act out his fantasy.'

'And what was that fantasy?' Whitestone said, very quietly.

'He wanted a woman who was telling him, *"No."* Not a woman who was pretending to say, *"No."* Not acting out some S&M panto. Not playing those submission and dominance games.' She hung her head. 'He wanted to take it to the next level, he said. He wanted authenticity. A woman who was being held against her will. He wanted a woman who did not want him.'

Whitestone's fist slammed down on the table.

'Rape!' she said. 'You're talking about rape!'

'Fantasy!' Ginger said. 'I'm talking about fantasy!'

'It's all a fantasy,' Whitestone said. 'Until they make it real.'

'Just give us a name, Ginger,' I pleaded. 'Last time of asking.'

I looked at Whitestone and she nodded.

'Give us a name and address and you can walk out of here,' I said.

'All right,' Ginger said. 'But he could be an innocent man.'

Whitestone laughed out loud.

'If there is one thing this bastard is not,' she said, 'it's innocent.'

We drove straight to a private road in Highgate.

It had the feel of an exclusive village.

Children off to the private schools in their uniforms. The girls in yellow and blue shirts and skirts, the boys in red and black blazers. And fathers off to work in Maseratis and Porsche 911s. Vanity cars for the man with everything. There were working women here too, plenty of them, but they got by without the vanity cars.

And there was an army of nannies – young East Europeans, older Filipinas, even one in a starched brown and white uniform that made her look like the ghost of a nanny from one hundred years ago. The nannies were loading small children into large SUVs and family cars. The inhabitants of this private road had lots of children. They had lots of everything.

The childminders were just the start. There was hired help galore, an entire servant class to walk the dog, clean the house, fuss over the large gardens, to fish a single fallen leaf from swimming pools that looked like they came from a David Hockney painting. And as the fathers roared off to sit in a traffic jam on the Finchley Road, they were waved off by mothers in their gym kit or dressed for their own high-flying gig in the financial district, walking to the tube in their Asics, their high heels in their bag, their phones in their hands. It was a world where privilege was in the air they breathed.

'What does the man with everything want?' Whitestone said as I parked the BMW. 'Some terrified woman chained up in a basement.'

The man we were looking for did not open his own front door. A housekeeper or maid in a black-and-white *Upstairs Downstairs* pinny opened it for him. Whitestone and I showed her our warrant cards.

'Mr Greenslade,' I said.

'Do you have an appointment?'

Whitestone held up her warrant card slightly higher. 'We don't need an appointment,' she said.

'Sir?' the maid called.

Greenslade was a tall, balding, overweight man who was dressed for work – there was a fat black leather briefcase stuffed with legal documents waiting by the door – and he was in a hurry. He was clearly irritated at this unscheduled intrusion until he realised who we were.

When he saw the warrant cards, his round, moisturised face seemed to crumble.

'I'll take care of it, Marilyn,' he told the housekeeper, the authority in his voice ebbing away.

We waited while the housekeeper had shuffled off to the back of the house. I could hear a woman's voice, children. The family was busy with breakfast, bustling to get another perfect day up and running.

I showed Greenslade the photograph of Jessica Lyle.

'Mr Greenslade, we're investigating an abduction and we think you can help us,' I said. 'Sir.'

He took us to the back garden where, through the floor-to-ceiling windows, we could see the family at table.

A good-looking woman in her middle years, three children, all very young, one in a high chair. Second or third marriage, I guessed. The summer morning was still cool in the garden but sweat gleamed on Greenslade's scalp and stained his pale blue business shirt a darker shade, as if the shame was seeping out of his soft, squishy body.

'You approached Ginger Gonzalez of Sampaguita looking for a particular service that she was unable to provide,' Whitestone said.

'I don't know what you're talking about,' he said.

'Listen,' I said. 'You need to think very carefully about how you play this, because denial is just not going to work for you. Denial is going to be very bad for you indeed. We know what you wanted from Ginger. We know exactly why you went to Chinatown.'

He glanced towards the house. His wife was watching him.

'Your wife,' Whitestone said.

'What about her?'

'She's beautiful,' Whitestone said. 'Why would a man with a beautiful wife, a man with all of *this*' – her gesture took in his family, his home, the private road, the army of servants, all of green, rich Highgate, this gilded life of plenty – 'want a woman who can't say no? Your wife not enough for you?'

He stared around the garden, seeing nothing. The stains on his business shirt grew larger.

'After the birth of our last child, she lost interest,' he said. 'In me.'

Whitestone nodded.

'Ah, that explains it then. It's the woman's fault. I knew it was the woman's fault. It's always the woman's fault. I just needed you to explain it to me.' A beat. 'Do you know what they do to rapists in prison?'

Tears of fearful self-pity sprang to his eyes.

'I don't want any trouble,' he said.

'You're already in trouble, Greenslade,' I said. 'We're trying to get you out of trouble. For the greater good. But you need to start telling us the truth.'

'It was just a fantasy,' he said. 'I saw it online. Men taking women. *Taking* them. And then it was the only thing I could see.' He ran a hand across his damp scalp, his eyes sliding away from us. 'The only thing that worked for me. The only thing that got me excited.'

'It all starts with a fantasy,' Whitestone said, very calmly, and I saw again that she was at her best during the morning. It was at night when the vodka took over, it was after dark when the horrors happened. I thought of the broken body of the scooter rider lying in the shadows of that abandoned car wash on a road that looked as empty as the surface of the moon, and quickly pushed the thought away.

'Every assault, every child abduction, every rape,' Whitestone said. 'Every act of cruelty starts off as the stuff of dreams. Always, it starts as a fantasy and then some idiot steps over the invisible line that skirts the stuff of dreams and dares to make it real – especially these days, especially now, where every vile impulse has got its own chat group, its own hundred dedicated pages on every social media platform – every sickness, every perversion, every twisted act of torture is made to seem somehow socially acceptable, as if everyone is at it, as if it is perfectly normal, as if you might actually get away with it. And then someone like us has to come along and clear up all the mess.'

She paused to watch him sweat.

'Where did you go after Ginger Gonzalez gave you a knock-back in Chinatown?' she said. 'Because it did not end there, did it?'

He licked his lips. His lips were very dry. Two detectives were sitting in his back garden, talking about his secret dreams. That is bound to give you cotton mouth.

'I didn't *do* anything,' he said. 'You have to understand that.' His wife was still watching him from the kitchen through those great glass walls. *What was this about? Who were these people? What had he done?* He turned his back to her and mopped the sweat from his forehead with the palm of his hand. 'I walked in and then I walked straight out. I swear on the lives of my children. There is a reason these things are fantasies. Because the reality is so ... unspeakable.'

His wife continued to watch. She was steering the children through breakfast, preparing them for a day at

school. And all the while her eyes never left her husband.
She knew something was not right. She knew that something was about as wrong as it could be.

'You found this place online?' I said.

He nodded.

'Someone in Ginger's line of work. But without Ginger's scruples.'

'We are going to need a name,' I said.

'Someone I found on the Dark Web,' he said. 'I never
saw their face. I never knew their name.'

'Someone on the Dark Web,' I nodded. 'It's the digital
version of a-man-I-met-in-the-pub.'

'But it happens to be true,' he said. 'Someone offering
this ... service ... is not going to be keen on publicity,
are they?'

'So you found what you were looking for,' I said.

He nodded, his eyes drifting away. We were all talking more quietly, we were all speaking softly and without
emotion.

'What was this place?' I said.

He breathed out, a kind of broken sigh.

We waited.

That was all we had to do.

'It was a basement room with a metal grille in the
doorway,' he said. 'A kind of cage.' He looked at us. 'It
looked like a cage.'

Whitestone was very still.

'But I didn't touch the girl!' he said. 'I gave them the money and I left.'

'We believe you,' Whitestone said. 'It's all right. We know you're telling the truth. All you have to do now is to keep telling the truth.'

I showed him the photograph of Jessica Lyle again.

He had hardly glanced at it the first time.

'Look at it,' I told him, my voice hard, and he did as he was told.

And so did I.

Jessica Lyle, smiling in a world that was good and kind.

'Is that the woman?' I said.

'I didn't see the woman.'

'Never lie to me,' Whitestone said, flaring up but keeping her voice low so that it would not disturb the children at their breakfast. 'Do you hear me, you piece of shit? If you ever lie to me then I swear to God that all of this comes crumbling down. The house. The family. All of it ends.'

'I'm not lying,' he said.

'Where was this place?' I said.

'One of those big houses that are left empty,' he said. 'In Belgravia. I'll give you the address.'

18

One hour later, the briefing room at West End Central was packed.

There were Specialist Firearms Officers from Leman Street police station, Whitechapel, in their grey para-military body armour, a few plain-clothes faces from SCD9, the anti-trafficking unit at New Scotland Yard, plenty of uniformed officers from here at 27 Savile Row, and our mob from upstairs at Homicide and Serious Crime Command. And every one of them was struggling to understand how sexual slavery could be happening in the most exclusive residential address in London.

Pat Whitestone was standing on a small stage in front of a massive HDTV.

She was as bright-eyed and lucid as I had ever seen her.

'We are looking at a £20 million house that nobody owns,' she told the room. 'A five-storey lateral conversion on the north side of Eaton Square that is among the frozen assets of an overseas national suspected of laundering dirty money by buying London property.'

She hit a button on her iPad and the cream-columned Regency terrace of Eaton Square appeared on the big screen behind her.

'The owner of the property is a mid-ranking civil servant currently living on a government salary of fifty potatoes a month back in the old country. The house is currently unused apart from the basement. And that's where we are going because we have had two separate reports that the basement is being used for the purpose of sexual slavery.' A beat. 'Eaton Square is a good choice,' she said, answering the unspoken question. 'Many of the local residents are older people who have spent a lifetime accumulating wealth and most of them have a place in the countryside or abroad or both.'

She glanced back at the cream-coloured terrace on the big TV screen.

'Many of the foreign owners are frequently absent,' she said. 'Eaton Square is just their London base. Those people – you can't really say they actually *live* anywhere. So Eaton Square makes sense for all those reasons. It's quiet, discreet and full of empty property. Perfect for a pop-up brothel. If these big mansions stay empty – and as far as I can tell, nobody has plans to fill them with the homeless – then we will see a lot more of them being used for illegal activities.'

She touched her iPad again.

Jessica Lyle's face filled the screen.

'This is Jessica Lyle, the woman who was abducted by two unknown assailants on a private estate in Hampstead. We believe Jessica is the woman they are holding in Eaton Square. I wish I could tell you more. I don't know if the men inside are armed. I don't know how many of them there are. And I don't know how much of a fight they are likely to put up when you go in there and point an assault rifle in their face. But I can tell you with total certainty that they are holding a young woman in there against her will.'

She nodded briskly.

'And we're going to get her out,' she said, and shielded her eyes as she stared at the back of the room. 'SFO Rose? Jackson?'

The tall, light-skinned black man I was standing next to pushed himself from the wall and strode to the stage.

Jackson Rose. The closest I had ever got to a brother. I had known Jackson longer than I had known anyone in the room. In fact, I had known him longer than I had known anyone in my life.

He addressed his Specialist Firearms Officers.

'We will be going in through the tradesmen's entrance at the side of the house where there is some kind of metal grille over the door. So our method of entry will be by Benelli rather than the big key.'

197

He meant they would blow the door open with a 12-gauge Benelli M4 shotgun rather than smashing it down with a battering ram.

'We understand there is at least one more metal grille inside the premises, so the big key will be used once we've gained entry.'

A woman's voice from the middle of the room. One of the SFOs in their grey paramilitary kit.

'What sort of grille is it, skipper?' she said.

'It sounds like a cage,' he said, his face impassive.

The audience reflected on that, everyone thinking about the woman who was being held against her will in there, and everyone wondering what kind of luck they would have when we went inside. Because even when you know with total certainty that you are about to face the scum of the earth, you never know a thing about your luck.

That's the great central mystery in the life of a police officer.

Your luck.

'Look after yourself and each other out there,' Jackson said, and then he nodded at Whitestone. He was done.

'Let's bring her home,' he said.

19

'There's some new poison in the world,' Jackson Rose said in the back of the unmarked drop-off van. 'It wasn't like this before our time.'

His shots were doing the final checks on their kit. You could smell the fresh gun oil on their Sig Sauer MCX assault rifles.

Jackson and I were next to the back doors, crouched by a small black-and-white monitor relaying images from the camera hidden in the roof of the van. The screen was split into nine live CCTV images. It is only two miles from Mayfair to Belgravia. With the blues-and-twos screaming, the world was getting out of our way.

'There were always places where women were sold,' Jackson said. 'Places where women were exploited, bullied, bought and sold. But there was never anywhere quite like this, was there? I don't understand it, Max. It feels like there is some new sickness in the world that was never here before. A place where men can buy a woman that doesn't want them, where men can buy a woman who is not for sale. I never thought I would live to see these things, but here they are.' He shook his head. 'It's like some sick fantasy someone decided to act out and I can't even begin to explain it to myself.'

'They call it behavioural contagion,' I said, glad to have him beside me, glad to have him to talk to, happy to face the world with him by my side. 'The head doctors,' I said. 'They call it behavioural contagion when people see some line being crossed – self-harming, starving themselves, hurting a woman – and they think it gives them permission to cross that line too.'

'But that still doesn't explain it,' said Jackson Rose.

'No,' I said. 'That doesn't explain it.'

The driver half-turned to call over her shoulder.

'ETA for entry team is one minute,' she said.

We turned into Eaton Square, and entered the stillness that you only find in the realm of serious money. Knocking on for the middle of morning, and nothing was moving out there.

And then I saw him.

The elderly concierge in gunmetal-grey uniform staring at the perfect sky.

He could not stop looking at the sky. It was another beautiful day. Another glorious day in the city. But there was something wrong with the summer sky.

I looked through one of the peepholes drilled in the side of the van and saw that a growing black cloud was staining the cloudless blue.

There was smoke pouring out of somewhere that I couldn't see, and it was turning the blue sky black, the shades of an old bruise.

And as we slowed for our target address, I saw the smoke was billowing from the basement of the £20 million house that nobody owned. I did not need to check the address because I felt my stomach twist with a terrible knowledge.

They had heard us coming.

The man came tumbling out of the smoke as the first of the SFOs were jumping from the back of the van.

'Stop! Armed police! Stand still!'

A tall, gangling streak of a man, pale-faced with panic, falling forward, his mouth gawping open with shock, as if the fire he had started had grown quicker than he'd been prepared for. Assault rifles were shouldered and aimed at his centre of mass but he kept on coming, falling more than running, more afraid of the fire behind him than the guns in front of him.

'Stand still now!' Jackson said, taking half a step forward.

The man went down to his knees.

Then he was being forced on his face by a couple of shots, and Joy Adams pulled his arms behind his back and snapped on the cuffs as another man came out of the smoke.

TONY PARSONS

This one was squat and broad with a nose that had been broken on multiple occasions and he had a petrol can in one hand and a cheap plastic light in the other, his thumb pressed down and the flame flickering in the early sunlight.

'*Kthehem! Kthehem!*'

Which is Albanian for *back the fuck up*.

Which is the first thing you learn in Albanian.

His mouth was still moving with the threat when a single shot split the day.

It went on and on, ringing in the back of my brain, the single Sig Sauer MCX round fired by SFO Jackson Rose, and the squat man with the petrol can and the plastic lighter went down, his eyes blank before he hit the ground.

The top of the can was off and he landed in a puddle of petrol that made a sound like a sudden rush of wind and, all at once, the flames engulfed him.

You could smell the flesh burning. Someone was screaming. It was the man who had surrendered, howling as he saw his friend's face turning black in the fire, attempting to get to his feet until one of the shots bounced the butt of an assault rifle off the back of his skull and he went down and did not move. And then there was the hiss of the foam from the fire extinguisher and, mixed up with that, there was new screaming coming from somewhere else.

Somewhere in the house.

A woman's voice.

*

202

I pushed past a pair of uniformed officers in PASGT helmets who were shouting something I could not understand as they emptied the fire extinguishers they were holding over the burning man. Then I was in the smoke, my left hand brushing the cream-coloured brick of the house, looking for the door, then finding the door, closed but unlocked after the men had fled their fire, the smoke thicker here, and all at once in my eyes and my throat and my nose, choking me, sickening me.

This is how you died in a fire, I knew. The smoke suffocated you before the flames ever had a chance to reach you.

I went deeper into the house.

The screaming had stopped.

The air was a black, churning fog. And then it was something else, an unbroken, unmoving mass. Blacker still, and thicker. I was moving down a corridor. I plunged deeper into the smoke and I did not want to die.

There were stairs down to what had once been a kitchen. I was at the top of them.

And through the smoke, thinning now that I was out of the corridor and the roof was suddenly higher, I saw that I was at the top of a staircase that led down to a dungeon.

I stopped halfway down the stairs, retched and cursed, wiped my mouth with the back of my hand and carried on to the basement.

I saw the flames licking the skirting board in the basement, burning it black, but the houses of the rich do not burn as easily as the houses of the poor and the basement had not ignited as quickly as the men had hoped and expected.

And now I saw what they had tried to burn.

There were three cages down here.

And I saw that in each of the cages there was a woman.

One was shaking the cage door.

One was on her knees, gagging on the smoke.

And one was not moving.

'*Ju lutem!*' the woman still standing begged me.

And that was Albanian too.

Please.

'*Get down! Get down!*' I shouted at them, because smoke rises, and the closer you are to the ground the more likely you are to find oxygen.

I tore at the nearest cage with my hands.

It did not move. I screamed into the black fog that covered the stairs.

'We need that shotgun down here now!'

Whitestone came down the stairs, her hands covering her streaming eyes.

When she took her hands away, she saw the women in the cages.

'Jesus Christ,' she said.

I shook the cage door and cried out again for help because I knew I could not budge it, I knew a battering ram or a Benelli shotgun was needed and I could feel the sweat streaming down my body inside the stab-proof jacket.

Then there were shots moving through the black smoke and into the basement and one of them carried the bosher battering ram, its red paint almost completely worn away by time, slamming it expertly against the lock of the first cage but only putting a deep dent in the metal bars.

Then there were shots everywhere, and one of them had a semi-automatic Benelli shotgun.

'*Firing!*' he shouted and fired his Benelli shotgun and took a pace left and shouted '*Firing!*' again, and then another pace left and the same warning, '*Firing!*' and each time he fired, a cage door sprang open.

And then there were more bodies around us, and I saw what Whitestone had seen.

One dead woman.

One dying woman.

And, as we watched, the third, the one who had spoken to me, began to collapse because smoke kills you quickly, because it only takes somewhere between two and ten minutes to die from smoke inhalation.

Three women under lock and key who were meant to burn with the rest of this place.

Three women in this corner in hell.

Three women.

But none of them was Jessica Lyle.

20

We sat on the steps of West End Central, Whitestone
and Adams and me, coughing up the black filth from
our lungs, dabbing at our raw eyes with bottled water,
craving fresh air and sky after being in that basement.

'I want to talk to them,' Frank Lyle said.

He stood before us with the look of a sick animal.

No, a dying animal.

Whitestone put on her glasses and squinted up at him.
There was a black streak on one side of her face.

I stood up.

'Mr Lyle,' I began.

He held up a large hand, ordering silence.

'I'm talking to the organ grinder, not the monkey,' he
told me. He nodded at Whitestone. 'The pimps and the
girls,' he said. 'I want to see them.' He looked towards
the lobby of West End Central. 'I know they're in there.'
He looked as though he had not slept well for a long
time. 'At least that stinking Albanian pimp must be,'
he said.

'There was no sign of Jessica in that building,' I said, and I kept talking even though he was still looking at the organ grinder and not the monkey. 'We found five Albanian nationals. Two men holding three women. One of the men was shot dead at the scene. One of the women we found in the basement was dead on arrival at the hospital. The surviving man will be interviewed when the translator arrives. He can't speak English.'

'I want to talk to the bastard *now*,' Lyle said. 'In one of the holding cells. I promise you he will be talking fluent English when I've done with him.'

Whitestone stood up, fumbling with her glasses.

The man had lost his daughter and she had cut him a lot of slack.

But the slack was running out.

'Mr Lyle,' she said. 'As far as we can tell, these two men were running some kind of improvised brothel that they had set up in an unoccupied building. There is no reason for us to believe that there is any connection between these men and these women and your daughter.'

He made to brush past us. I stood before him.

'Please listen to what we are telling you,' I said.

'None of them speak English, Mr Lyle,' Whitestone said. 'Not the man we're holding. Not the two surviving women.'

He snorted with disbelief.

'You don't buy that, do you?' he said. 'Every little Third World wide boy who just jumped off the back of a lorry speaks English.' He jabbed an angry finger at the glass doors of West End Central. 'Either *they* know something,' he said, 'or *you* know nothing. Either these evil bastards have something to tell me or you have been chasing false leads all this time. Which is it?'

'We're doing all we can,' Whitestone said, and I saw her visibly sag, as if she knew how feeble it sounded to a man who only wanted his daughter home.

'I'll beat it out of him,' Lyle said, making it sound so simple, pushing past me and going up the steps.

We let him go, too tired to argue. Let someone else deal with him. He wasn't going to be waved in by the duty sergeant today.

'Those girls,' Joy Adams said, her voice soft with disbelief. 'That place.'

Then we sat in silence, still dabbing at our eyes with the bottled water, until two uniformed officers came out with Frank Lyle walking between them. A man and a woman officer, they spoke to him in professionally calm, soothing voices. We stood up and Whitestone glanced at me and I knew she felt it too.

Something that could only be called shame.

Lyle was one of those old-school coppers who was always ready to lose his rag, and I had expected him to put up a fight.

But he went quietly today, and the touch on the arms of the two uniformed officers slowly steering him to the street was gentle. They escorted him down the steps and let him go.

We made way for him.

He did not look at us as he set off along Savile Row, as shuffling and round-shouldered as a very old man. He stopped outside one of the bespoke tailors to cough something into his hand and then stared at what he saw there.

Then sank to one knee, and we all ran to him as if he was still one of our own, and would always be one of our own, and I caught a glimpse of what he had on his hand.

The blood from Frank Lyle's lungs was black now.

Tommy answered the door to the Lyle home, staring at me as if he had never seen me before in his life. And maybe he hadn't.

I held out my hand. That was a mistake. He looked at it for a while and then shook it limply, glancing anxiously away.

'Remember me, Tommy? DC Wolfe. You were playing football in the garden.'

'You're looking for my sister.'

'That's right.'

'Is this about finding her?'

'This is about your father.'

'Oh, but he's in the hospital. Someone called my mum.'

'I know he's in the hospital. Can I see your mum, Tommy?'

'Is my sister coming home?'

'I hope so,' I said.

Then I looked at his big, open face framed by the mass of untamed curls.

'You missing your sister, Tommy?'

'Sometimes,' he said. A secret smile. 'But I was always told I needed to be more like her. Always, always, always, always, *always*.' He beamed at me, and it was the same wide white smile as his perfect sister. 'So it's nice to be a bit alone, too. Because then they can't tell me to be more like her, can they?'

'What do you think happened to Jessica?'

His face clouded.

'I *know* what happened.'

'What's that?'

'Some bad men took her,' he said. 'Because she's so pretty.'

Jennifer Lyle was in the kitchen, the big windows to the garden behind her, the Wendy house lit by the golden light of a summer's day that was reluctant to end.

'Thank you for taking my husband to hospital,' she said. 'I was just about to leave to see him.'

'DCI Whitestone was in the ambulance with him.'

'And what was Frank doing at West End Central?'

'He wanted to talk to someone we have in custody. He believes the man has information about the abduction of your daughter.'

'And does he?'

I shook my head.

'And that's why I wanted to see you, Mrs Lyle.'

'Jennifer.'

'Jennifer. Your husband needs to trust us, Jennifer. He needs to take a step back from our investigation. When he comes home, could you please ask him to do that? Because it's not helping us find your daughter.'

'But my husband was a policeman himself and he knows how it works. He knows that the police sometimes try very hard to find someone.' Her face creased with sadness. 'And sometimes you don't try very hard at all. It's true, isn't it?'

She was right. I thought of the girl that Snezia had told me had gone missing from the Western World. Minky? And I wondered who was looking for Minky today, and how hard they were looking.

'Sometimes you act like you don't give a damn,' Mrs Lyle said, not unkindly, not angrily, just explaining it to me. 'My husband has been in those briefing rooms where you decide if you are going to keep looking forever or if you are going to stop looking or if you are not going to look at all.'

'We're doing all we can for you. And for your family. And for your grandson.'

And suddenly I was aware of the child's absence.

'Baby Michael is in the garden,' Jennifer Lyle said. She bit her lower lip as her eyes slid away from mine. 'With his father.'

I stared at her, not understanding. And then I saw them on the far side of the Wendy house.

Harry Flowers with baby Michael in his arms.

I let it sink in. And I turned to Jennifer Lyle, letting out a breath ragged with disbelief.

'Jessica and Flowers were lovers?' I watched him cradling the baby in his huge arms, trying to make sense of it. 'But why the hell didn't you tell us?'

There was a steely look of defiance in her eyes.

'Because if my daughter was some ex-drug dealer's mistress, you would not be looking quite so hard,' she said. '*Would you?* She wouldn't be such a beautiful MOP then, would she?'

MOP is police slang for a member of the public. She knew all of our secret language, and she also knew how we worked, and how we thought.

'If you knew the truth, Jessica would have been portrayed as something horrible,' she said. 'Some gangster's moll. And that wouldn't have helped bring her home.'

'Does your husband know about Jessica and Flowers?'

'Frank just found out. He always believed that Lawrence – our daughter's late fiancé – was Michael's father.
And Jess and I decided to let him believe it, especially
with all the medical issues Frank was going through.'

Medical issues, I thought. Coughing up black blood.
Collapsing in the street. Terminal lung cancer.

'I recently told my husband the truth about Michael's
father,' she said. 'And as soon as I did, Frank went for
Harry with a hammer. And that is exactly why I did not
tell him before. Because I knew Frank would want to
kill Harry.'

Harry, I thought. It's *Harry* now.

I shook my head.

'You should have told us, Mrs Lyle,' I said. 'It matters.
You know it does.'

'But exactly how would the truth have helped Jessica?'
she said. 'Or Michael? You think my husband is the raving
maniac and I am the reasonable one. You're dead wrong,
Detective. I am quite happy to be as unreasonable as I
need to be. I just want Jessica back. I just want her safe.
That's all I care about. And I just want you to *do your job.*'

'I'm trying,' I said, and I went out into the garden.

'I should knock your front teeth out,' I told Harry
Flowers.

'Why would you do that?' he said.

'For withholding information,' I said. 'For withholding so much information from the police that you

213

obstructed our investigations.' I shook my head. 'For treating us like mugs. For hiding the truth. For deserving to have your front teeth knocked out.'

'I didn't stop you doing your job,' he said, rocking the baby. 'I let you get on with it.'

We both stared at Michael's face. The baby smacked his lips in sleep and burrowed deeper into the arms of Flowers.

'So what happened, Harry? Help me to understand. You're on one of your scheduled twice-weekly visits to see your mistress and then you take a shine to her flatmate? Is that what happened?'

He shook his head.

'It was already over with Snezia and we both knew it. These things wear out. And Jess was at a low point in her life.'

'Because her fiancé died.'

'I mean long before Lawrence died.' He glanced back at the house. 'Her parents like to think of Jess and Lawrence as some great love affair, but it wasn't like that at all. They were just two kids who had more or less grown up together. Jess was starting to wonder if she really wanted to spend a lifetime with a guy who was not much more than her childhood sweetheart.'

'And you were the exit door out of this difficult relationship?'

'I was more than that.'

'Help me with the timeline here, Harry. Jessica moved in with Snezia two years ago. When did it begin with you and Jessica?'

'It began the first time I looked at her. It began the moment I saw her face. It didn't start then – the way you mean it – not for a long time. But for me, at least, it began the moment I saw this incredible young woman who was moving into the flat. I had never seen anything like her. And I have seen them all over the world.'

'Jesus, Harry. Who would have thought it? You're an old romantic.'

'Everyone loves Jess,' he said, and I wondered how many people had told me exactly that.

'I can understand the attraction for you. But what did she see in you?'

I watched his rich man's vanity bridle. But he shrugged. 'Search me.'

'Must have been the size of your budget, Harry.'

'Sneer all you want.'

'I'm dead serious. What did Lawrence do? He was a teacher, right? And then you swan in with your flash car and your property portfolio and your big promises. Is that what happened?'

His mouth tightened but he said nothing, concentrating on his baby boy.

'So – leaving love at first sight to one side for the moment – there was a period when Jessica was sleeping

215

with you and the fiancé?' I said. 'I understood that she and Lawrence were still engaged when he died.'

He hesitated. 'There might have been some overlap.'

'And are you sure that you're Michael's father?'

He stared hard at me. 'Maybe I should knock your front teeth out.'

'And Lawrence died just before the baby was born.'

'Yes, he died horribly. Knocked off his bike riding home and the police' – he allowed himself a bitter little smile – 'the police could not even find the driver who hit him. It was a tragedy.'

'Well, it was a tragedy for him, but it worked out quite well for you. Your young rival was taken out of the picture.'

And now I saw the older man's wounded pride.

'Lawrence wasn't my rival.'

'But Jessica kept a photograph of him by her bedside.'

'Of course! She still loved him. But not in *that* way. They had practically grown up together. In the end, she loved him like a brother.'

'Then he was gone. So no more overlapping. No more sharing Jessica. Poor young Lawrence. But lucky old Harry.'

'You think I had something to do with Lawrence getting knocked off his bike?'

'With your history of violence, Harry? I would be remiss if I didn't consider it a strong possibility.'

He looked sick to his stomach. 'You know how many cyclists get killed every day on our streets? You know how many thousands are seriously injured every year? Lawrence was hit by some drunken moron in a sports car who never stopped. You think I could arrange that?'

'I don't know,' I said, the anger rising in me. 'But I know that you are lying bastards. All of you. The Lyles. You. Snezia. You all acted as though Jessica had her future snatched away from her when her fiancé died. That's what you were all happy for the police – and the press, and the public – to believe. But his death could not have been more convenient. Certainly not for you.'

And for her, I thought.

For Jessica.

If it was true. If she wished the unwanted fiancé gone and a new life with an older, richer man. But was that what she really wanted? I realised that I knew next to nothing about Jessica Lyle apart from the fact that every-one she met seemed to fall in love with her.

Everyone loves Jessica. But who did she love?

'If I had wanted to kill the lad,' Flowers said, 'a car is the last thing that I would have used.'

And although I said nothing, I believed him. A hit-and-run is not an exact science. Getting knocked over by a car is as likely to leave the victim crippled as killed.

And if Harry Flowers wanted someone gone, I thought, he would be more likely to set them on fire. Less room for error.

But still – the death of Jessica Lyle's childhood sweetheart would not have broken his heart.

He looked from his baby's face to me.

'None of it is very complicated,' he said. 'None of it is hard to understand. We're all just animals looking for a home.'

'But they didn't take the wrong woman, did they, Harry? Because they never wanted Snezia in the first place. Whoever snatched Jessica, they knew what they were doing, didn't they?'

'Yes,' he said. 'It feels like they knew exactly who they were taking.'

I shook my head, still taking it all in.

'Because Snezia was on the way out and Jessica was all set to be your latest bit on the side.'

Sudden fury blazed in his eyes. 'Jess will never be *anyone's* bit on the side.'

'Call it what you want. But you chose not to share that vital information.'

'Would you have tried harder to find her if you knew we were together?' he said, repeating the line I had heard in the kitchen, and I saw that this had been discussed, this had been endlessly hashed over when Frank Lyle was having his lungs drained at the hospital, when Harry

Flowers and Jennifer Lyle had sipped herbal tea at the kitchen table and rocked baby Michael to sleep and worked out how best to play it.

And how best to bring Jessica home.

'Would you be throwing the full resources of the Met at this if you had known?' he said. 'Even with all of Frank's friends on the Force? Do you think all those old coppers would have broken sweat if they had known I was in love with the woman who was taken? Despite Frank's thirty years. I don't think so, do you?'

He had me there.

'Maybe not. So who knew the truth about you and Jessica?'

'Nobody,' he said. 'Well, Snezia knew. We weren't going to hide it from her. And Jessica's mother knew after Jess found she was pregnant. The fiancé – Lawrence – never knew about us.'

'You sure about that? He never saw any text messages from you on her phone, he never caught the pair of you fluttering your eyelashes at each other? Snezia never told him? These things are hard to hide, Harry. Even for a smooth operator like you.'

'Jess never told him and he never found out.' He thought about it. 'And now her father knows.'

'Yes, I remember dear old dad after he got the happy news. Trying to beat your brains out with a hammer.'

'Frank will get used to the idea before he dies,' he said, and some cold light in Harry Flowers' eyes offered a glimpse of his pitiless criminal's heart. He looked at Michael as the baby stirred from his sleep and began to grizzle. 'Children are the great healers.'

'Who else knew? If Jessica was the target, then we need to know who knew about the pair of you.'

I thought of the clothes being thrown from the window. The shoes, the suits, the vinyl. All his good stuff.

'Your wife,' I said. 'Did she know about you and Jessica?'

'No, Charlotte only just found out about Snezia. The wife is usually the last to know.'

'In your long experience.'

'Yes,' he said. 'In my long experience. But nobody else knew. Jess and I nearly bumped into Junior one night when we were at some tapas bar on Great Portland Street. But he didn't see us – because he was with his mates and they were all rat-faced and trying to get off with the waitresses. And the rest of my family never knew.'

I remembered Meadow Flowers turning up at the Western World with her hen party pack to torment Snezia. It felt like the Flowers family were playing catch-up with Harry's sexual adventures, always one relationship behind.

Then, tucking the baby against his side, he took a match folder from his jacket pocket and turned it over in his hand. It was one of those little folders of matches that he used as a business card. *Auto Waste Solutions*, it said on the cover. His company where old cars go to die.

He handed it to me.

'Open it,' he said.

I took it. I opened it. Michael had stopped grizzling, soothed by the arms that held him, and suddenly I had no trouble at all believing this was Harry's son. On the inside of the match folder someone had quickly scribbled a car registration number.

'Do you know what that is?' Flowers asked me.

I shook my head, but I felt my insides fall away.

Because I knew with total certainty that it could only be the registration number of Pat Whitestone's car. The car that had hit the boy on the scooter. The car that had needed to be repaired before anyone saw.

But someone had seen.

And someone had told.

'Nobody's above the law, are they?' Flowers said. 'Apart from you lot. Apart from the law themselves. Why do you think so many people hate you? Because you think the rules don't apply to the police. And you are dead wrong, mate. You are about as wrong as you can be.'

I gave him back the match folder. I couldn't stand to touch it.

'What do you want, Flowers?'

'Nothing.'

There was an old car blanket draped over the porch of the Wendy house. He took it, spread it on the grass and gently, gently laid Michael on top of it.

Then he tore off a match, struck it and held the sudden flame to a corner of the *Auto Waste Solutions* folder. It caught, the old cardboard burning slowly until it reached the match-heads and then suddenly flaring.

Flowers carried on holding it, both of us watching the match folder burn in the soft light of the dying summer afternoon, and then, just as the flames were about to reach his fingers, he dropped it on the porch of the Wendy house, kicking it far away from where the baby was sleeping.

From the big windows that looked on to the garden, Mrs Lyle and Tommy were watching us.

I was still waiting to hear what Harry Flowers wanted.

'Bring her home,' he told me, his voice choked with feeling. 'Bring her home or I swear to God I will burn the lot of you.'

21

Someone had done a good job on Pat Whitestone's car.

I stood outside her home, a terraced house on a quiet street off the Holloway Road, and slowly walked around it.

I looked at the registration plate and it was the same number that I had seen scribbled inside a match folder that said *Auto Waste Solutions*.

The last time I had seen this car, parked under a street light directly below our loft, it had been a mess – the driver-side headlight caved in, a dent in the front bumper and paint torn from the side where something had hit the car at speed. That damage had all been made good. Almost too good. I lightly touched my fingertips to the car, as if the paint might still be wet. The headlight and the paint looked box fresh, with none of the wear and tear that was on the rest of the car.

You would never know she had been in an accident, I thought. Not unless you knew what you were looking for.

The door of the house opened and Whitestone's son Justin came out with his assistance dog, Dasher, a three-year-old Labrador-Retriever mix.

'Justin,' I said.

'Max,' he said. It wasn't a question.

He came down the path, a tall good-looking kid, the beautiful Dasher tracking by his side. The gangling awkwardness of Justin's teenage years had gone and he was now a fine-looking young man. A couple of years ago he had been blinded in one of those meaningless eruptions of violence that can happen to young men in any city. A quiet kid who had been in the wrong bar at the wrong time with the wrong people. But he was not letting that monstrous bad luck define his life.

There was the same quiet courage in him that was in his mother.

He smiled as he reached me. He had ditched the dark glasses that he had worn when he first lost his sight and I saw the scarring high on one cheekbone where the bottle had hit him.

I held out my hand and Dasher gave it a desultory sniff.

Yes, I know you, pal, but don't get too excited.

Dasher was working and the two-year training that every assistance dog receives is largely about learning to never be distracted. Dasher's days of jumping with joy at the sight of some old friend were behind him.

Dasher had a job to do. The dog was deeply loved, but he was not a pet.

'Still thinking of joining the family business?' I asked Justin.

The Metropolitan Police has thirteen thousand civilians working alongside thirty-one thousand officers. There had been a time, in the black months after his accident, when Justin had talked about possibly one day being one of them. That was the plan at the worst of times when he could not get out of his room or out of this house and he was struggling to find his way forward.

But now he laughed and shook his head, as if it had been a childish fancy, like being an astronaut, something that he had grown out of. He leaned down to soothe Dasher and the dog settled, waiting for his instructions.

'My mum tried to talk me out of joining the police and she's done a pretty good job. I'm studying PPE.'

'Personal protection equipment?'

'Politics, Philosophy and Economics, Max.'

'What can you do with that?'

'You can do anything.'

'That sounds good.'

We shook hands and I watched him until he had gone around the corner with Dasher and then I went up the short garden path and rang the bell.

Whitestone did not look surprised to see me. She was stone-cold sober and I was glad about that.

She was going to need to be stone-cold sober from now on.

'They're keeping Frank Lyle at the hospital to drain his lungs,' she said. 'At first they thought he had had a stroke. But it's the lung cancer, getting worse.' She looked at me for a long moment. 'And what's the bad news, Max?'

'I went to Frank Lyle's house,' I said.

'OK,' she said.

'I went there to ask Mrs Lyle to get him to take a step back from the investigation,' I said. 'Because he's not helping anyone.'

She nodded, steeling herself.

'And Harry Flowers was there,' I said.

She shook her head, trying to make sense of it.

But it made no sense at all.

'Flowers was having an affair with Jessica,' I told her. 'The flatmate of his mistress. Flowers is the father of baby Michael. I don't even know if *affair* is the right word. They were seeing each other. They were in a relationship. They were sleeping together. That's why Frank Lyle tried to take Flowers' head off with a hammer. Because he just found out. Jessica's mother has known for a while, but it was breaking news to the old man. And he wasn't thrilled to bits.'

She thought about it. 'So Flowers was ready to move on from Snezia and he took a shine to Jessica?'

I shrugged. 'Maybe it was the other way around. Maybe he took one look at Jessica and he was ready to move on from Snezia. You've seen photographs of Jessica. You've heard the way everyone talks about her. Everyone who meets her is crazy about her.'

I saw the spark of triumph in her eyes.

From the very start she had liked Flowers for the abduction.

'Flowers wanted Snezia gone but she was reluctant to move out of the love nest,' Whitestone said. 'Flowers wanted her out – out of the apartment, out of his bed, out of his life. And whatever goons he hired snatched the wrong woman.'

I shook my head. 'I can't buy it,' I said. 'If he wanted to press the eject button on Snezia, he didn't need the heavy mob. He didn't need to kidnap or kill her. He just needed his chequebook.' I hesitated. 'And we have to tread lightly with Flowers, Pat.'

She laughed out loud.

'Tread lightly? Why's that?'

I took a breath.

'Where did you get your car repaired?' I said.

She shook her head, running through that night in her mind.

The panic. The guilt. And the feeling that she had managed to put it behind her. But it wasn't behind her.

She looked at my face.

'No,' she said. 'Harry Flowers can't possibly know what happened that night.'

She was seeing it all in her head. The delivery driver on a scooter coming out of nowhere. The collision over before she knew what was happening. And the terrible moment come and gone when she had to decide if she was stopping.

And I had my own memory of that night. Whitestone standing at my door, the desperation all over her face. And later, driving up and down that empty road alone until I saw the stolen phones scattered across that lonely road north of King's Cross.

She found her bag, dug deep inside and took out a yellow match folder.

Auto Waste Solutions.

'He knows your car was in an accident,' I said. 'He knows you hit something you should not have hit.' I took the match folder from her. 'I don't know how much else he knows, but I watched him burn one of these things with your registration number on. I'm betting he will have photos of the car and maybe even CCTV of you bringing your car in. He *knows*, Pat. Or at the very least he suspects you hit something and never reported it. Think about it. His yard must have contacts with every garage in the city, maybe even the entire south-east of England. I've seen the place. It's huge. It's a giant graveyard for cars that have had their time. Where did you get it repaired?'

'Where I always go. A pair of Greek-Cypriot brothers off the Holloway Road.'

'Do they know you?'

'They know me because I go in there for petrol, service and MOT. A packet of Pringles and a newspaper on Sundays.'

'How many people work there?'

'I don't know. It's just a family-owned business on the Holloway Road. There's the brothers. The mechanics. A girl on the reception desk. And one of those car washes that employs twenty blokes from Kabul or Baghdad who just jumped off the back of a lorry.'

'Maybe it was one of the brothers who told Flowers. Or one of the blokes who just jumped off the back of the lorry. My bet? It was whoever fixed your car, some grease monkey who knows you're a cop. Or maybe it doesn't work like that. Maybe that garage – and every garage – clocks the registration number of anyone who drives in looking sweaty and desperate and asking for some urgent cash-in-hand repairs, fast as you can do it. And then they hand the information on to Auto Waste Solutions to check out the owner later, to see if it is someone that they can bleed dry. I bet it happens all the time. A good revenue stream for anyone in the wrecked car business. And they got lucky with you.'

Behind her spectacles, I saw her pale blue eyes blaze with anger.

'This is what the bastard does. This is how he buys your soul. This is what his business was built on. Harry Flowers finds your price. If it's money, if it's pouring petrol over your children – whatever it takes to make you bend the knee. He finds your soft spot and then he makes you his creature. When I was in uniform I saw decent policemen whose lives were trashed because they took his shilling. Good people who did the hardest of time, Max, the kind of hard time that ruins you forever, decent coppers who became the shoe-scrapings of prison life, just because Harry Flowers bought them. What does he want?'

'He wants us to find Jessica Lyle. Or her body. And he says that's enough.'

She laughed bitterly.

'Harry Flowers can never have enough of you,' she said. 'He thinks I'm his creature now. He thinks he has me for life.' She buried her face in her hands. 'What am I going to do, Max? I can't live with this hanging over me. I can't be one of his bought coppers.'

I could suddenly feel it all unravelling.

'Listen to me, Pat. You're going to do your job. We're going to find Jessica Lyle. And you are never going to be on Harry Flowers' payroll, OK? That's not you and it will never be you. We're going to find Jessica and, if she is still alive, we're going to bring her home to her family. And if she's dead, then we will bring them her body.'

She nodded, steeling herself, and something was settled in her mind.

I watched her turn the yellow match folder in her hands.

'OK, Max, that's what we'll do,' she said.

She pulled off a match and struck it, placing the flame against the folder. It caught, flared and began to burn. We watched the fire advance to her fingers.

'And then I will finish it with Harry,' she said. 'Finish it forever.'

22

Snezia Jones was moving out of her apartment.

In the soft light of the summer evening, a procession of dark, unassuming men of Anglo-Pakistani descent were toting cardboard boxes out of the apartment block in Eden Hill Park and loading them into the back of a removal van. The cousins. It was taking a while. The van was filling up and the cousins were sweating, but they kept going back inside. I suspected Snezia was a bit of an Imelda Marcos when it came to accumulating stuff.

The men were being instructed by Mo, Flowers' driver, and every one of them could have been his family member. Perhaps they really were his cousins. Mo saw me watching from the BMW and gave me a polite nod. I nodded back. I had always liked Mo.

Snezia came out of the building, a dozen designer bags hanging from her arms. I got out of the car and approached her.

'You never told me you got dumped,' I said.

She bristled with professional pride, her Gucci and Louis Vuitton bags jiggling with irritation.

'I *wasn't* dumped. I have *never* been dumped. *Nobody dumps me.*'

'But you knew that Harry Flowers was seeing Jessica. You knew they were in a relationship. *You knew she had his baby.* And yet you didn't tell me.'

'My relationship with Harry was over before he began with Jessica,' she said, reluctant to move on from the dumping issue, her professional pride piqued, wanting to get this important point clarified. 'So I was never *dumped*. And I have never been dumped. And I never will be dumped.' She smiled proudly. 'I have never met a man who did not want me again in the morning.'

'You should have told me that Jessica was involved with Harry Flowers.'

'I was told not to.'

'You don't have to follow Harry Flowers' orders, Snezia. You really don't get it, do you? Have you ever heard of Obstruction of Justice? It's the legal term for withholding information from the law. And it is bad news. You can do twenty years.'

'Or you can get a small fine, depending on the offence. Don't you have to prove – what do they call it? – specific intent to obstruct justice?'

'Did Harry tell you that? Flowers is just some old career criminal, Snezia. You should stop confusing him with Yoda.'

'But I always wanted to help you find Jess, didn't I? And I never tried to obstruct justice, did I?'

'Don't try to get smart, Snezia. It doesn't suit you.'

'Look, I have never wanted anything but for Jess to come home safely. If I ever had something important to tell you, then I would. But Jess was terrified of her father finding out about her and Harry. When it comes to his daughter, that man is a maniac. Jess made me promise never to tell *anyone* about her and Harry. She thought her father would try to kill Harry if he knew. I mean – like *literally* kill him. And she was right, wasn't she? If he wasn't such a sick old man, he might have succeeded. An honour killing. Is that what they call it? That's what Jess was afraid of, because she knew her father would never accept Harry. She was always the golden girl in that family. There's not much competition. There's only her and that retarded brother.'

'Tommy Lyle has learning difficulties.'

She nodded. 'Retarded, like I said. So it was almost like she was the only child with all parental hopes riding on her. She thought that getting knocked up by Harry was not what her father planned or wanted or would ever accept. And she was right.'

A beautiful young man with elaborate, swept-back hair came out of the building, carrying a magnificent kettle. He placed a long, wet kiss on Snezia's mouth, put the kettle in the back of the van and went inside. He wasn't knocking himself out. He wasn't working up a sweat like Mo's cousins. But then he had his hair to think about.

Snezia looked at me as if she had proved a point.

'You moved on,' I said.

She glanced towards the glass doors that the beautiful man had just swished through.

'I always move on,' she said.

'But it has to hurt,' I said. 'Getting dropped for your flatmate.'

'I told you – it was all over between Harry and me before Harry and Jess began.'

'Yes, you told me and I don't believe you. But I do believe that Harry Flowers loves her. He's crazy about her.'

She inhaled deeply. 'Jess might have *thought* it was serious, but that doesn't make it serious.'

'Harry seems to think it's serious. They have a child. That's about as serious as it ever gets. But help me with the timing, Snezia. The dead fiancé – Lawrence – got knocked off his bike six months ago. Jessica hadn't worked up the nerve to end it with him at the time of his death. So she was cheating on Lawrence when Flowers was cheating on you.'

'You're so sweet,' she said. 'Harry never cheated on me. A man can't cheat on his mistress. Someone once told me that. Somebody's wife.' She smiled. 'And Jessica never cheated on Lawrence. Not really. They were like brother and sister towards the end. Isn't that the way it always ends up between men and women, if you leave them together long enough?'

'Harry Flowers would disagree.'

'Look, Harry is always very keen at the start. He was keen on *me* at the start. Then his interest wanes. Then his eye wanders. He is a man of limitless sexual opportunities, and that kind *always* get bored in the end. Just as Harry would have got bored with Jess. Even if he is too pussy-whipped to know it right now.'

'Nobody blames you for feeling bitter.'

She shook her head. 'I wish none of this had ever happened. I wish Jess was still here. I think about what might have happened to her and it rips my heart out. But I'm *not* bitter. Look at my boyfriend,' she said proudly. 'Do you know what he is?'

'A hairdresser?'

'He's *age appropriate*. And there's a lot to be said for it.'

'No regrets?'

'The truth is that Harry and I were glad to see the back of each other. We were both relieved that it ended so painlessly. Jessica was the way out for both of us. I had already met Josh. And you don't cheat on Harry Flowers.'

A small white van entered Eden Hill Park and took a long slow loop around the estate. The private security guard. What was his name? Modric. He looked at me and nodded. I didn't nod back.

Modric parked the van and got out, watching Mo and the cousins carry the boxes. An ineffectual little man, I thought. I could understand how easy it must have been for him to bottle it the night Jessica Lyle was taken. I could understand why Whitestone hated him. I turned to Snezia.

'Were you and Jessica still friends on the night she was taken?'

'Of course! Listen, if it worked out for Harry and Jess, then I was happy for her. Happy for him. Happy for both of them. But come on! How *could* it have worked out? Harry has a wife who he will never leave. And who will never leave him. Oh, Christ on a stick.'

A silver Mercedes-Benz was entering the estate. At the wheel was Ruben Shavers. Derek Bumpus was beside him, his broken arm in its blue plaster cast resting on the open window.

And in the back seat was Meadow Flowers.

'Guess who gets the apartment next?' Snezia said, her eyes not leaving the silver Merc. 'Daddy's daughter and her new husband. It's a wedding present.'

Josh came out of the building carrying a contraption made of chrome, tinted plastic and extractor blades, a smoothie blender so complicated it looked as though it might have been designed by NASA.

Meadow Flowers buzzed down her window.

'Put it back, bitch,' she told Snezia.

The Merc came to a halt directly in front of the removal van. Shavers switched off the engine. He got out of the car, relaxed, calm, his default charming smile on his handsome face, his arms hanging loosely at his side.

Bumpus also got out, not quite as smoothly, and stared at the fine-looking young Josh and then at Mo and lastly Mo's helpers, who had all suddenly come to a dead stop.

'I didn't know the al-Qaeda did removals!' Bumpus said.

Nobody moved. The big engine of the Mercedes ticked and clicked as if tut-tutting at the unauthorised removal of the smoothie blender.

Meadow was still sitting in the back seat, like a monarch about to wave to the crowds. But finally she got out, sighing with exasperation.

'*Put. It. Back. Bitch*. What part of *put-it-back-bitch* don't you understand?'

Josh turned to carry the blender back into the house.

'Stop,' Snezia said. 'No, it's not right. It's mine. I paid for it with money I earned.'

'On your *back*,' Meadow smiled, which got a laugh from Bumpus, whose smile vanished and face reddened as Josh started to carry the tug-of-love blender to the removal van.

Bumpus roared one word.

'*Don't!*'

And that was when the security guard began to move.

He had parked his vehicle at a respectful distance from the removal van, but now he was jogging towards it, reaching for his phone, his eyes never leaving the large man with the broken arm and the flushed face glaring at the young man carrying the smoothie blender.

And all at once I got it.

The men who took Jessica Lyle had said one word to the guard, and it was enough to unman him, and it was enough to seal her fate.

Don't, they had told Modric.

And he didn't.

But he was going to make up for it now.

'That's *them*!' he shouted at me, still moving towards Bumpus and Shavers, still fumbling with his phone. 'The men who took the woman!'

And Shavers was laughing, his massive scarred hands spread wide, making no move to run, but Bumpus was already climbing clumsily into the driver's seat of the silver Merc and gunning the engine. Shavers called his name, telling him to stop, but the car was moving and Shavers snatched at the open passenger door and threw himself inside, the door flapping wildly as Bumpus swung the car around, driving with his one good hand, gravel flying and tyres screaming as he sped away.

Straight at the guard.

Modric held up his hands, and he said one word which may have been 'Stop!' before the car drove through him, crumpling his legs just below the knees and violently bouncing him first off the bonnet and then off the windscreen of the big Mercedes.

I heard glass crack and bones break. Someone was screaming. And then the Merc was gone.

I bent down to look at the young security guard, his smooth, unformed face a bloody mush, and I touched the shoulder of his silly uniform, because I wanted him to know.

He had not been a coward today.

And then I went after them.

23

I ran up Hampstead Grove, and it was more like a country lane than a road in central London, the day suddenly twilight under the thick canopy of trees, and the road always getting steeper as I climbed towards the highest point in the city.

I heard what sounded like an explosion not far ahead of me.

The silver Mercedes had stopped on the wrong side of the road, the front of the car caved in, the hood lifted and folded in on itself, the guts of the engine spilling out and smoking.

There was no one inside. I kept running, not noticing the car it had hit until I was almost past it.

There was an old grey Mini trapped between the crashed Merc and a lamppost. The driver's side was sheared off, steam or smoke billowing from under the hood. There was an elderly woman behind the wheel. She had the look that I had seen before in the victims of sudden trauma. As though time had suddenly stopped stone-dead, but they couldn't understand why it had happened.

I gently eased the woman out of the car. She could walk so I led her away from the wreck, calling 999 with my free hand. Her face was impassive but drained of all colour or awareness.

'You're safe,' I told her. 'But you're in shock. I need you to breathe for me. Can you do that?'

No response.

I quickly felt her back, neck and head, keeping one eye on the wreck. I didn't like all that smoke. She had no obvious injuries so I helped her to lie down on the scraggy grass verge by the side of the road and used my jacket to elevate her feet by about 12 inches.

Then I went back to the wreck.

The Merc and the Mini were almost welded together. Both the engines were still running. I turned off the ignitions and switched on the hazard lights. Then I went back to the woman. The sirens were already coming but I crouched beside her and stayed with her until the ambulance arrived.

And when the paramedics were attending to her, I went on.

I stopped at the top of the hill, slowing my breath, uncertain which way Bumpus and Shavers had run.

On both sides of the road, separated by a large pond glinting in the last of the sunlight, Hampstead Heath unfolded. Eight hundred acres of woodland, grasslands, meadows, heathland and ponds. You could get lost here. You could hide.

If they went east, to the great green and wooded mass of the Heath, they had more chance of losing me. They would be spoilt for choice when making their exit. They could leave the Heath via the landscaped gardens of Kenwood to the north or the bathing ponds or Parliament Hill and then out to the crowded streets around South End Green to the south.

I stood there panting and thinking. There were sirens in the air but they didn't seem to be getting any closer and they were not going to help me.

If they went in the other direction, I thought, looking off towards the long slope down to West Heath and then Golders Hill Park, they had a mile or so of thick woodland to cross before reaching Golders Green. I could not see Bumpus and Shavers camping out beneath the stars.

So I went west, jogging down a steep dirt lane and then turning into the thick woods. I walked for a few minutes, watching the trees for movement, and to my right and high above me there was a building that looked like a palace that had been abandoned long ago. Time-stained columns covered with climbing plants ran the length of the empty halls.

The Pergola, I thought. One of the prime residences of Edwardian London, left to rot for a hundred years.

And that is where I saw him.

Ruben Shavers, walking slowly through one of the Pergola's halls, as if out for a stroll.

No sign of Derek Bumpus.

I ducked behind a tree and let Shavers walk on and then I climbed the steep hill to the walls of the Pergola.

No Dogs, said a sign on a gate. *Not even yours.* I listened but I could hear nothing. Even the distant sirens seemed to have stopped. I clambered over the gate and dropped into the Pergola.

Shavers was walking slowly between the stone columns, walking in circles, I saw now, but still looking as if he was strolling, touching at his forehead, looking at the blood on his hands.

'Get on your knees,' I said.

He turned to look at me, woozy from the crash, maybe concussed.

'Listen to me,' he said.

'*On your knees.*'

He remained standing but held up his hands as if in surrender. There was a livid gash above one eyebrow. Could I take him? He was a big man, but it had been a long time since I saw him fight in York Hall. I fancied my chances with his head split open and possible concussion kicking in.

I walked towards him, taking my time.

'Down,' I said. 'Last chance, Shavers.'

He slowly got down on his knees.

244

'Listen to me,' he said. 'It's not what you think. I know who took her. And I know why they took her. And I know what happened to her.'

People lie to me all day long.

Perhaps people lie to everyone all day long. But if you are a policeman, lies are the air you breathe. People lie so they will not be punished. They lie because they are afraid. And they lie because they are guilty.

'You took her,' I said. 'You and that fat ugly bastard.'

'Not me. Bumpus maybe. But not me.'

'Where is she?'

'I can help you. I can take you to her. She's safe. She can go home to that little baby of hers.'

I had my phone in my hand, ready to call it in.

But I nodded to him, telling him to keep talking if he had something to say.

'It's like this,' he said, and I saw his eyes flick beyond my shoulder just as Bumpus hit the back of my head with what felt like half a brick.

It doubled me up, my vision a mass of black stars, like the end of the universe. The pain made me sick to my stomach.

But Bumpus had not knocked me over, I was still just about standing, so he grabbed my hair and forced me to the ground. On my knees and then over on to my back and his large fleshy head was above me and he was kneeling on my chest, a sliver of drool coming from his mouth as he wrapped one hand around my throat.

For a guy with one arm in a cast, he had a pretty good grip.

He began to choke me with his good hand.

'Your daughter,' he said. 'That sweet little girl. That beautiful thing. I know where she lives. What does her bedroom look like? I have thought about it many times.'

And I could not speak because the stink of him filled my nose and throat and lungs and he was my darkest nightmare made real, a man who wanted to do my child harm, real harm, the worst kind of harm imaginable, and I knew that it would give him nothing but pleasure, nothing but sick joy.

'How old is she?' he said. 'Is she ready for me?'

'*I will kill you*,' I told him, and he laughed at me.

Shavers cursed behind him.

'Del, do you really want to top another one?' he said.

'Yes,' Bumpus said. 'I want to top one more. This one. This pig who broke my arm. Him more than anyone. Top him. Then pay a visit to his daughter.'

Then Bumpus was releasing his grip on my throat to turn and stand up and shout at Shavers. A disagreement among professionals.

I tried to sit up but the nausea from the blow made me lie down again. The back of my head was pulsing with pain. I closed my eyes and when I opened them to the sound of their voices they were standing with their faces pressed together, awkwardly shoving each other.

One man with blood streaming down his face and the other with a broken arm.

I fought for air, the feel of those fingers still embedded in my throat, trying to think.

Do you want to top another one?

Bumpus looked down at me and laughed.

He had seen something change in my eyes.

Top another one?

'Oh yeah,' he said. 'You dumb pig. Oh yeah. You don't think you'd be my first, do you?'

Sirens again.

Getting closer.

In the silence of that abandoned palace, the three of us paused to listen to them for a moment, as if discerning their meaning.

Then Ruben Shavers was tugging at his partner's good arm.

'Del,' he was saying. 'We have to go.'

But Bumpus was not finished with me.

'Do you want to find that bitch?' he said.

He could not resist. He just could not resist. Sometimes they can't resist rubbing your face in the mess they have made of someone's life. He kicked me in the face. More flashing black stars. The universe ending all over again, that last moment for all things flashing on and on for eternity.

'Try looking in the graveyard,' Bumpus told me.

24

Frank Lyle slept sitting up, the sleeping position of the dying man in a hospital bed, a transparent oxygen mask over his nose and mouth, his face dark with stubble. I had only ever seen him with his face clean-shaven, I realised. But everything was changed in here.

There was a plastic sheet surrounding his bed like an oversized shower curtain, separating him from the other men in the ward. Some of them slept deeply, the bottomless sleep of opiates, while some twisted and moaned in the night, somewhere between sleep and waking.

The old cop stirred, writhing with a sudden spasm of pain, and then he was staring at me, as if unsure whether I was only in his imagination.

'Christ Almighty,' he said, peering closer at the raw scuff mark high on one cheekbone. 'You look worse than me.'

We both smiled at that.

'And when someone in a cancer ward tells you that you look rough ...' he said. Then he winced with a sudden stab of pain.

'Frank,' I said. 'We know who took Jessica.'

He waited, and I could hear his laboured breathing.

'Two of Flowers' men,' I said. 'Ruben Shavers and Derek Bumpus. We assume they were freelancing for a third party.'

'Are they in custody?'

'Not yet. They ran. But we'll find them.'

He thought about it, his eyes shining with helpless tears in the twilight of the hospital ward. Then he shook his head.

'So – what? They were bought by some business rival?' he said. 'Or an old face from long ago who has waited a lifetime for payback?'

'Looks like it,' I said.

He held back the tears but he could not stop his voice from cracking with emotion.

'There are only two real possibilities,' he said, as if we were working this case together. And I guess that in a way we were. 'They took her and killed her immediately. Or they took her ...'

He waited for the breath to come, and when it finally came there was still not quite enough of it.

'And then they raped her,' he said. 'And then they killed her. Anything else you can think of?'

'No,' I said. 'But if we don't have a body then she could still be alive. Somewhere, somehow.'

I resisted the urge to touch his arm.

He was not the kind of man who had much use for a reassuring pat.

'We'll keep looking,' I said. 'For Bumpus and Shavers. For Jessica.'

Look in the graveyard, Big Del had boasted, just before he kicked me in the head.

Was Jessica Lyle really buried in a graveyard? But what graveyard? And how the hell was I ever going to find it?

'My only child,' Lyle said.

Was his mind wandering? Perhaps it was the painkillers. The medication would be heavy duty by now.

'But you have a son,' I gently reminded him. 'You have Tommy, don't you?'

He laughed bitterly, remembering.

'Oh yes. My son.' His eyes flashed with irritation in the twilight of the hospital ward. 'I meant – my only daughter. That's what I meant.'

His back arched with a sudden slash of excruciating pain.

There was a scarred metal box on his bed for calling for help.

'Frank,' I said. 'Do you need some more morphine?'

But he shook his head, his face still twisted by the pain.

'Not yet,' he said. 'I'm rationing the hard stuff. Or it will only be much worse later.' He stared at me, panting for breath like an overheated dog on a summer's day. 'You've been in a place like this before, haven't you?'

I nodded. 'My parents,' I said. 'Both of them. And my grandmother. My nan.'

I didn't like to say the word. Even now, half a lifetime on from losing my family, I hesitated to name the thing that had killed them.

So Frank Lyle said it for me.

'Cancer,' he said. 'Some of the men in here, some of them are younger than you, I bet. And somewhere else – in some other hospital – there are children with cancer. So what do I have to moan about? I tell myself that I have had a life. Some of them in this ward, like him in the next bed, their life hasn't even started. I try to count my blessings. But it is the hardest thing in the world, trying to understand the good luck you have had. What happened with your folks?'

'They died within twelve months of each other when I was a kid,' I said. 'Lung cancer. Smoking-related, although they had both stopped for years. Same thing with my nan. She looked after me when my mum and dad were gone. I reckon there comes a point where it's not worth giving up. My old man didn't tell anyone he was dying, like it had slipped his mind.'

'Maybe he was trying to protect you and your mother,' he said, harder now, a touch of the tough old cop returning. 'That ever occur to you?'

'Later,' I said. 'That's what I thought maybe happened a lot later. And he was like you. A hard man.'

Frank Lyle snorted in his hospital bed.

'Maybe he just wanted to deal with it alone,' he said. 'But I think, more than anything, your father, he just couldn't find the words. I don't know how you find those words to tell people you love you're not going to be around. That's what is hard.'

'It was all different with my mum,' I said, 'because we knew from the start. But in some ways, it was just the same, at the end.'

'That must have been tough,' he said, softening. 'Losing them so close together.'

'You ever meet people who lost both of their parents in the same car crash?'

'A few,' he said, then thinking about it. 'A lot.'

'Me too. Because married couples travel in cars together. They do it all the time. And so – some of them – they die together. It was a bit like that with my parents. I was like one of those kids who lose their folks in a car crash. You are living one kind of life and then suddenly you are living another kind of life.'

I watched him stop thinking, overwhelmed by the pain now, the pain of the tumour that was growing inside him and killing him.

I indicated the metal box. 'Morphine,' I said. 'It will help you sleep.'

'I don't care for the stuff,' he said, as if he was talking about Marmite. 'It puts a fog in my head. It turns you into somebody you're not.'

'It will take the edge off the pain,' I said, although I knew he was right about the morphine fog. 'Until you get a bit better.'

'They don't put you in here to get a bit better,' he said. 'They put you in here to die.'

But the agony was all-consuming and he reached for the metal box on his bed and called for a nurse. I stood up when she whipped back the curtains and began to administer to him, as jovial as a nursery school teacher.

I got up to go.

'What happened to you?' he said. 'After your parents were gone?'

'I was lucky,' I said. 'Because I had my grandmother. You only really need one person who loves you.'

We were silent.

'Like my grandson,' he said. 'Like Michael.'

'Yes,' I said. 'Like Michael. He's lucky too.'

Whitestone was standing outside the main doors of the hospital.

A skeletal patient in a dressing gown sucked hungrily on a cigarette with one hand and steadied his oxygen tank with the other. Whitestone sipped from a vending machine cup of coffee that was too boiling hot to drink and she did not really want. But she sipped it anyway.

'How's the security guard doing?' I said. 'How's Modric?'

'Modric will live, I reckon,' she said, not making it sound like that was necessarily a good thing. 'He's in a medically induced coma. They're trying to protect his brain. He has a cerebral haemorrhage from where his head hit the car or the deck. Tubes coming out of every bit of him. I saw his wife outside the ICU. They've got two little kids. She can't stop crying.'

I looked back at the hospital.

'Maybe I should talk to his wife,' I said. 'Tell her how well he did.'

'She knows,' Whitestone said flatly. 'And with that and two quid, she can buy a cup of coffee.' She nodded at me. 'Tell me what happened again,' she said.

She had done the hot debriefing while they were patching me up in Accident and Emergency, but they always liked you to keep telling the story. Just in case it was different.

'I saw Ruben Shavers in the Pergola and as I was arresting him I was struck from behind by Derek Bumpus,' I said. 'And as Bumpus was attempting to strangle me, they argued and Shavers said to him, *Do you want to top another one?*'

'Another one after killing Jessica Lyle.'

'And maybe also Lawrence, the fiancé that got knocked off his bike. Pat, I am really struggling to believe that was just another accident statistic.'

'Shavers and Bumpus have worked for Flowers for years. They could have bodies buried all over this town. What else?'

She watched me hesitate and knew that there was something I had censored in the hot debriefing. But I told her now.

'Bumpus talked about Scout,' I said.

'How does he know about Scout?'

'He saw her the first time Flowers came to see me after Jessica was taken. And the first thing he said to me was – *How old is your kid?* And he talked more when he had his hand around my throat. He said he was going to pay her a visit. He said he knows where we live.'

Her face was impassive in the glow of the vending machine.

'He asked me about Scout's bedroom, Pat.'

'He's taunting you. He's getting under your skin.'

'Yes, all that,' I said. 'But I think he means it, too. I think he means every word. There are men like that in the world. We have busted enough of them. Men who want to do things to children. And Derek Bumpus is one of them. And he has this thing, Pat, this obsession with Scout.'

She was silent. And then she nodded.

255

'Then what happened?'

'Bumpus wanted to kill me but the sirens were coming and he ran out of time. But he could not stop himself from taunting me. Wanting to show me – I don't know – that he thought he had somehow won. *Look for her in the graveyard*, he told me. And then they fled.'

Whitestone thought about it. She sipped at the scalding brown liquid pretending to be coffee and then, with a grimace of disgust, poured it into the vending machine's little silver drain.

'How many graveyards are there in this city?' she said.

'We can't dig up all of them.'

'Then it's a false lead. He wants us chasing our tails instead of him.'

I wasn't convinced.

'But if you want to bury a body that will never be found,' I said, 'then where better than a graveyard?'

25

Late morning on a glorious summer's day, the sky an unbroken blue, perfect for a white wedding. The Flowers house was waiting for the bride and groom, the manorial gates wide open and adorned with bows of white silk.

We parked on the other side of the road, waiting for the father of the bride.

From the road you could see the marquee that had been erected in the back garden – actually more of a real building than a marquee, with high white walls and pretty, white-framed windows. On the lawn black-clad waiters and waitresses stood to attention as they were given their instructions by the caterers. Music was playing inside the marquee – the romantic end of R&B. Guests were beginning to arrive in their own cars, the women in their hats and summer dresses, some of the men dressed in morning suits, even a top hat or two, really pushing the boat out, all of them turning to look at the convoy of police vehicles on the road. Some of them giving us the finger.

I was in my BMW X5 with Whitestone and Adams. Behind us there were two large vans full of uniformed officers and a smaller, unmarked van containing Jackson Rose and a team of Specialist Firearms Officers.

One of the guests buzzed down the window of his green Porsche 911 to spit at one of the police vans. I saw the face of Junior Flowers, his smooth face twisted with loathing.

'On my sister's wedding day,' he bawled. 'The disrespect of you people! Un-fucking-believable!'

More cars were arriving back from the church.

'How much for a wedding like this?' Whitestone said. 'Fifty grand? A hundred?'

I shrugged. I didn't know much about weddings.

'Recycling dead motors doesn't pay for a do like this,' Whitestone said. 'Used cars don't pay this kind of bill.'

I was looking in my rear-view mirror. 'Here they come,' I said.

The Bentley Bentayga led the way, followed by a black Mercedes and then a Rolls-Royce Silver Cloud with a white ribbon tied to the hood. Harry and Charlotte Flowers were in the back of the Bentley with Mo at the wheel. Another middle-aged couple were in the Merc – the parents of the groom, I assumed. And in the back of the Rolls-Royce were the happy couple, Meadow Flowers smiling among a mass of white lace with a handsome young man by her side.

We let them pass through the gates.

Whitestone gave the nod and we followed them inside.

They were still getting out of their cars when the uniformed officers piled out of their vehicles and went quickly into the back garden. Joy Adams went with them. Jackson and a dozen shots got out of their van but stayed on the driveway, their short Sig Sauer MCX assault rifles held at the 45-degree angle. With their grey body armour and their Glock 17 handguns, they looked like an army from the future.

Wedding guests came from the garden to gawp at them, flutes of champagne in their hand. Meadow Flowers, a riot of white, was helped from the Silver Cloud by her groom, with one hand in his and the other laid instinctively across the gentle swell of her belly, that gesture of instinctive reassurance and protection that I remembered Anne making when we were waiting for Scout to be born.

Nobody was spitting at us now.

'We're looking for your men,' Whitestone told Harry Flowers.

He stared at her, long and hard, as if she had some nerve, as if he had never expected to see her again. He was sweating inside his light grey morning suit.

'Dad?'

Flowers glanced at his daughter and her husband.

'Do you need the whole family?' he asked.

'Just you, Harry,' I said.

'Go,' he told his family.

They hesitated, all of them, his wife and his son and his daughter. Then something flamed in his eyes and they obeyed his instructions.

We stood on that gravel driveway, just us and Harry Flowers, with Jackson and his shots at a discreet distance around the back of their van, and Beyoncé singing 'If I Were a Boy' drifting to us from the garden.

'Where are your men?' I said. 'Where are Shavers and Bumpus?'

He mopped his sweaty brow and snorted with disbelief.

'You think they're going to be handing out the canapés? That pair are *not my men*. Not any more. And it looks like they haven't been my men for a while.'

'I thought they might still be your men,' Whitestone said.

He turned on her. There was cheering from the garden. The bride and groom were making their big entrance at the party.

'How could those Judas bastards still be my men?' Flowers said.

'Here's a theory for you,' Whitestone said. 'Jessica Lyle was dumping *you*. She had had enough of her well-heeled bit of rough. You were a rebound thing after she started feeling a bit stuck with her fiancé, Lawrence.

260

You were a sympathetic listener on a big budget. And effectively her landlord, of course.'

'I was not her landlord. She was Snezia's flatmate. I was nobody's landlord.'

'And Jessica was bailing out,' Whitestone continued, ignoring him. 'And you couldn't stand it. Some men – and some women too – they think they are the only ones who are allowed to do the dumping. They think that they can never be the one who gets rejected. And then it happens to them. And it hurts.'

He shook his head.

He muttered something under his breath.

Whitestone cupped a hand to her ear. 'Louder?'

'I said – *I love her.* And I can prove it to you. Come on.'

We followed him into the house, flowers everywhere, and into his office. Behind a framed photograph of Winston Churchill smoking a cigar and carrying a machine gun there was a wall safe. He tapped in the code, opened the door and reached inside.

He took out a phone.

'A second phone,' Whitestone said, as he turned it on. 'A dedicated phone only used for your screwing around outside the marriage, right? My ex-husband had one of these. So you had a second phone dedicated to Jessica Lyle? It doesn't prove a thing.'

He scrolled through the phone's photographs and, finding what he was looking for, held it up for us to see.

261

Harry Flowers and Jessica Lyle in a hotel room at a room service table, raising a wine glass and smiling.

'Look at the date stamp,' he said.

We looked. It was the night she had been abducted.

'Does that look like someone who was unhappy?' he said. 'Does that look like a woman who wants to get out of a relationship?'

Whitestone chuckled.

'Christ, Harry! Women can fake bigger things than a smile for a selfie! Your secret scrapbook doesn't prove a thing.'

From the window I could see the uniformed officers moving among the guests, asking questions, taking notes. The music was still playing. Somehow the party was going on as the Met made their enquiries.

'Harry,' I said, watching the garden. 'Either they took Jessica because you ordered them to, or somebody hired them to do it. Which is it?'

He shook his head bitterly, as if he had nothing more to prove to us.

'I can believe it of Bumpus,' he said. 'He is unstable. He has always been unstable. Devoted to me – at least he was once – but always borderline psychotic. Maybe a bit over the borderline.'

'Then why was he on your payroll?'

'Because people are scared of a madman,' he said. 'You know – the Ronnie Kray effect? Sometimes it is not enough to be harder than the rest. You need that element of madness. You need genuine lunacy – the feeling that anything could happen. That it wouldn't end in black eyes and broken bones, but someone might get their nose bitten off. Or killed. And back in the day, before I went straight, Big Del Bumpus gave us that. I know he didn't like Mo and the cousins being on the payroll. Big Del wasn't very broad-minded when it came to living in vibrant, multicultural society. He felt he was being pushed out.'

'What about Shavers?'

'Ruben was always moaning about money. Always blowing cash he didn't have to impress the women. Back in his boxing years, he thought he was going to be on the earnings of Anthony Joshua. And although he didn't make it, he never made that adjustment in his head, he never reduced his expectations. You know what I think? I think that Bumpus had hurt feelings. And Ruben was a greedy bastard.'

'Who hired them?'

'My guess is they did it off their own bat.' He gestured towards the wedding party. 'You're not going to find them here.'

Joy Adams appeared in the doorway.

Flowers stared at her as if he was seeing her for the first time.

'But you should look for Shavers in Tottenham or Brixton,' he said. 'That's where Mo's cousins are looking. Ruben still had contact with the old neighbourhoods.' He was still looking at Joy. 'They never really leave, do they? And Bumpus is from Manchester way, but he grew up in care so there's nobody to run to up there. They haven't gone far. And if I find them before you do, I will personally bring them to West End Central.'

Whitestone nodded, unimpressed.

'Let me ask you, Harry – how does a glorified grease monkey pay for a wedding like this?'

'You save up.'

Then he smiled at her, shaking his head, genuinely amused.

'Oh, DCI Whitestone. I can't believe you would come to my home on my daughter's wedding day.'

'You think you're some kind of no-go area, Harry?'

'Just do your job,' he said, jabbing his finger at her face, his voice suddenly cracking with rage and grief. 'I want them *found*. I want them found and then I want them hung in their cells. I know that you can arrange it because we all know that it happens all the time,' he said. 'There's still capital punishment in this country, it never went away, but now it happens in police custody. Another tragic suicide in police custody. That's what I want for the men who took Jessica. *Get it done*. Make it happen or you will wish you had never been born, Whitestone.'

'Excuse me?'

He took a step towards her, starting to lose it, his mouth pulled out of shape with outrage.

I stepped forward, took a fistful of morning suit lapel and shoved him back.

'Don't you get it?' he told her, shrugging me off but knowing enough to keep his distance. '*You belong to me now.*'

I looked across at Joy and nodded.

She headed for the front door.

Whitestone took a step towards Flowers.

She lowered her voice, so it was just between the pair of them.

'You think I'm afraid of you, Harry?' she said.

'Not as much as you should be.'

'I don't think you have anything on me,' she said, stepping back, attempting a smile, making light of it. 'Maybe some old lag clocked me. But that's it. No CCTV. No photos. You played your cards well. But that's it. Bluffing.'

'Try me.'

'Maybe I will, Harry.'

As we were leaving he poured himself a drink, needing to steady himself before joining the party in the garden. But he called my name at the door.

'You were the last person to see them,' he said.

'Yes.'

'What did they say?'

'Bumpus told me to look in the graveyard,' I said.

*

Whitestone and Adams returned to the car, but I lingered by the back door, watching the wedding party. Charlotte Flowers approached me with a flute of champagne in each hand. I thought she might throw it in my face. But she offered me one of them and I declined.

'Is this where you say you're on duty?' she smiled.

'How did you end up here?' I said.

Her smile grew wider.

'At this wedding?'

'In this house. In this life.' I looked towards the closed door of Harry Flowers' den. 'In this marriage.'

She sipped from one of the champagne flutes.

'My father died when I was ten. My mother – a great beauty in her day – remarried. The man had sons. Older sons. Three of them.' She sipped her drink and seemed to be listening to the music from the garden for a moment. 'And it was hell,' she said, still smiling. 'And then I was a few years older and I was this privately educated party girl from central casting. And I was around a lot of drugs. I mean – *a lot.*'

I looked at her fresh, untouched face. And I found it hard to believe she had ever taken anything stronger than a protein shake.

'You have to stop all that before you're seventeen, of course,' she said. 'Or it shows forever. And my mother didn't like it very much – and my stepfather liked it even less. And he told my mother that it was me or him. She chose him – no contest – and they threw me out. And then I met Harry – already making a lot of money – and I wouldn't sleep with him. Because I suspected that, with a man like Harry Flowers, that's what it would take to seal the deal. And so it proved. And so here we are.' She chuckled. 'And there are policemen with assault rifles at my daughter's wedding!'

'I'm sorry we had to come here today,' I said. 'We have no intention of ruining your daughter's big day. But we're seeking information on two men who are on the run. Information for what could turn out to be a murder investigation.'

'And there was me thinking that you had just come here to intimidate my husband.'

She had finished one flute of champagne and started on the one that she had offered me. And for the first time I could see her as one of those party kids who come from a home where there is plenty of money but not much of anything else worth having.

'Intimidation is a part of it,' I said.

I remembered her on the day she had found out about Snezia, hurling her husband's possessions out of a first-floor window, and I wondered how much she really knew about her husband's other life. About the petrol can emptied over the Mahone family. About the

267

dedicated phone, the mistresses, the flat in a good neighbourhood that he had kept for years.

The uniformed officers were leaving now. Through an
open window, decorated with white ribbons, I could see
them filing past the side of the house and heading for their
vans. Someone cheered. The volume of the music went up.
Alicia Keys at her most achingly romantic. And something
about Alicia's voice – promising that there was no real life
and no real happiness without you, singing in a way that
made you believe her – unlocked something inside me.

'How can you stand it?' I said. 'Living with a man
like your husband?'

Charlotte Flowers smiled at me, as if she was a woman
who could survive anything.

'There's nothing you can tell me about my husband
that I don't know – or can't guess – already,' she said.
'So he has some little bit of a girl on the side. Or two
or three – or even his own private harem.'

Charlotte Flowers was the kind of woman who would
say *harem* rather than *whorehouse*. Even if they had never
loved her, someone had spent a small fortune on her
education.

'Do you think that compares to twenty-five years of
marriage?' she said. 'Do you think he's with them on
Christmas Day? Even if some little hussy attempts to
trap him by getting pregnant, do you really think it
compares with raising a family?'

With a half-empty champagne flute, she gestured towards the garden, taking it all in – the marquee that looked as though it was built to last and the romantic music that had been carefully chosen and the river of champagne.

I saw that Harry Flowers was out there now, happy again, red-faced with pride and alcohol as he greeted his guests.

Charlotte Flowers watched me watching him.

'Whatever he's done, it's nothing next to all this,' she said. 'Are you *sure* you can't have one drink to toast the bride?'

'Enjoy your day,' I said. 'And I am sorry if we spoiled it.'

'Nothing could ever spoil today,' she smiled.

The shots were stretching their legs at the front gates. The uniformed officers were getting back into their vans. Joy Adams was in the BMW, checking her messages.

And Pat Whitestone was in the back of the small unmarked van with Jackson Rose, staring at the Glock 17 he held in his hand.

They both looked up at me, their faces unreadable.

And then they shut the doors.

A cheer came from the back garden.

The father of the bride was dancing with his daughter.

26

Fred's gym.

There was a svelte forty-something woman who looked like she should be running through her yoga asanas banging seven bells out of the heavy bag. There was an old man in glasses with a blood-pressure monitor attached to his upper arm and the latest Asics on his feet walking steadily on a treadmill, taking his time, as if he planned to live forever. There were a couple of young men in their twenties who looked like cage fighters but who worked in the City, pumping the free weights that were all printed with one word.

Fred's

And Fred was in the middle of it all, silver hair pulled up in a topknot, counting down someone's reps, then fussing with the music, looking for a soundtrack that matched the mood to perfection, and always urging encouragement.

'You're so lucky to be training,' he told me, as he put on some Chic and I whaled away at the heavy bag until a buzzer went and I got down on the floor for ten burpies and ten press-ups. By the time I got up from the press-ups and burpies the minute's break between rounds had almost gone by and Fred was waiting for me with curved Lonsdale punch mitts on his hands.

'On the bell – double jab and move away,' he said. 'Recover while you work.'

On the final buzzer, Fred tossed the punch mitts aside and went off to change Chic to The Jam on the sound system, Nile Rodgers somehow not quite hitting the spot. And as I was waiting for him to return, Jackson Rose appeared before me, watching me, already in his training kit, black-and-yellow protective wraps on his hands.

'Put some gloves on,' I told him, putting the punch mitts on my hands.

Jackson slipped on a pair of red Cleto Reyes 16-ounce gloves, the old Mexican leather cracked and worn.

'Double jab, straight right, left hook,' I told him.

He threw out the combination I had called, his punches hitting the pads I held up with a whiplash crack, his left hand drifting away from his chin with the final punch, dropping down by his hip.

With my right hand, I slapped him hard across the left side of his face.

271

'Keep that guard up,' I said. 'Triple jab, straight right, two left hooks.'

He did as he was told, his punches harder now, the light brown skin on one side of his face reddened by the pad.

This time he kept his guard up.

'You are not doing Pat Whitestone any favours,' I said. 'Double jab and move away.'

He threw out two stiff jabs. They rocked me back an inch.

Jackson was not a natural boxer but he had what the old-timers called heavy hands. He hit hard.

'I don't know what you're talking about,' he said.

We began circling each other. Jackson held his guard up in peekaboo fashion, and I had the pads held loosely by my side. When I showed him one of them, lifting it to head height, he smacked it as hard as he could.

'You're meant to be on her side, Max.'

'I am on her side,' I said, showing him the left pad. He hit it with a straight right and kept hitting it until I pulled it away. Nobody was listening to us but I lowered my voice anyway. 'If you provide her with a firearm, you'll be getting her into more trouble than she already has.'

'Who said I got anyone a firearm?'

He dropped his guard and I clobbered him around the left side of his face as hard as I could with the pad in my right hand.

There was the slap of hard leather on flesh and bone and, at last, the first sign of real anger in his eyes.

'Pat Whitestone thinks that Harry Flowers is trying to own her,' he said. 'Like he has owned dozens of good cops. Men who are now behind bars because they took his money or did him a favour or looked the other way or tried to stay on his good side.'

I held up both pads and Jackson struck them with a furious combination.

'You want that to happen to her, Max? You want Flowers to own your friend?'

'Nobody's going to own her. Have you tooled her up already, Jackson? What is she – a hitman all of a sudden? What's she going to do? Blow his brains out?'

'Maybe someone should.'

We had both forgotten the pad work.

We stood facing each other in that crowded gym, Paul Weller singing 'Eton Rifles' on the sound system.

'She's got a teenage son, Jackson. You dumb bastard.'

'Do it again, Max. Go on. Call me a dumb bastard again.'

'She's bringing her boy up alone. Great kid. Justin. Can't see. Lost his sight in some stupid bar attack. What happens to him if his mother goes down because some dumb bastard got her a gun?'

And finally he lost his rag.

'I remember Justin. I remember his mother kept seeing the scumbag who blinded him. What were they called? Oh yes – the Dog Town Boys. She ever have any problem with any of the Dog Town Boys these days? And I remember that swaggering little sack of shit who hit Justin with a bottle. What was his name?'

'Trey N'Dou.'

'Trey N'Dou. If it wasn't for me, Trey N'Dou would still be wandering the streets where they lived as if nothing had happened. And I remember we went up to see him. You remember any of that, Max?'

I remembered it well.

I remembered the desperation of Pat Whitestone at seeing her son's attacker wandering the streets as if nothing had happened.

And I remembered driving north with Jackson one hot summer's night two years ago.

Whitestone wanted the scumbag gone. Not dead. Not the score evened up – because the score could never be evened up. But she wanted Trey N'Dou gone. She was sick of looking at the face of the man who had blinded her son. So Jackson and I went to see Trey N'Dou. But reasoning with him didn't work. Even threatening him didn't work. So Jackson got him on his back in a car park on Liverpool Road and made Trey N'Dou wet his baggy jeans by firing two shots between his legs.

'Am I dead?' Trey N'Dou had said.
And that worked.

The idea had been that Jackson was going to watch my back while I sorted out this problem.

But Jackson had done more than that.

He had made the problem go away.

'This isn't the same thing, Jackson, and you know it.'

'I remember that Dog Town Boy – I remember he laughed in your face. And I remember that I had to deal with it. I had to clean it up. Just as I have been cleaning up your mess all your life, Max.'

I punched him in the face.

It really hurts to be hit with a punch mitt.

They are not nicely rounded like boxing gloves. The side of the things have a thick, hard edge and that was what connected with Jackson's gap-toothed mouth. He took the blow and then swung back at me, all discipline gone, lashing out with a wide haymaker that I had time enough to roll away from.

But then he was on me, punches raining down on the top of my head as I covered up and started digging the hard ridge of those punch mitts into his lower ribs.

It was all pretty even.

I was always tougher than him.

But he was wilder.

He had that touch of madness that Flowers had talked about with such admiration.

Then Fred had both of us by the scruff of the neck and was pulling us apart.

'I could sell tickets to you two,' he laughed.

And I saw that TDC Joy Adams was standing by Fred's side.

'We've found Ruben Shavers,' she said.

27

The short row of shops had been burned out in the last riots.

They were blackened and boarded up, their steel shutters down and stained with fading graffiti. The *For Sale* signs on every one of them looked overly optimistic. The small flats directly above the shops were all unoccupied, vacant rooms above a torched ruin, their broken windows cloaked with net curtains that were grey with time and the smoke of burning buildings.

From the BMW, we watched the flat above the end shop. Its name had been lost in the flames but there was a drawing of an Afro-Caribbean woman carrying what looked like a basket of fruit and veg on her head. There was a red, gold and green awning above the shop, its colours faded, the fabric scorched by the flames of the riot and worn thin by time.

'What was that place?' Whitestone said.

'It was a Jamaican supermarket,' Joy said from the back seat. 'Jamaican and British produce all mixed.

Ackee and callaloo and Aunt May's Bajan sauce and saltfish, as well as your Hovis and HP sauce and Heinz Baked Beans.'

'It was the owner who called us,' Whitestone told me, her eyes not leaving the window. 'At first she thought it was kids in there, but then she saw a man at the window. A tall, good-looking black man.'

'What are we waiting for?' I said.

'Shavers has got a wife and two kids in the neighbourhood. They may be in there. It would be easier for everyone if they went home for their tea.'

A florist's van was parked outside the row of shops. On the side was a sign promising *'Beautiful' Blooms of Barking*. And inside it were SFO Jackson Rose and a team of shots out of Leman Street police station, Whitechapel, base of SCO19, the specialist firearms unit of the Metropolitan Police.

A flock of children turned the corner and gathered in the doorway of a burned-out shop.

The younger ones were on bikes and in school uniform. The older boys wore hoods that gave them the appearance of Tolkien's elves. All of them were black. One of the older boys produced a matchbox and heads leaned in to examine its contents. Most of the group began to move away in the direction they had come. The boys on bikes lingered.

In the back seat, I heard Joy Adams exhale.

I turned to look at her. 'Recognise any of them?'

'The smallest one,' she said. 'The one who looks little for his age.'

Now Whitestone turned to look at her too.

'He's my brother,' Joy said.

'Bring him here,' Whitestone said.

Joy hesitated for just a moment. Then she got out of the car and the boys on the bikes all turned to look in her direction. They quickly pedalled off, scattering in all directions, making themselves impossible to follow.

Only the one who was small for his age remained.

Joy spoke to him and then turned back for the car. He slowly followed her. The pair of them got into the back seat, the boy nervously looking at his bike leaning in the doorway of a dead shop.

'What if someone nicks my bike, man?' he asked his sister.

'Nobody's going to steal your bike,' she said. 'Jordan, this is DC Wolfe and DCI Whitestone.' She appraised the child in school uniform, whose eyes flicked nervously from our faces to his bike and back again. 'And this is my brother Jordan,' she said.

'Hello, Jordan,' I said.

'Wagwan?' he said in greeting. *What's going on?*

Joy shook her head. '*Wagwan?* You Jamaican now, are you? Our people are from *Kumasi*, Jordan. You know where Kumasi is?'

'Ghana, innit?' he said. 'West Africa. Gold Coast. Where the slave ships came from. I tell you, man, I'm dead worried about that bike.'

'Jordan?' Whitestone said. 'Please show me the matchbox.'

'What matchbox is that, miss?'

She held out her hand. The boy reached into his school blazer and took out a matchbox. Whitestone looked at the contents and then gave it to me. Maybe a dozen blue pills, identical, all with a sleeping emoji face stamped on the front. Two flat-line slits for the eyes, one flat-line slit for the mouth.

These were the tranquillisers that Harry Flowers had sold when Ecstasy was old hat.

Loopers were back.

I gave the matchbox to Joy and she looked inside.

Then she slapped her brother around the top of his head.

'Stupid, stupid, stupid,' she said. 'Why do you let these big kids use you? Why don't you stand up for yourself?'

She grabbed the collar of his school blazer and shook him. He pulled away from her, his eyes bright with tears.

'I haven't done nothing, Joy,' he said.

'I wonder if you would do me a favour, Jordan,' Whitestone said calmly.

We were all silent.

Jordan glanced anxiously at his bike. 'Yes, miss?'

'What I want you to do,' Whitestone said, pulling out a £10 note, 'is to go over the road and buy a pizza.' We all looked at the fast-food shop across the street. *Pizza Paradise.* The only business around these parts that had survived the riots.

'Then I want you to take it up to the flat above this first shop,' Whitestone said.

'Them flats are empty, miss,' Jordan said.

'Maybe,' Whitestone said. 'And maybe not. But if you ring the bell and say you have a pizza delivery, then I am not going to ask you to empty the pockets of your school blazer. How does that sound?'

She smiled at him. Jordan did not smile back.

He was thinking about what he had in the pockets of his school blazer. Did he have more than the ugly great zombie knife that all the kids were packing these days? Probably not. No gun. No acid. Just a big, bad knife. But it would be enough to get him in more trouble than he could handle.

'Then I can go, miss?' he said, and I realised he addressed Whitestone as if he was talking to a deeply feared teacher.

'You do that little favour for me,' Whitestone said, 'then you're a free man.'

He took the tenner.

'What kind of pizza you want, miss?'

'A Margarita will be fine.'

We watched him cross the road to Pizza Paradise.

'Nice kid, your brother,' Whitestone said.

'There are no nice kids around here, ma'am.' Joy said. 'As soon as they're old enough, nobody lets them be nice.'

Within minutes Jordan was back with a steaming 12 x 12 box. Whitestone nodded encouragement and the boy went up the stone staircase by the side of the shops. A few minutes later he came down without the pizza.

I buzzed down the car window.

'He kept the pizza,' he said. 'He's a hungry man.'

'What did he look like?' I said.

Jordan glanced up at the flat above the shop.

'Like that boxer in the olden days, man. Muhammad Ali. Can I go, miss?'

Whitestone nodded. 'Thanks for your help, Jordan.'

Without looking at his sister, Jordan mounted his bike and pedalled off at top speed. Whitestone was already speaking to the wireless radio microphone on her lapel.

'Delta 1, we have positive visual ID on Bravo 1,' she said, dead calm.

And then there was white noise and a familiar voice in my earbud receiver.

'Copy that,' Jackson said. And then, to the men and women in the back of that florist's van. 'On my command ...'

The back doors of the florist's van parked outside the abandoned Jamaican supermarket flew open and they came out in their body armour and their PASGT helmets, assault rifles already going to their shoulder. They headed for the stone stairs but even before they reached the top, glass had begun to fall into the street.

The window of the flat above the burned-out shop was being kicked out.

'Your little brother,' I said to Joy. 'He tipped him off.'

Ruben Shavers leaped out of the first-floor window just as we were getting out of the car. He must have got caught on some broken glass as he was jumping out because he twisted in the air as he fell.

The plan must have been that the red, gold and green awning above the supermarket would break his fall.

But that awning had been there for a while, in all kinds of weathers and in quite a few fires, and Ruben Shavers went straight through it as if it was made of wet tissue.

He hit the ground with enormous force, howling with pain as Joy cuffed him. Whitestone told him his rights. I helped the big man to his feet as Jackson's face appeared at the first-floor window, grinning down at me.

'Can you walk?' I asked Shavers. He didn't answer me.

His face was busted up pretty bad but nothing seemed to be broken. He hung his head, as if something was over.

We started back to the car.

Across the street, outside Pizza Paradise, a crowd had gathered. It was the children we had seen with Jordan but now they had been joined by older men and women.

They crossed the road and began shouting and screaming and spitting at our feet and in our faces.

Most of their hatred seemed to be directed at Joy.

'Pig! Pig! Pig! Pig! Pig!'

'Go,' Whitestone told me. 'Go, go, go.'

I started shoving my way through the crowds, the ignition keys in one hand, the scruff of Ruben Shavers' shirt in the other.

I threw Shavers in the back seat. He was a big man, much stronger than me, but far too banged up to resist. Joy climbed in beside him. Whitestone got into the passenger seat but a man stopped her shutting the door. Someone was beating on the roof. And then someone was standing on the roof. Angry faces appeared at the windows, all the windows, twisted with hatred, banging on the glass, and all around me I saw the palms of hands slapping against the glass. I started the engine but I couldn't shut the door because bodies were in the way, their hands clawing at me. Every door, I realised, was still open. People were attempting to pull Shavers out of the back seat. I stuck the car in drive and eased forward, trying not to hit anyone, the doors all still open, bodies everywhere now.

'Pig! Pig! Pig! Pig! Pig!'

Then I put on the blues-and-twos. The sudden flare of light and noise made the mob back off for just a moment.

And a moment was all I needed.

We got out of there, the doors flapping, the sirens screaming, the flashing blue lights the brightest thing in that ruined neighbourhood.

I glanced in the rear-view mirror.

Ruben Shavers was doubled up and moaning.

Joy Adams stared straight ahead, her face wet and gleaming, although you could not tell where the spit from the mob ended and where her tears began.

28

'Where is she?' Whitestone said.

Ruben Shavers looked at a point somewhere over her shoulder, as if he knew but he could not bring himself to say.

'I remember you well now,' I told Shavers. 'I must have seen you fight a few times. You were so fast for a heavyweight.'

'Phase one,' he laughed, staring at the table, as if quoting from the police handbook. 'Establish rapport.'

He examined the back of his hands and stared at the round white scars on the dark skin where someone had gone to work on him with a hammer for taking the wrong wife – or daughter, or mother, or sister, or girl-friend – to his bed. The professional hazard of the compulsive womaniser.

'You danced,' I said, and although he knew I was buttering him up – establishing rapport with the suspect, as he said, like they told you in all the police textbooks – for me it was more than that. Because I truly wondered.

How did someone with that much talent go down such a wrong road?

'Like Muhammad Ali before they stopped him fighting because he wouldn't go to Vietnam,' I said. 'Like a big Sugar Ray Leonard.'

'I was no Ali,' he said. 'There's only one Ali.'

'I didn't say you were as good as Ali,' I said. 'And I didn't say you were as brave as Ali. And I didn't say you hit as hard as Ali. I said you were fast for your size like Ali.'

And just like Muhammad Ali, Ruben Shavers was one of those men who would never be short of sexual opportunities. There was no need to tell him that. He knew already. That's what had happened to his hands.

He still hadn't looked at me.

He sat on the other side of the interview table, his handsome face scuffed and bruised from the fall, his young female lawyer flipping through paperwork by his side.

The lawyer glanced at her watch, as if the day was running out and she had somewhere else to be. But Ruben Shavers sat there with his arms folded across his chest, as if aware that he would have nowhere else to be for years and years and years.

'What happened to you, Ruben?' I said.

Now he looked at me.

'You still trying to bond with me?' he said. 'How's that working out for you?'

'No bonding in here,' I said. 'Just trying to work out how you wasted your life.'

He exhaled, and placed his hands on the table, as if he would never really grow used to the sight of the dark skin stamped with all those circles of white scars.

'Who did that to your hands, Ruben? Did Flowers ruin your hands? Is that why you hate his guts?'

'The hands have got nothing to do with it,' he said. 'It was some old boxing big shot who was rich enough to get a young wife but not man enough to keep her happy. He's long dead. So is she, as it happens. No great mystery. Nothing to see. Move on.'

'Where is Jessica Lyle?' Whitestone said.

We call it an interview, but it is nothing like an interview. An interview implies a degree of mutual respect and polite interest.

What the police conduct are interrogations.

He shook his head and Whitestone glanced at me. He knew but he wasn't saying. Dead or alive or somewhere in between, he knew exactly where Jessica Lyle was right now.

'Did she die immediately?' I said.

'Or did you and your steroid-sucking friend Bumpus have a little fun first?' Whitestone said.

He looked affronted. 'Do you think I need to assault women?' he said. 'That's not me.'

'Your friend Bumpus told me to look in the graveyard,' I said. 'What graveyard was he talking about,
Ruben?'

Now he looked at us.

'If she really was in a graveyard, do you think he
would be stupid enough to tell you?'

'Yes,' I said. 'I do. I think your pal Big Del is that
stupid. Who do you think you are exactly? Stephen
Hawking? Frankly, I don't see either of you as criminal
masterminds, Ruben.'

'And who killed Jessica Lyle?' Whitestone said. 'You
or Derek Bumpus?'

The lawyer languidly stirred. 'My client is not charged
with murder,' she said with a pained little smile, as if it
was socially awkward to mention it.

Whitestone stared at her, letting the silence build.

'Not yet,' she said.

Then she turned back to Shavers.

'At this point, your kind are usually blaming their
partner for everything that went wrong,' she said. 'You're
not going to do that? You're not going to put it all on
your friend?'

'Derek Bumpus is not my friend.' He paused, wanting
to tell us something. 'We had a row.'

'What did you row about?' I said.

He took a breath.

'Everything,' he said.

'Why, Ruben?' I said. 'That's what I don't get. Did someone hire you – some old enemy of Harry Flowers, or some new business rival – or did you do it because you just wanted to get back at him? Is that what it was? Pure spite?'

'Disgruntled employees,' Whitestone said with a twisted smile. 'You're a cliché, Ruben, do you know that? The disgruntled employee who lashes out at the wicked boss.'

'You don't take a woman because you've had a bad day at work,' he said.

'Then why did you take Jessica Lyle?'

He shook his head, as if it was a mystery to him too.

'The big man's scared,' Whitestone told me. 'He's terrified! He knows the old story about Harry Flowers and the can of petrol. He knows about the visit to see the Mahone family when they were having their Sunday lunch.'

'I really must object,' the lawyer said, not seeming that outraged.

Whitestone paused, as if something had just occurred to her.

'Or was it *you* who went to see the Mahone family with Harry Flowers?' she said. 'Were you the mystery man with the petrol can, Ruben? Were you the hired hand who soaked that family – Mahone and his wife and those small children – in petrol and threatened to set it alight?'

The lawyer said nothing. It was Shavers who spoke first.

'Harry says that never happened,' he said quietly. 'Not the way that people talk about it.' He looked Whitestone in the eye. 'And I wasn't there.'

'Ruben here has lied through his teeth about everything else,' I told Whitestone, who was still watching Shavers. 'Why would he tell the truth about that?'

I took a matchbox out of my pocket.

I took one of the pills inside it and held it up between my thumb and index finger, the sleepy emoji facing Ruben Shavers and his lawyer.

'You know what that is, Ruben? It's not a vitamin pill. This is what your boss built his business on. Loopers, they're called. Very powerful, very addictive. They don't get you high. They just get you out of it. They just put a glass wall between you and the world. Take one of these and you just don't care about anything any more.'

'It was long ago,' Ruben said. 'In a galaxy far, far away. You think Harry Flowers is still dealing Loopers that someone cooked up in their basement? He's a legitimate businessman. You've been to the yard. You've been to Auto Waste Solutions.'

I was still holding up the pill with the sleeping emoji.

'If you're depressed before you take them, you'll be suicidal on the morning after,' I said. 'Kids like them.

291

Young people with all sorts of problems. Bad skin. Exams. Trouble at home. Anxiety. Low self-esteem. Loneliness. The usual stuff. The standard shopping list of human misery. These magic pills promise to make it all go away. The anxiety. The stress.' I put the Looper back in its box. 'You've got children, haven't you, Ruben?'

'What we suspect is that your boss is not quite as respectable as he is cracked up to be,' Whitestone said. 'And maybe some other drug-dealing low life wants him to back off. So they hired you and your fat friend to kill the thing that Harry Flowers loves most. Just to send him a message. Just to let him know that they are deadly serious in any negotiations. Or just to even the score.'

He shook his head, and there was something final about the gesture.

'But why not tell us everything?' I said. 'You know how it works. The more you help us, the more you help yourself. You're going down – nothing can stop that.'

He glanced at his lawyer.

The lawyer studied her files.

Whitestone laughed.

'Your brief can't help you, Ruben,' she said. 'Because she knows you are going to get a life sentence for the abduction and murder of Jessica Lyle. It's up to you if that really means a whole life tariff with no possibility of parole. You understand what a whole life tariff means?'

'It means dying inside,' he said.

'It means it is up to you how hard you go down,' I said. 'Tell us what happened – who hired you, why they hired you, what you did to Jessica Lyle and where the body is buried – and maybe one day you will walk in the park with your grandchildren. How old are your kids?'

For the first time there was some real emotion on his face.

I never saw a hard, heartless bastard in an interview room who was not capable of self-pity.

'Louis is six and Lilly is eight.'

'You know you're not going to watch them grow up, right? That's over. Forget about watching Louis and Lilly grow up. If Louis and Lilly see you before they are fully grown, it will be on visiting days at a high-security prison. So that's all gone. You are going to watch Louis and Lilly grow up from behind bars. But twenty years from now, there *might* be a chance to get out. *If you come clean.* You know how many people there are inside who are considered too dangerous to ever be let out? Sixty-one, Ruben. That's all. Just sixty-one. You have to ask yourself – do you really want to be number sixty-two?'

He shook his head, almost too tired to move it, and folded his arms tightly across his chest, as if shutting down.

293

I smashed my fists on the table.

It didn't make any sense.

'*Where is she?*' I said, one last time.

'I can't,' he said, and it was hard to believe that such a big man could have such a small voice, a voice so shrivelled with terror.

'Why the hell not?' I said.

'Because my family will burn,' he said.

29

The holding cells below the Old Bailey lead directly up to the courtrooms and so Ruben Shavers appeared in the dock as if by magic, not there one second and there the next, a large man in handcuffs flanked by two police officers in blue short-sleeve shirts and black stab-proof jackets. They were both carrying assault rifles. One of them was Jackson Rose.

There was a shocked silence at Shavers' abrupt appearance that was broken by a suppressed cough from the public gallery.

I looked up and saw it was Frank Lyle, leaning forward to stare as if in disbelief at one of the men who had taken his daughter. The old cop was painfully thin now, as if all his meals were fed into his arm by drip, and he had the ragged stubble of the long-term hospital patient. Sitting between his wife Jennifer and his son Tommy, holding their hands, he looked as though he been carried from his hospital bed. But terminal cancer was not going to stop him seeing justice done for his daughter.

Further along the same row were Snezia Jones and her boyfriend. She wept soundlessly and shook her head, as if coming here had been a mistake.

And in the back row on the end seat, looking like he was ready to make a quick getaway, was Harry Flowers.

They sat surrounded by the usual occupants of the public gallery at the Central Criminal Court, that odd mix of the curious, tourists, and journalists who had not been able to find a place in the crowded press box. They all watched Ruben Shavers while he stared blankly at a random point on the wall, his thick arms limp and useless in handcuffs.

Jackson caught my eye and nodded.

There were two more SFOs at the back of the public gallery, two at the rear of the courtroom and more around the main entrance of the Old Bailey, highly visible in their helmets, goggles and body armour, their assault rifles in that at-ease 45-degree angle.

'All rise,' the bailiff said.

Court Two of the Old Bailey rose obediently to its feet as an elderly woman in the scarlet robes of a high court judge entered, her shoulder-length wig more mouldy grey than white. She took her time settling in her seat.

Ruben Shavers was asked to confirm his name and the charges against him were read out.

The kidnapping of Jessica Lyle.

The false imprisonment of Jessica Lyle.

The murder of Jessica Lyle.

The judge peered at the defendant, her eyes bright and beady over the top of her reading glasses.

'How do you plead?'

Shavers cleared his throat.

'Not guilty, My Lady.'

I heard a broken whimper from the public gallery. I thought it was the family of Jessica Lyle. But the faces of Jessica's parents and brother showed no visible emotion. The moan had come from a woman of about forty, her skin the light orange tan of the long-term sun-bed addict.

I had taken her for a tourist. Now I saw her tears and knew this had to be the partner of Ruben Shavers, the mother of Louis, six, and Lilly, eight.

The day's proceedings were over in a few minutes.

Ruben Shavers was remanded in custody and would come back around two months from today for his trial.

'All rise,' the bailiff said, and I could feel the sense of anticlimax in the public gallery but I had been in enough courtrooms to know that there would be no drama today.

And then it happened.

As the judge was turning to leave, Shavers swung his handcuffed wrists left and high, catching the armed officer next to him full on his chin and putting him down. Jackson, on the other side of Shavers, had a split moment to react and stepped back against the side of the dock, rolling with Shavers' clubbing blow that caught him on the temple, hard enough to spin him around but not enough to put him on the ground.

And enough for what Shavers wanted.

Suddenly he was over the dock and in the well of the court. I made a move towards the exit, expecting him to make his break for freedom.

Because the only alternative was dying in this courtroom.

And I saw that was exactly what Ruben Shavers wanted.

He was crossing the courtroom, away from the exit door and any hope of escape, his long strides taking him past the parallel desks of the defence counsel and crown prosecutor, their backs towards him, but the lawyers turning to look, their faces aghast at the sight of the defendant on the loose. The court registrar and court reporter were directly facing him but they shrank back behind their shared desk, paralysed, willing him to go straight past them, and he did, brushing past the bailiff standing there white-faced with shock, and the grey-wigged old judge in her red robes finally turning to look down at Ruben Shavers over the top of her glasses as he made a mighty leap, taking one step off the front of the bench to propel himself upwards and seizing the hem of her robe with his manacled hands.

'Stop – armed police!' Jackson said, stone-cold with calm, and his warning seemed to echo around the room as the armed officers at the exit door of Court Two of the Old Bailey called out the same warning a split second later.

Shavers still had a fistful of the judge's red robe in his hand when the single shot rang out, brain-piercing in that confined space.

The judge, slipping out of her robes, squirmed away and was gone into the door in the wall behind her.

You can't hear a shot fired that close to your head without cowering and it felt like the entire courtroom ducked our heads as one as Ruben Shavers slid to the floor, the scarlet robes of the judge still held in his dead hands.

There are Family Liaison Officers for the victims of crime.

Some FLOs are ineffectual, all of them are well-meaning, but none of them are there for the relatives of those who commit the crimes.

That was why I found Mrs Ruben Shavers sitting alone on the pavement outside the Central Criminal Court, overcome with shock, stupefied by it as the world rushed on around her, the police and emergency services hurrying towards Court Two while the lawyers in their wigs and robes ran for their lives in the opposite direction.

'Mrs Shavers?'

I had my warrant card in my hand. I told her my name.

'I'm sorry for your loss,' I said.

Then I held out my hand.

And she took it, limp and weak and too stunned to refuse.

'What's going to happen to our children?' she said.

I drove her home.

Her name was Lilly – like her daughter – and she was a former ring girl at York Hall, one of the beautiful young women who hold up the round number as they parade the squared circle.

They still have them in boxing rings, professional beauties with nailed-on smiles, wearing minimal outfits whatever the season, but you don't see them in many other places these days. She had met Ruben Shavers when she was eighteen and had been with him ever since.

'On and off,' she told me as we crawled through the traffic. 'On and off and sometimes somewhere in between.'

She did not weep for her husband. Not yet. Sometimes our tears have to wait a while.

*

The flat was empty. It was a former council property in Finsbury Park that had been sold off when politicians were encouraging people to own their own homes. And although the flat was modest, it felt like a home. You could smell the musky stink of some pet rodent, a hamster or guinea pig, brooding in its little cage. Lilly Shavers was one of those women who build a home for her children even if the man of the house comes and goes, even if their relationship is on and off and somewhere in between.

There was new tech everywhere – iPads, a couple of laptops, a giant HDTV. No toys, I noticed. Perhaps children don't play with toys any more. The children, she said, Lilly and Louis, were staying with her mother. She sat in the living room, staring at the switched-off HDTV, while I made two cups of tea. I loaded three sugars into her cup without asking how she liked it.

I sat in silence as she sipped her tea. I waited until she had finished it. Her breath was changing, her eyes were brighter. There was panic there now, and grief, and emotions I could not place. Lilly Shavers was coming out of shock. Her sunbed tan was a shade darker.

'Did you find anything?' I said.

She looked at me as if surprised to find me in her home. As if seeing me truly for the first time.

'When your husband was arrested,' I said. 'When we took Ruben. You knew he wasn't going to be coming home for years and perhaps never coming home again. Most wives – all wives, I suspect – they would look through their husband's personal belongings. They would try to make sense of this life they shared and maybe knew nothing about. Some men keep secrets from their wives. But all wives want to know the truth, don't they?'

We had drunk our sweet tea. Too much sugar, Max.

'So did you find anything?' I repeated.

She laughed and shook her head.

'You bastard,' she said. 'And I thought you were being *nice*. I thought you were being *kind*.'

'Who was kind to Jessica Lyle?' I said. 'Who was nice to her?'

We stared at each other.

'I found everything,' she said.

She had it spread out on the marital bed, as if it was evidence for a prosecution that was never going to make it to court.

There was a lot of paperwork. Most of it seemed to be credit card bills that she had scored with bright green marker pen.

'There are receipts for presents that he never gave me,' she said. 'Nice presents. Jewellery, mostly. Bags.'

She gave me a bitter look.

'The things that women like,' she said.

The paperwork spilled off the bed and on to the carpet.

On the bedside table there was a photograph of Ruben Shavers grinning in hospital scrubs, a new-born baby in his arms.

'There are hotel bills for rooms that I never slept in,' Lilly Shavers told me. 'I had looked at his phone, of course, but he was too experienced to have anything incriminating on there. But I found this.'

Near the pillow of the bed there was an old-style BlackBerry. I had not seen one of those in years. It gave me a mild pang of nostalgia, like seeing a steam train or a Spitfire.

'Plenty of photos on there,' she said, nodding at the old-style BlackBerry. 'Some of them adult in nature. Do you know what I mean, Detective?'

She held it out to me, this dedicated phone that she had never seen before, and I remembered the second phone of Harry Flowers, and I wondered if they had both come up with the idea independently, or if one unfaithful husband had recommended a second phone to the other, an illicit dating tip.

'What is heartbreaking is that you learn to suspect *everything*, don't you?' she said. 'I wonder if he had any feelings for me at all. I wonder if he had any love for our children. Or if all he cared about were his whores.'

She was crying.

'What was Ruben scared of?' I said.

Defiance and pride in her now. 'Nothing,' she said. 'You ever see him fight?'

It was not true. There was something that terrified Ruben Shavers. It made him too afraid to talk. And it made him too afraid to go on living.

I gestured at the bed covered with all its paperwork of betrayal.

'Is this all of it?' I said.

'Almost,' she said.

She went to the bedside table that displayed the picture of Ruben as a proud father.

She opened the bedside drawer and took out a set of keys.

She held the keys out to me.

'I'm a widow, aren't I?' she said. 'Wow. How can I be a widow? How did that happen?'

I was looking at the keys.

'What do they open?' I said.

'God only knows,' she laughed.

I took them from her.

A Yale and a Chubb, the brass worn smooth with time.

A set of keys to the secret life of Ruben Shavers.

30

If DCI Pat Whitestone was still drinking, then she showed no sign.

My boss was working in MIR-1 before anyone else arrived, and she remained at her desk when Joy Adams and I headed home. But Whitestone seemed weary to me, and distracted, as though the search for Jessica Lyle had worn away something inside her, and when TDC Joy and I stood before the giant map of London that covers the end wall in MIR-1, Whitestone showed no inclination to join us.

'It's really hard to hide a body,' I said. 'Even in a city this big. Even in a city that stretches for thirty miles either side of a river that is two hundred miles long.'

Joy and I stared at the map in silence.

More than any other major metropolis in the world, the map of London is splashed with green and blue.

'Even here,' I said, 'among all these parks, woods and commons and with all those canals, rivers and reservoirs – it is so hard to hide a body.'

'Because bodies decay,' Adams said. 'And because killers are stupid.'

'If Jessica Lyle died soon after they took her,' I said, 'then Ruben Shavers and Derek Bumpus were almost mad with the adrenaline that comes with the terror of getting caught. If they disposed of the body in a rush – in some basement, or some skip, or some pond – then we would have found her by now.'

'Because killers are stupid,' Adams repeated. 'And bodies decay.'

'So to bury her in a graveyard makes perfect sense,' I said. 'What Bumpus told me – *look in the graveyard* – doesn't seem like some dumb taunt. It would be perfect – to have a grave dug and ready to use as soon as they took her.'

We stared silently at the map.

And then Whitestone laughed.

'Just how hard did Bumpus kick you in the head, Max?' she said. 'You're really going to build an investigation around the word of a villain? Good luck with that.' She glanced at her watch. 'I'm checking in with forensics down on the third floor. The CSIs found some female DNA in Bumpus's flat. They already know it didn't belong to Jessica Lyle, but an ID would be handy.'

After she was gone, Adams and I continued to stare at the map of the city.

306

'Maybe the boss is right,' Adams said. 'Maybe Bumpus was giving you a false lead. Maybe he wants us chasing our tails.'

'I don't think so,' I said. 'He was goading me with something he knew and I didn't. The trouble is, this is a city of graves. When Sir Christopher Wren was rebuilding St Paul's Cathedral after the Great Fire, he dug up layer upon layer of graves, burial grounds 18-feet deep that went back more than a thousand years. Pagan dead. Roman dead. Saxon dead. Norman dead. Generations of the dead who the world had forgotten. And when they built the tube at the start of the last century, they had to drill through catacombs with walls that were made of the bones of plague victims. This is a city of ghosts.'

'But he told you *a graveyard*,' Joy said. 'He wasn't talking about some Roman burial ground, Max. He said a *graveyard*. And I guess that means one of the big cemeteries they built in the nineteenth century when the churchyards were overflowing with the dead. And how many of them are there?'

I thought about it. 'Over a hundred,' I said.

'But how could they hope to get away with burying her in a graveyard?' Adams said. 'That's what makes no sense. It doesn't matter if the grave was already dug and waiting to be used or if they did it on the night – a freshly dug grave that wasn't meant to be there would be seen as soon as the sun came up.'

307

'The only way to get away with it,' I said, 'the *only* way, would be to bury the body in a graveyard that is closed to the public. And there is only one of those.'

I pointed to a patch of green in the top left-hand corner of the giant map.

'Highgate?' she said uncertainly.

I nodded, and my skin crawled at the memory of my own personal history with Highgate Cemetery.

I remembered the night that two men had attempted to bury me alive there. I recalled the rustle and crack of the bones that were already inside the coffin they placed me in, and I could once again smell the moist soil mixing with the expensive cologne of one of the men, and I remembered thrashing like a wounded animal in a trap inside the sealed box as the shovels above me in the land of the living dropped dirt that went *splat-splat-splat* on the wooden ceiling inches from my face.

Most of all, I remembered the taste of my fear.

I pushed the memory away.

'When people think of Highgate Cemetery, they think of the big stone monument at the grave of Karl Marx,' I said. 'But Marx is buried in Highgate East Cemetery. That's open to the public. The other side of the road is Highgate West Cemetery. You ever been in there?'

'No.'

'Highgate West is like a graveyard in a dream. These huge vaults and crosses and mausoleums that have been swallowed up by nature and time. All these huge, crumbling Victorian monuments surrounded by jungle. And because so much of the architecture is fragile, Highgate West is only open to small guided tours and for burials.'

'Wait a minute – it's closed to the public but they still bury people there?'

I nodded.

'Highgate West is still a working cemetery,' I said.

'How easy is it to get in there? When it's all locked up?'

'It has high walls and locked gates,' I said. I thought about it. 'There are anti-climbing spikes on the iron gates at the front. But no guards. The guy who owns my local gym – my friend Fred – grew up next door, in Kentish Town, and he once told me how he and his mates would sneak into Highgate Cemetery on summer nights. It was also popular with Fred and his crowd on Halloween. You can get inside if you really want to.'

Joy Adams looked at the patch of green near the top of the map.

'Then it would be perfect,' she said.

Our torches piercing the darkness, we climbed the steps that lead the visitor to Highgate West Cemetery up to the roof of the city.

On either side of the steps there were giant redwood trees. Among the thick undergrowth of the ancient forest, stone angels wreathed in ivy watched our progress.

'I'm glad we didn't have to climb those bloody gates, sir,' Adams said. 'Excuse my French.'

'Me too,' I said.

It had been easy getting inside Highgate West, but only because we had phoned ahead. When we pulled up outside, an elderly man with a gentle smile and a halo of white hair – one of the Friends of Highgate Cemetery, the unpaid volunteers who care for this special place – was waiting for us.

As he opened up, I had stared at the tangle of sharp metal spikes on top of the front gates and felt the doubt creeping in. I knew from my personal experience that there were other points of entry around the perimeter of the sprawling cemetery, but nobody was going over those metal spikes in a hurry.

And as we tramped through the darkness, Adams felt it too.

'This is nuts,' she said. 'I mean, it's a beautiful place, sir – I've never seen anywhere remotely like it – but this has to be nuts, doesn't it? We don't even know what we're looking for.'

We paused at the top of the steps.

I stared off into the thick wild wood. In the light of our torches and the moon, there were graves marked by massive stone figures, ten times life-sized. A lion. A dog. A horse. All of them curled up and sleeping for eternity. And hosts of stone angels, some of them with the features

310

of their face worn off by a century or more of time and weather. And everywhere the great tangled jungle of Highgate West.

But Adams was right.

This was nuts.

Yet I could not shake the feeling that, if you were going to bury someone without the world noticing, then this was the best place to do it.

We stepped on to Egyptian Avenue where the great stone catacombs, vaults and tombs were cut into the hillside and stretched off into the distance. Beyond Egyptian Avenue there was a winding path leading downhill and back to the entrance and it seemed to urge us to go home and end this madness.

'It was worth a shot,' I said. 'Let's thank that nice old man and all go home.'

We started back towards the chapel that marks the entrance to Highgate West Cemetery.

And we were almost there when I saw it.

A new grave, modest and modern, the stone still pure white, light years from the colossal grey tombs with their giant animals and angels swallowed by nature.

'Dr Stewart McGlenny,' Adams read.

It was a tombstone that remembered a beloved husband, father and grandfather. He had been a doctor in his long working life and he had been an old man when he died. In his late eighties. A long life, a good life, a life filled with love and work and family. And a privileged life, too, for it is not an easy task to get permission to bury your loved one in Highgate West Cemetery.

The dates were freshly cut on the simple white stone.

The date he was born.

The dash that in the end is all that remains of a lifetime.

And the day that Dr Stewart McGlenny died.

'Do you see that date?' I asked Adams. 'The day he died?'

'It's around a week before they took Jessica.'

'It's *exactly* a week. And as most funerals take place seven or eight days after a death, Dr McGlenny's funeral must have been very close to the night they took Jessica Lyle. My guess is that his loved ones buried him the next day. And never knew that somebody had already been buried in his grave.'

'I'll check the date of Dr McGlenny's funeral,' Joy said, her phone already in her hand.

'And then get me an exhumation certificate,' I said. 'Because they buried her here.'

Our twin torch lights shone on the grave.

The wreaths and bouquets of the old doctor's funeral had been cleared away now. All that remained, propped up against the pure white headstone, was a small bunch of wild flowers tied with a hairband.

And a pink pair of ballet shoes made of satin and leather.

31

'Open it up,' DCI Whitestone said.

The yellow bulldozer's diesel engine howled as its digger sank into the surface of the old doctor's grave.

The lights of the CSIs encircled the site and drenched it in a dazzling white glare. Uniformed officers and the blue-suited CSIs hung back behind the lights, all of them staring at the grave. The top part of the bulldozer turned sideways, thick clumps of earth falling away from the overflow, and dumped its load of soil to one side. Already a hole was opening up in the grave. The bulldozer emptied another load. And then another.

And then it slowed and stopped.

Ropes were lowered into the grave.

A coffin was lifted out.

Shockingly, the wood was untarnished and the brass handles still gleamed like a picture in an undertaker's brochure. It still looked brand new.

Whitestone did not look at me. It was impossible to look away from the grave that was being opened up before our eyes.

'Don't be wrong, Max,' she told me, still not looking at me.

I stepped to the edge of the open grave. Six feet deep but showing nothing but earth. The bulldozer moved forward again, struggling for traction on the cemetery's steep sloping path. It sank its digger into the open grave and clawed away only a scraping of dirt.

'Stop,' I said. 'We need shovels.'

Whitestone gave the nod and two suited CSIs in their facemasks and blue nitrile gloves and boots eased themselves into the grave with their shovels. They tossed just a few loads of dirt on the side of the open grave and paused.

'There's something down here,' one of them said.

And now we were all at the edge of the open grave.

All of us staring down at what had been buried beneath the coffin.

A patch of white plastic, picked out by a dozen torchlights.

'Get *back!*' one of the CSIs was shouting, suddenly furious, and then they were pulling the soil away with their gloved hands until what was revealed was another kind of coffin.

We don't call it a body bag.

We call it an HRP – a Human Remains Pouch – and this one had black webbing handles that the CSIs used to pull it away from the earth that held it. More hands reached down to help take the load.

The HRP was pulled from the open grave.

And Whitestone looked at me again.

'This was never just an abduction, Pat,' I said. 'This was always a hit. The plan was never kidnap. The plan was always murder.'

And then Frank Lyle was pushing through the crowds, his face drained of life under those pitiless lights.

'Jessica!' he said. 'Jessica! What did they do to you? What did they do?'

I took him in my arms.

'Listen to me,' I said, but there was nothing to say to him, and there was nothing reassuring for him to hear.

And so I held him close and I let him weep, and he pressed his face into my chest so that the world would not witness his tears.

And as the CSIs carried the white plastic HRP down to the waiting mortuary van with its blacked-out windows, the black van looking self-consciously staid surrounded by all the swirling blue lights of our vehicles, I was grateful that this broken man would be spared one last horror.

The task of identifying his daughter.

Because by this time there would no longer be enough of a beloved daughter for him to identify. It had been too long. That young woman had gone forever. Dental records and DNA would be enough to spare them from that terrible goodbye. The parents of Jessica Lyle would not be asked to look upon her face one last time.

How long had she been gone?

It was less than a month but it felt like more than a lifetime.

'Everyone loved her,' her father said.

'I know they did, Frank,' I said.

And as I held Frank Lyle against me, his face buried in my chest, I could feel the metal in my jacket pocket, the keys to the secret life of Ruben Shavers, digging deeper into my flesh.

32

In the morning DCI Whitestone and I made the ten-minute walk from West End Central in Savile Row through St James's Park to the Westminster Public Mortuary on Horseferry Road.

The black Bentley Bentayga was parked on a double-yellow line outside.

Mo Patel saw us coming and quickly tapped on the rear window, a nervous little Buddhist monk of a man.

Harry Flowers got out and came towards Whitestone. I put myself between them.

'Don't do anything stupid,' I told him.

'I just want to see Jess,' he said, his voice cracked with grief. 'I need to see my girl.'

'Not going to happen,' Whitestone said.

I pushed him away and we carried on into the mortuary.

Flowers shouted after us. 'Don't forget who owns you,' he told Whitestone.

I turned back to him, but she took my arm.

'Not now,' she said.

We signed in at the desk for the Iain West Forensic Suite.

And as we got into the lift for the basement, I could see Harry Flowers on the far side of the plate glass, staring at us.

DCI Pat Whitestone did not look at him.

But she knew he was still there.

'You ever work a stalking case?' she said.

I nodded. 'Some.'

'It's never over, is it?' she said. 'Not until someone is dead.'

We stood in our blue scrubs and hairnets, the temperature in the Iain West Forensic Suite as always just one degree above freezing, and we waited for the verdict of Elsa Olsen, forensic pathologist.

There was a single stainless-steel bed in the room.

But it held nothing but a metal bowl.

Elsa smiled with polite apology, like a dinner party hostess whose main course is going to be unexpectedly delayed.

'The body I have examined is too far gone to tell us the full story,' she said, no trace of her native Norway after an adult lifetime in London. 'It has been in the ground for – I would estimate – somewhere between three weeks and a month.'

I felt my stomach fall away.

How long have we searched for you, Jessica?

A shade over three weeks.

We waited.

'Nature is very efficient at breaking down a body that has been buried in soil,' Elsa continued. 'Inside a coffin, any coffin, decay would take a lot longer. And many years longer in a coffin made of something like oak, like the coffin of Dr Stewart McGlenny. But the body you found beneath Dr McGlenny's coffin was in a thin HRP and so nature worked a lot faster, although nowhere near as fast as if the body had been left above ground or in water. But the more advanced decomposition, the harder it is to answer the four questions of death,' Elsa said. 'Cause? Mechanism? Manner? Time? I can take a good guess at the time because a body begins to decompose four minutes after death and then follows the same four stages wherever it is buried – autolysis, bloat, active decay and skeletonisation. After around one month, between stages three and four, the body starts to liquefy. And that is what is happening to this body. Which is why a visual ID is impossible.'

'But the rate of decomposition is consistent with the time of Jessica's abduction?' Whitestone said.

Elsa nodded. 'But cause, mechanism and manner are impossible to gauge from the autopsy. There was no visible skeletal damage that could have been caused by a weapon. The skull was intact. No ribs were broken. But after autolysis – the initial decay, the chemical breakdown of tissues and cells – we lose a lot of the story because there is so much less to analyse. The heart stops pumping and blood stops circulating and the cells are deprived of oxygen and the dead lose their voice, or at least they find it much harder to tell us their story.'

I shivered in the freezing room.

'I can no longer look at lividity, rigor mortis, body temperature, cadaveric spasm, the contents of a stomach or what I find in the fingernails,' Elsa said. 'No skin cells, no blood, no semen. The usual clues have all evaporated into eternity. In the end, there is only decay. At first the dead speak very clearly to us. But then they slip away.'

The newly dead do not go far, I thought.

'But – just to confirm, Elsa – the timing works perfectly for us?' Whitestone said. 'Just give me that, will you?' She shook her head. 'Why can't you say it?'

'Because even the timing becomes problematic after a corpse is this old,' Elsa said. 'It could be three weeks old. It could be six. But the internal organs decay in a very specific order. The very last to decay is the uterus in a woman and the prostate gland in men. The organs that bring life are the last to decompose in death. And the uterus in the body you found is the only internal organ that is still intact. I can say that the subject is a young female in her twenties who died within seven days of the night that Jessica Lyle went missing.'

I looked at Whitestone and she nodded.

What else did we need for identification?

'But there is one big problem,' Elsa said. 'I have the dental records of Jessica Lyle. Her parents went to a lot of trouble to take care of her teeth. She didn't have one cavity.'

'What does that mean?' I said.

'The body you found had a poor person's teeth,' Elsa said. 'There are fillings, gaps, a broken crown. And one of these.'

With a long thin pair of tweezers, Elsa reached into the stainless-steel bowl sitting on the stainless-steel bed and extracted something.

She held it up for us to see.

A single white tooth with what looked like a grey metal screw on the end.

'This is a dental implant,' Elsa said. 'From the cheaper end of the market. My lab tells me it was made in Riga.'

'Latvia,' I said.

'But if the body wasn't Jessica Lyle,' Whitestone said, 'then who was it?'

And suddenly I saw it clear.

'Her name was Minky,' I said. 'She was a dancer at the Western World. She went out with Derek Bumpus and then she went missing around the same time that they took Jessica.' I turned to Whitestone. 'That female DNA they found at Bumpus's apartment? We need to check it out again.'

I remembered Snezia telling me that Minky had probably gone home or landed a rich man or simply moved on.

'The truth is that nobody cared about her,' I said. 'They looked for her. But they just never looked hard enough.'

33

We picked up Joy Adams from West End Central and drove out to Harry Flowers' home.

The last time I had seen it, the house was full of wedding guests and there was a marquee on the lawn. Now the house was shuttered and the marquee was gone and the only sign of life was Mo the driver cleaning the black Bentley on the gravel drive.

Whitestone and Adams stayed in the BMW when I got out to talk to Mo, and he paused from his cleaning to watch me coming. He looked at me and then up at the house.

'They've gone away,' he said. 'There's nobody home.'

That wasn't strictly true. I could see a group of men in loungers by the swimming pool, staring at their phones, billowing clouds of smoke coming from their vapers.

More of Mo's cousins. New help to replace the old help now that Ruben Shavers and Derek Bumpus were off the payroll.

'That's OK, Mo,' I said. 'Because it's you I want to talk to.'

He placed his wash mitt on the edge of his bucket.

'You always got on well with Ruben Shavers, didn't you?' I said.

He nodded cautiously, running the palm of his hand over his shaven head, leaving a few soapy suds on his gleaming scalp.

'Because Ruben treated you like a human being,' I said. 'So you liked him. That's human nature, Mo. We like the people who like us. But Derek Bumpus bullied you and made fun of you and was rude to you.'

'I try to get on with everyone,' Mo said.

'But I saw it myself,' I said. 'Bumpus – Big Del – called you Osama bin Laden. He called you a Paki.'

I indicated the men by the swimming pool, who were all watching us. 'When Snezia was moving out and Meadow was moving in, I heard him say that he never knew al-Qaeda did removals.'

'Bin Laden was a Saudi,' Mo said. 'They were all Saudis, those men on that day. It was nothing to do with my people. I tried telling him that. But he was an uneducated person and he did not listen. None of them ever listen. Saudis attack America and Bush and Blair send their armies to Iraq. But Iraqis didn't cause 9/11.'

He picked up his wash mitt and nervously wrung it out.

324

'But Ruben wasn't like Big Del,' I said. 'When he was alive.'

'No,' he said, and his eyes shone with a stab of pain. 'Ruben was a good man. Under it all.'

'Ruben liked you too,' I said. 'He spoke to me about you once.'

'He did?'

I nodded. 'When I went to the yard. Auto Waste Solutions. That's where Ruben talked to me about you.'

Mo lifted his head, waiting.

I nodded at the Bentley. 'Ruben told me you let him use the car on special occasions,' I said.

The driver glanced anxiously at the empty house.

'Don't worry, I'm not going to tell anyone,' I said. 'But it's true, isn't it?'

'He took good care of the car. And he was my friend.'

'And Ruben Shavers liked women, didn't he?'

'Many women!' Mo said, grinning with admiration.

'And what I think is, on these special occasions that you let him have this beautiful car, he wanted to impress some woman.'

'It didn't happen very often. Only with a special lady.'

'But it happened?'

'Yes.'

'And Ruben couldn't bring the car back to you, could he? He could never return it to you. Because then the boss would have known that he borrowed it.

And then both of you would have been in big trouble, right?'

He nodded.

'So I am guessing that, if Ruben couldn't bring the car back to you, then you had to go and collect it from him.'

'Yes.'

'And I think – just like Harry Flowers – Ruben had a place where he would see his women without his wife knowing.'

He was guarded now.

'And do you know what, Mo? I think I've got the keys to this place.'

We stared at each other.

'And you're going to take me there,' I said. 'Ruben Shavers' secret flat.'

Mo looked at Whitestone and Adams watching from the BMW.

'And if you don't, Mo, then what I am going to do is arrest you as an accessory for murder.'

'I didn't hurt anyone!'

'Doesn't matter, Mo. Doesn't matter a damn. If the law thinks you aided and abetted someone guilty of murder, then it's as if you committed the murder yourself.'

I let him think about it for a while.

He didn't have to think about it for very long.

'I'll follow you,' I said, heading back to the BMW. 'You take the Bentley.'

We drove from that leafy little corner of the suburbs to the Broadwater Farm estate, Tottenham.

The Bentley idled at the foot of a monstrous tower block that had begun to rot from the moment they put it up. Ten years after it was erected, back in the Seventies, the authorities decided that the only thing to do with it was demolish it. But somehow, they never did. So it had stood here rotting for the last forty years.

A flock of young kids on bikes checked us out. They were unimpressed.

Because they had seen this car before.

And although they were unimpressed they still lingered, waiting for something to happen.

The tower block was within walking distance of the home that Ruben Shavers shared with his family. It could not have been more convenient for a secret life.

Mo buzzed down the window of the Bentley and it didn't make a sound.

'Top floor,' he said. 'The last flat at the end of the corridor.'

The keys were in my hand now.

'Did you ever go up there?' I said.

He shook his head.

327

'No, but Ruben told me. He was proud that he had the top flat. Good view. He called it the penthouse.'

We all looked up at the concrete block of flats stabbing itself towards the sky.

Joy Adams almost smiled. 'Penthouse,' she said. 'Nobody has a penthouse in this neck of the woods.'

'You can go now, Mo,' I said. 'We'll be in touch.'

The Bentley drove away, escorted by the flock of small boys on bikes.

'Do we want back-up?' Adams said.

I shook my head.

The keys to the secret life of Ruben Shavers were in my hand.

'Nobody up there is going to hurt us,' I said.

We came out of the lift on the top floor.

The wind whistled down those walkways, as it had for a lifetime, and as it would until they finally tore this place down.

We walked to the end of the corridor.

I took out Ruben's keys and slipped them into their locks.

First the Chubb.

Then the Yale.

We pushed open the door and went inside.

A long, lithe woman was looking out of the window, the palms of her hands pressed into her back, trying to relieve the aches and pains of a dancer.

For a moment I could not speak. I was suddenly aware of my heart in my chest and the only sound was the distant buzz of the traffic far below and the blood in my veins.

'Jessica,' I said, and the young woman turned. 'We're police officers.'

She stared at us as if she might be dreaming. I saw the blue and white packets of prescription medicine scattered across the coffee table. Xanax.

'Where's Ruben?' she said.

Whitestone looked at me.

Ruben.

'Shavers can't hurt you,' Whitestone said.

'Ruben was never going to hurt me,' Jessica said.

'Ruben Shavers is dead,' I said. 'But you're safe now. Nobody can hurt you now.'

'No,' she said.

It was not a denial of his death. It was a denial of her safety.

We stared at Jessica Lyle, still not quite believing it was her, and yet somehow having no doubt, and she looked at us and then past us, as if Ruben Shavers might walk through the door to his secret flat.

I took a breath and let it out.

'The night they took you,' I said. 'What happened?'

'They drove to some graveyard,' she said. 'But there was a police car parked outside. So they kept driving. And took me to the fat man's flat.'

329

It must have seemed like the perfect crime.

A grave beneath a grave that had been freshly dug and would never be found after the weeping mourners had gone home. A grave beneath a grave that nobody would even know about.

And like most perfect crimes, the plan fell to pieces almost immediately.

Because a squad car was routinely parked outside Highgate Cemetery, there to watch for speeding cars on Swains Lane and put off kids who fancied partying in the graveyard. And that one parked squad car meant the kidnappers suddenly had to improvise.

'They were arguing,' Jessica said. 'Ruben and the fat man. Ruben wanted to call it off – to let me out of the car. I was trying to talk to him. I told him I had a little boy. He seemed – he seemed like he was listening to me. He was looking after me.'

And I took her in for the first time. Yes, she was a woman that people would look at. They would look at her twice, and they would look at her for far too long. Because you can never quite believe it, that rare beauty. She had the bluest eyes I had ever seen in my life – eyes like frozen fire. But is that what all this grief and death had been for? A pair of blue eyes?

'The fat man was calling Ruben all sorts of names. They were hitting each other. It was horrible. We went to the fat man's flat, and I was trying to talk to Ruben

330

and the fat man was telling me to shut my mouth, and calling me names, and there was a woman there. The fat man's girlfriend. Ex-girlfriend. I don't know. She had a key and she had let herself in. She wasn't meant to be there. She was collecting some things – these awful cheap, tarty clothes. And she saw me and she lost her temper with the fat man.'

In my mind I saw Minky attacking Derek Bumpus, her fists flying.

'The fat man hit her. She went down and she wasn't moving. I don't know what happened to her after that because then Ruben took me away. And brought me here.'

Whitestone exhaled.

Because we knew what happened after that.

Minky had died.

Either Minky died when her head hit the floor or Derek Bumpus killed her before she could leave. The actual cause of death had dissolved long before Elsa had a chance to examine the body at the Horseferry Road mortuary. But either way, Minky had seen Jessica Lyle and it was her death sentence.

The freshly dug grave had been meant for Jessica Lyle.

And then there had to be a change of plan.

'Ruben brought me here,' she said. 'And he said he had children too. And then he went away and when he came back he said he had told his boss and the fat man that it was all taken care of.'

She was wearing a man's white shirt.

I remembered three evidence bags in West End Central and what they contained. A sweatshirt, a pair of yoga trousers and a pair of pants. All black apart from the slogan in lurid pink on the sweatshirt.

Last Chance to Dance.

'Your clothes,' I said. 'Someone sent us your clothes.'

'Ruben's idea,' she said. 'To make them believe that it had been done. That I was gone.'

Whitestone touched her arm.

'Did Ruben Shavers assault you, Jessica?'

'Oh, no.' She shook her head, appalled at the idea. 'He would never hurt me that way. He would never try to touch me. I think ... I *know* he liked me.'

She looked at us with her blues eyes.

Everyone loves Jessica.

'And now he's dead?' she said.

'Yes,' I said. 'An armed policeman shot him.'

There was sadness in those huge blue eyes. But she had no tears for Ruben Shavers.

'But, Jessica,' Whitestone said. '*Why didn't you try to escape?* Why didn't you smash the door down, break the windows, scream the roof off? Why didn't you come home? What about your baby? What about Michael?'

'Because Ruben told me that the person who hired him and the fat man would hurt my family,' she said. 'Ruben said that if they knew that I was alive, then my family would all be hurt. Even Michael. Even my baby boy.' There were tears in her eyes now. 'He said my family *would all be burned.*'

'The pills,' I said, indicating the coffee table. 'Did Shavers make you take them?'

'Oh no,' she said. 'He didn't *make* me. He said they were good for my panic attacks. Because at the start – it was very hard.'

A regular supply of Xanax and terror, I thought.

That would make anyone a willing prisoner.

'My little boy,' Jessica said, her voice racked with sorrow. 'My parents. They must have thought ...'

The tears came now and Whitestone went to her, wrapping Jessica Lyle in her arms. They stood like that for a while. I waited until the two women broke their embrace and then I smiled at that perfect face.

'Let's take you home to your family,' I said.

34

In summer it was never too early to get up.

Our little family woke and stretched and rose from our beds and dog basket as the sky lightened and poured through the wall-to-floor windows of the loft.

We brushed our teeth and pulled on our clothes and went down to the old BMW X5, Stan dozing on Scout's lap as we drove north to Hampstead.

At the top of the hill above Hampstead village, we parked behind Jack Straw's Castle and crossed the road to walk through the thickly wooded Vale of Heath to the big green meadow beyond, the day still so new that the entire meadow was teeming with rabbits.

Scout slipped Stan off his lead and, endlessly tolerant to all living creatures, he trotted hopefully towards the rabbits, ready to play, but they stood on their hind legs at our approach, their noses twitching at the presence of human and dog and danger, and ancient instincts sent them scurrying to their burrows, so fast it felt like a disappearing act. And then we were alone.

It was still too early for the serious runners, and even too early for the other dog walkers. Even the young yoga woman who came to the meadow to perform her surya namaskar, her daily salute to the rising sun, had not yet arrived.

Having the Heath to ourselves always felt like a winning Lottery ticket.

We walked deeper into the Heath, Scout and Stan and I, and all three of us knew those trees and paths and fields as well as we knew our own home. Without discussing it, we turned right into the thick woodland of East Heath, cool and dark under the canopy of trees, and came out on Pryor's Field, the series of linked ponds in the distance glinting like a string of pearls. We headed for the dazzling water, watched by a solitary kestrel gliding high above us.

By the time we got to Hampstead High Street, they were just opening up at the Coffee Cup, and we ate pancakes with blueberries and maple syrup at one of the outside tables, Scout slipping Stan morsels of pancake under the table as we watched the world wake up. Our walks on the Heath were always the best part of the day.

There are churches all over Hampstead, up on Heath Street and down on Church Row, and two of them on either side of Pond Street leading down to the Royal Free Hospital, and a small Roman Catholic church

335

tucked away on Vernon Mount and a large white church on the corner of Downshire Hill and Keats Grove.

And as I was paying the bill at the Coffee Cup, they all began to ring their bells at once.

I looked at Scout. Her eyes were closed and her lips were moving.

She felt me watching her and opened her eyes.

'I'm not making a wish,' she said.

I shook my head. 'Don't let me stop you wishing, Scout,' I said. 'I would be very sad if I thought that I had stopped you wishing when you hear the sound of the bells. OK?'

'OK,' she said, closing her eyes.

My phone began to vibrate.

JOY ADAMS CALLING, it said.

'I'm at Broadmoor Hospital, sir,' she said. 'The doctors called me and asked me to speak to Liam Mahone.'

Liam Mahone — the only surviving member of the Mahone family.

Little Liam who was four years old when someone came to his house one Sunday lunchtime with a can of petrol and emptied it over Liam's family before threatening to set them all alight.

Liam Mahone who had been catatonic for all of his adult life.

'I thought Liam didn't talk,' I said.

'He's talking now, sir. He saw a face on TV. And it brought it all back. All of it.'

'Can't you get a statement?'

'You are going to need to come down here, sir,' Adams said. 'And the boss. Now.'

I looked at my watch. Broadmoor Hospital is a forty-mile drive from London.

'We have a press conference at West End Central at ten a.m.,' I said. 'The boss wants to tell the world that we found Jessica Lyle.'

After we had found Minky's body, the mood had turned sour against the police. There were disapproving hashtags on social media – #WrongBody, #DumbPigs, #HighgateGaffe – and an online petition for us to prioritise missing children instead of missing adults.

Because in the end they always lose faith if we search in vain. Give it long enough and the press and the public and the social media sites who were initially so keen for us to find the missing one – the angelic child, the beautiful woman – in the end they lose patience with a fruitless search, and they give up on us, and they give up on the special missing one, and they complain about the wasted money and wasted time and the wasted effort and, above all, the rank stupidity of people like me.

'The press conference is the boss's idea,' I said. 'She wants to tell them all – the press, the public, the snowflakes with their hashtags and online petitions – that we found Jessica Lyle.'

I could hear Joy Adams breathing.

And in the background, beyond the sound of her breathing, I could hear a man screaming.

'Cancel it,' she told me.

Broadmoor Hospital.

The big, sprawling red-brick Victorian building that sits beyond the green, gently sloping hills of Crowthorne, Berkshire, and high walls of razor wire. Whitestone and I passed through two full body searches and into the hospital's inner courtyard, and then under an arch where the old red brickwork of the Victorian lunatic asylum finally gives way to newer buildings.

Broadmoor is not a prison.

But it is more secure than any prison I ever saw.

Two massive guards led us down long corridors the colour of buttercups.

Heavy reinforced doors were opened and then closed and locked behind us before the next door was opened. That was the sound of Broadmoor. The sound of doors being slammed shut. And distant sounds of deep distress.

Finally we came to the Paddock Centre where a man wearing a personal attack alarm was waiting for us with Joy Adams.

'Professor Tomlinson,' he said. 'I'm Liam's clinician. He's waiting for us.'

We followed him further down the bright canary-yellow corridors, and the massive set of keys attached to his waist jingled softly in a quiet that was broken only by the sound of a TV programme about the pros and cons of moving to the countryside.

The corridor opened up into a communal space where a group of men sat under the TV set. They were all massively overweight. They showed no interest in us, or even awareness of our presence.

Beyond the TV area there were doors with no windows.

'Isolation cells,' Professor Tomlinson said, and beyond one door I heard a low moaning sound. 'Patients stay in these when they become over-excited. Liam is resting in one of these cells right now. As I explained to TDC Adams, he has been a little upset by what he saw on the news.'

At the end of the yellow corridor, a huge guard waited outside a locked door.

Professor Tomlinson gave him a nod and he opened it up.

Inside, a slightly built man sat watching a TV set that was not turned on.

He was uniquely thin in that place of morbidly obese men.

'Good morning, Liam,' Professor Tomlinson said in his soft sing-song voice. 'You remember TDC Adams – Joy. And these are her colleagues. DCI Whitestone and DC Wolfe. Pat and Max. If it is all right with you, Pat and Max would appreciate it if you could tell them exactly what you told Joy.'

'Hello, Liam,' I said. 'I'm happy to meet you.'

Liam Mahone sighed.

He lifted his right arm and he sniffed it.

'What's he doing?' Whitestone asked Professor Tomlinson.

But we knew what Liam Mahone was doing.

He was smelling the petrol that he had been doused with at the other end of his lifetime.

I tried to picture him as a four-year-old child, and I tried to imagine the terror that had come calling that day. But that child was gone now and there was only this damaged man.

'Hi, Liam,' Joy said. 'Remember me?'

He exhaled again, not looking at us. He gave his arm another tentative sniff, as if making sure the imagined stink of death was still there.

'What exactly is wrong with Liam?' I quietly asked Professor Tomlinson.

'DPSD,' he said. 'Dangerous and Severe Personality Disorder. Many psychiatrists dislike the term because it is not a clinical diagnosis. It covers a group of patients who are considered to be a danger to the public.' He crouched by the side of Liam Mahone. 'Do you feel like talking, Liam?'

Liam continued to stare at the TV without seeing it. I crouched by his side.

'Look at this picture, Liam,' I said.

He moved his head to stare at the A4 printout of Derek Bumpus, the tip of his index finger warily tracing the four creases where it had been folded inside my jacket. Bumpus's great round face stared belligerently at the camera in the police mugshot.

'Joy told me you saw this man's picture on TV and you became very upset,' I said. 'And I think that's because this man once threatened to hurt you and your family. Have I got that right, Liam?'

Liam Mahone looked at Joy. Then he looked at Professor Tomlinson. And finally he looked at me, then quickly looked away. He sighed and nodded.

'What did you tell Joy?' I asked.

'That man said that he was going to *burn* us,' Liam Mahone said. 'My brothers. My sisters. My mum and dad. And me. He meant it, too! He wasn't just saying it! He was going to burn us up and he poured this stuff – the stuff that you set fire to and it burns you – all over us. And then the woman with him struck a match and said she was going to do it.'

I looked at Joy.

She nodded.

'Liam,' I said. 'You mean *the man.*' I showed him the print of Derek Bumpus. 'You mean the other man with this man in the picture. The second man. The man who was in charge. Harry Flowers. That's the name of the other man. The man who gave the orders. You mean the man in the picture – Derek Bumpus – was with the other man. Isn't that what you mean, Liam?'

He frowned with impatience.

And then he sniffed his arm, more forcefully this time.

'The *woman* was in charge,' he said. 'The lady told him what to do and he did it. Anything she told him, he had to do or else. This man' – indicating the mugshot of Derek Bumpus – 'he did what she told him to do.'

And at last Liam Mahone looked me in the eye.

'It was the *woman,*' he said.

Then he sighed more deeply than he had sighed before, and closed his eyes, as if ready to slip into a heavily medicated sleep.

And I understood now that a lot of people hated Harry Flowers. But nobody – not the Mahone family, not his embittered employees, not any business rivals, not any abandoned mistress – hated him quite as much as the woman who had helped to build his empire, and stood by his side, and turned her face away from every betrayal.

Nobody hated him quite as much as his wife.

35

Snezia Jones was ready to run.

There was a black cab waiting for her outside the small modern block of flats overlooking Highbury Fields.

She came out of the apartment block's lift with a small travel bag in either hand and suddenly stopped dead, staring at us through the tastefully tinted glass doors.

Joy cancelled the cab. The driver angrily flicked on his yellow *For Hire* sign, not happy at all. We went inside. Snezia led the way into the lift. Joy took her travel bag. She wasn't going to need it after all.

It was a beautiful flat. We paused to take in the view across Highbury Fields. The remains of a Mexican take-away for one was scattered on the coffee table. The roadside chicken tacos had hardly been touched. No sign of the boyfriend.

'Anyone else at home?' I asked.

Snezia shook her head.

'Most people can't do it,' Whitestone told her, looking out at the rolling green field that stretched to Highbury

343

Corner like a dream of the countryside. 'Take a life, I mean. People say — *I'll kill you*. But it's not that easy.'

She turned to look at Snezia to make sure she was paying attention.

'I never ...' she began. We waited. But she could not finish the sentence.

'They can't take a life and then carry on with their own life as though nothing has happened,' Whitestone said. 'Most people normal can't do it. And when they do — if they do — then it stays with them forever. Always there. Every day. In their dreams. And that is what happened to you, isn't it? No matter how much you may have hated Jessica Lyle.'

Snezia sank into a white leather armchair, so new that it still smelled of the showroom, and shook her head briefly, a final half-hearted denial of everything.

This is what they do in the last ditch, when they have realised that their life is about to change forever.

Not me, Officer. I didn't do it. It was someone else.

I gave Joy the nod.

'You are under arrest for Conspiracy to Murder,' she told Snezia.

Adams smoothly lifted Snezia from the sofa, spun her around, snapping the cuffs on behind her back, remembering her training. *A formal arrest will always be accompanied by physically taking control.* Because some people go fighting mad when the end is near. At Newgate prison, when they had the public hangings that Charles Dickens watched, the corridor that led from the holding cell became narrower as it got closer to the gallows, because the condemned can fight for their life with an inhuman strength.

But that's not what happened with Snezia. The fight went right out of her. And that can happen too, when the end is near. There are also people who are meekly led to their fate.

Snezia hung her head, and a tendril of her white-blond hair fell over her exhausted face.

'You do not have to say anything,' Adams said.

'What happened to the ballet shoes?' I asked.

Snezia blinked at me, not understanding.

'But it may harm your defence if you do not mention when questioned something you later rely on in court,' Joy said, checking the locks.

'When Jessica Lyle was taken,' I said. 'You showed me a pair of ballet shoes. Remember? When we were in the old flat. What happened to them?'

She shrugged. 'I must have lost them during the move.'

'No,' I said. 'You placed them on a fresh grave in Highgate Cemetery. Because you thought it contained the body of Jessica Lyle.'

Her head jerked towards me. *You thought . . .*

Because she did not know. She still did not know.

'Anything you do say may be given in evidence,' Joy said.

There was a massive HDTV on the wall facing the sofa.

I picked up the remote and turned it on and scrolled through the guide for BBC News.

And the return of Jessica Lyle was the top story on the rolling news.

She stood on the doorstep of her family home, her baby son in her arms, her parents pressed against her on either side, her brother holding on from behind, a tangle of arms and love, and they were all one flesh. Her mother was smiling, a broad smile that seemed fixed to her face with stunned disbelief. Tears rolled down the haggard cheeks of Frank Lyle, and the old cop pressed his face into his daughter's shoulder to hide them from the watching world. And Tommy laughed and baby Michael stirred in his sleep.

And I wondered what she told them. I marvelled at the conversation that I would never hear.

Did Jessica tell her family about the diet of Xanax and fear that had kept her from their side when their hearts were being shredded because they thought she was dead? Did she explain the unexpected mercy of Ruben Shavers? And I could not help but wonder – did they know that Jessica had been seeing another man at the time of her fiancé's death? Did they think that their perfect girl was painfully human after all? Did they look into those blue eyes and wonder if they really knew her at all?

Or perhaps she told them none of it. Perhaps they just held each other and wept. Perhaps the presence of her was miracle enough for now.

And I was happy for them. Because the family of Jessica Lyle looked restored, intact, and happier than they'd believed they would ever be again.

And Snezia sank back into her new leather sofa, the handcuffs making her arms rise awkwardly behind her, unable to take it in.

Staring at a ghost.

'Yes, she's alive and kicking,' said Whitestone. 'And as gorgeous as ever, isn't she?'

'They didn't put Jessica Lyle in that grave,' I said. 'They put a body in there, under the coffin that it was dug for. But it was not Jessica. Bumpus buried Minky in there.'

'Minky?'

I nodded. 'There was no sudden return home for Minky. There was no rich sponsor who discovered her at the Western World. Jessica Lyle was meant to die that night. But Minky died in her place.'

Snezia shook her head. It was not possible.

'Change of plan,' I said. 'Because the original plan fell apart from the start. Who do you think came up with the plan, Snezia? A team of nuclear physicists? The people who do these things, Snezia, they are not smart people.'

'No,' she said.

Not to the team of nuclear physicists, but to the idea that the plan could have gone so catastrophically wrong.

'The open grave was waiting at Highgate Cemetery,' I said. 'But when Shavers and Bumpus arrived with Jessica, there was a squad car parked outside the gates. Because you know what, Snezia? There often is. It's parked there to discourage the local youth from party- ing among all those precious old tombstones. And it's there to watch for drivers using their phones at the wheel. And it's there because it's a good spot for a couple of tired coppers to park up and take a breather. So they kept driving to Bumpus's flat in Camden, where the ex-girlfriend who still had a key was collecting some stuff.'

'Minky.'

'Minky. Poor Minky. And she was unhappy when they walked in with Jessica – this stunning new woman – and Bumpus was unhappy that she had seen them with Jes- sica. A witness. The plan would not work with a witness. And somewhere between all that sexual jealousy and all the fear of getting arrested, Minky got hurt and then she died. Jessica went home with Ruben Shavers and Minky went into the grave. But you didn't know that when you left the shoes and the flowers, did you? You thought the plan had worked. You thought Jessica Lyle was dead and gone.'

She still couldn't take her eyes from the TV.

'You set her up,' I said. 'Your friend in your car. You made it look like someone wanted to abduct you. And for what? Because you got dumped for someone younger and prettier? We all get dumped, Snezia. You know what happens after that? We find someone better. Nicer, hotter, kinder. That happens to everyone in the world.'

'Speak for yourself,' Whitestone said. And then to Snezia: 'You actually wanted Jessica Lyle dead just because she took Harry Flowers from you?'

Snezia's milk-white face twisted with contempt.

'I didn't care about losing my *boyfriend*,' she said. 'Is that what you think? I can always get another *boyfriend*. I can always get another *sponsor*. I cared about losing *my flat*.' Her eyes teared over. 'I really loved that flat.'

We stared at her in disbelief. Now it was our turn to stare in wonder.

'That's your motivation for Conspiracy to Murder?' Whitestone said. 'The housing shortage?'

And I saw it was true.

For a woman like Snezia, it was easy to find a boyfriend in the city.

But almost impossible to find somewhere decent to live.

Adams began to lead her away.

'It wasn't my idea!' Snezia said, desperate to tell us everything. 'I would have found another flat! I would have got another sponsor! But *she* told me – *she promised me* – that things could stay the same only if Jess was gone.'

Whitestone placed a gentle hand on Snezia's arm and I saw the same bleak light in her eyes that had been there when Jackson showed her the handgun in the back of that van.

'We know, sweetheart,' she said, a soft reassurance, almost maternal, as if all debts were about to be paid.

'Jessica was my friend,' Snezia said, something else on her face now, getting over the initial shock. 'But she was the kind of friend who gets everything she ever wants. She was the kind of friend who is in a different league to you. Look at her! Just look at her!'

We all looked at the Lyles as they retreated back into the family home, the press calling questions and the cameras flashing and the uniforms holding them all back. Even as the family passed through the door, Jessica still held baby Michael in her arms and her parents and her brother still held her. I never saw a family look so complete, and I never saw a woman so loved.

'Bitch,' Snezia said.

36

There were leaflets in the waiting room of the Harley Street clinic and I read their titles while we were waiting.

Give In to Your Exhaustion. Involve Your Partner. Don't Suffer in Silence. Get Your Partner to Give You a Soothing Massage. Talk to Your Partner.

Good advice to prepare you for your new life, your changed life, and the new life that was coming into the world.

The receptionist glanced up at us, wishing us away, embarrassed by the uniformed officer who could be seen through the frosted glass of the clinic front door, determined to act as if it was another day at the office.

And I remembered the special day my wife and I – and Anne was still my wife then – came to a place like this for her twelve-week scan, and I remembered how we held hands and prayed silently and believed with all our hearts that if we could just get through this day then we could face anything. It was so vivid in my mind

— Anne on her back, flinching and laughing as the nurse applied the cold gel to her bare belly, and the white knuckles of our held hands and our eyes no longer just for each other, our gaze now fixed on that black-and-white monitor, and lit by a cone of light coming down from above, illuminating the unborn baby, shining down on our daughter.

'Have you got any names?' the nurse asked.

'There's only one name,' Anne said. 'Scout.'

'Like the book,' the nurse said. 'To Kill a Mockingbird. I love that book.'

And we smiled in the darkness, our eyes never leaving the screen, and our grip on each other had tightened as though we would never let go.

'Here they come,' Whitestone said.

A door opened at the end of the thickly carpeted corridor that was more like a hotel than a hospital, and Meadow Flowers and her husband came out, smiling with relief and joy. I remembered that feeling. It was the best feeling in the world.

Their smiles faded when they saw us waiting.

And Mrs Charlotte Flowers came behind them, holding a black-and-white photograph of her unborn grandchild, and she smiled at me with that same polished charm she had shown on her daughter's wedding day, she presented me that same charming mask, and it did not begin to slip until I spoke.

'Snezia told us everything,' I said. 'You have to come with us now, Mrs Flowers.'

And I was prepared for denial, that was what I was expecting, that would have been the standard response from the ordinary sociopath.

But there was nothing ordinary about Charlotte Flowers.

And even as her mouth was still turned into an almost-smile, she came at me without warning and pressed her thumbs into my eye sockets, trying to blind me.

And now the receptionist was struggling to pretend this was just another day at work because Charlotte Flowers and I were writhing on the floor in a tangle of thrashing limbs, my hands on her arms as she tried to gain leverage to push my eyes into the back of my brain. Then I had her off me and I was on my feet again, but her mouth was snapping at me, attempting to bite off my nose, my ears, my lips, her jaws and teeth so close to my face that I could smell the floral bouquet of her lipstick. Whitestone and Adams were pulling at her limbs and a uniformed female officer had come in off the street but Flowers fought with a strength that came from some-where other than muscle and bone. And even when she was in cuffs she kicked and she spat and bit and cursed us all to hell.

But in the back of the car to West End Central she began to weep. We thought she was crying for herself, for the life that was ahead of her, which is why they usually cry, but that was not why she wept. While resisting arrest, and attempting to push my eyes out the back of my skull, she had lost the photograph she had been carrying.

And that was the only time I ever saw Charlotte Flowers cry.

Tears that were not for herself, but for the grandchild who was waiting to be born.

Charlotte Flowers sat in the interview room at West End Central.

The chair beside her, the chair for a lawyer, was empty.

'Before the start of this interview, I must remind you that you are entitled to free and independent legal advice either in person or by telephone at any stage,' I said.

I paused. She was smiling at the black-and-white photograph in her hands. The receptionist had found it and handed it to a uniformed officer. We had given it back to her in her holding cell. Now it felt like the image of that unborn child was more real to her than an interview room in West End Central.

And I could not tell if she was at peace or insane.

'Do you wish to speak to a legal advisor or have one present during the interview?' I said.

She looked up at me and smiled and shook her head.

'Out loud for the tape, please.'

'No.'

Charlotte Flowers did not want a lawyer.

She wanted to talk.

And so we let the tape roll.

'She doesn't want to see Harry,' she said, unable to resist a smile, her voice thick with triumph. 'I saw the news. She's with her family, isn't she? Harry was just a rebound thing. After her fiancé died. Harry did not understand the deal. You see, Harry is one of those men who has had a lot of women – a *lot* of women – but who doesn't understand the first thing about them. But with this one – he doesn't understand that she doesn't need his money. Not really. She can make her own money. And her family can look after her. And she can find a man her own age – look at her! She's stunning! She's a ten! She will be spoilt for choice. Harry doesn't understand that it's nothing for a woman to bring up a child alone these days.' She nodded at me. 'Maybe nothing for a man.'

'But Michael is Harry's child,' I said. 'Harry wants to bring up his son. It's the most natural thing in the world.'

She chuckled.

'That baby is not Harry's son. Because it *can't* be. After Junior was born, Harry had himself done.' Her long fingers made a snip-snip scissors gesture in the air. 'Harry had a vasectomy because it was just so hard – on both of us – with Junior. Our son started crying when he was born and he never really stopped. On and on

355

and on! A most demanding child. Two children was enough. Two was plenty. I insisted. So the baby must belong to the boy on the bike. The boy who died. Her fiancé. Lawrence?'

'Perhaps Harry doesn't care who the father is,' I said. 'Perhaps he is so crazy about Jessica Lyle that, given the chance, he would be happy to bring up the boy as his own.'

She sighed, as if that was a technicality, but I saw her mouth twist with suppressed rage.

'Perhaps. But the baby is *not* Harry's baby. OK? And he knows it.' Again with the snip-snip gesture. 'And so does she.'

'Can't you say her name?' Whitestone said. 'Can't you call Jessica Lyle by her name?'

Charlotte Flowers stared at her with haughty contempt, the amusement fading, like the lady of the house confronting an obdurate servant, and I saw the steel in her.

'I think she's quite enjoying her new-found fame, don't you?' she said. 'She doesn't need Harry any more. Harry's out. Cut off. Dropped. Dumped from a great height. Services no longer required, thanks very much. And Harry thought he was the tough one in that relationship!'

Whitestone glanced at me. Charlotte Flowers was acting as if she had won. And my boss was wondering if she was insane.

'Mrs Flowers, you should have a lawyer present,' Whitestone said.

She shook her head, as if it made no difference.

'Oh, Charlotte,' I said, and she took her eyes from the photograph in her hand to look up at me. 'All this for just another one of his girls,' I said. 'All these lives ruined. And for what? For just another one of Harry's women. One among dozens. Hundreds.'

She sneered at me.

'You're wrong,' she said. 'This one was never just another girl. This one was never going to be content with being a bit on the side. Exclusive fucking rights for a nice apartment and a generous allowance – that was never going to be enough for this one, a sponsor who has to be home for Christmas, weekends and all the major holidays. This one was never going to be grateful for the usual deal. *She* was special.'

'That's right,' I said. 'Everyone loves Jessica.'

Charlotte Flowers stared at me levelly. 'When did you first know?' she asked me. 'It was before Snezia started opening her big mouth.'

'Not until we met with Liam Mahone,' I said. 'Liam saw that picture of Derek Bumpus on the news and something stirred, something he had buried deep, something that had been eating away at him for a lifetime.'

She raised a wry eyebrow.

A smug smile began creeping across her face.

357

'Liam remembered that it was a woman who came to see his family at that Sunday lunch,' I said. 'A woman who gave the order for the Mahone family to be marinated in petrol. A woman who made them believe they were going to be burned alive. Harry's reputation – and his business – was built totally on fear. People were – are – terrified of him because of what he threatened to do to the Mahone family. But Harry Flowers never threatened to burn the Mahones. *Because you did*. Harry wasn't even there that day. It was you and some hired goon. My guess – Derek Bumpus, back when he was a damaged kid from care, probably a clinical psychopath, and half in love with you, and ready to do anything for you.'

She pouted. 'Big Del was only half in love with me? You're such a hard man, Detective!'

She smiled at the memory and gazed fondly at the image of her daughter's unborn baby, as if they were sharing a happy moment they would treasure forever.

'You played it very well,' I said. 'The pantomime of throwing Harry's clothes out of the window. Playing the hurt wife. It was all very convincing. It certainly convinced me. As if you didn't know about Snezia Jones. As if you didn't know about Jessica Lyle. As if you didn't know that your husband has had something going on the side for years. When a woman as smart as you, Charlotte – you would have known all along.'

'It's difficult to hide infidelity these days,' she said. 'Especially for a man as stupid as my husband. We're all so connected, aren't we? Some of them — men like my husband, unfaithful tart-shagging bastards like him — think that a second phone and deleting a few racy text messages will keep it a secret. But there are no more secrets. Not any more. Everything comes out in the end.'

'The wife and the mistress teaming up to rid themselves of the threat to the status quo,' Whitestone said. 'There's a first.'

Charlotte's mouth twisted with contempt.

'We didn't *team up*,' she said. 'Snezia was my employee, not a partner.'

'Then it was your idea,' I said. 'To have Jessica Lyle killed.'

'I made mistakes,' she said, and I saw Whitestone was right.

Charlotte Flowers could not say Jessica Lyle's name.

'Using those two apes, who Harry has been debasing for years, that was a mistake,' she said. 'One of them — big black Ruben — always short of cash for a lifestyle he could never afford. And the other one — bat-crazy Derek — resentful that Harry's workforce were starting to reflect our multi-racial society. And then involving that stupid stripper who Harry was trading in for her younger, fitter flatmate. But it seemed so right at the time! They were all so unhappy with Harry. His boys, Shavers and Bumpus. His bit on the side, Snezia. They have all suffered endless humiliations, just as anyone around my husband will. Harry has a roving eye, you see. And a roving cock, of course. Always on the lookout for something better! But I thought our little task force would be enough to rid us of that skinny bitch who threatened everything. I thought Snezia might be the weak link. The stupid stripper. But it turned out to be Ruben. Going soft on her! I should have seen that one coming. And I should have done it alone. What's the old saying? Never work with hired thugs and hookers. That was my mistake, wasn't it?'

She again looked fondly at the photograph of her unborn grandchild, happily drifting away.

'You made your big mistake long before you decided to kill Jessica Lyle,' I said. 'You made your mistake when you doused the Mahone family in petrol and didn't tell your man Bumpus to drop the match. Because those children were always going to grow up. And whatever the world did to them, they were never going to forget you.'

Her thumbs worked at the edges of the photograph, as if she was trying to soothe the baby, caress it, rock it to sleep.

'Boy or girl?' Whitestone said.

'Girl,' she said. 'Thank Christ.'

'But why did you want Jessica gone?' I said. 'It had happened before. Harry had always had his women on the side, probably since you expanded the business for him and the serious money started rolling in. What was so different this time?'

Pat Whitestone and Charlotte Flowers looked at me and then looked at each other.

And for a long second there was a real closeness between them.

Mrs Flowers took a deep breath and gently placed the image of her grandchild on the desk of the interview room.

'This one just had to go,' she said. '*Jessica Lyle*. There – I said her name. Happy now, are we? This one had to *really* go. Because this was something no wife on the planet could ever forgive. This was a special kind of humiliation. This was *new*. There was no coming back from this one. This time was different from all the other times – from all those other women in all those other rooms on all those other nights *because this time my faithless, whore-fucking husband fell in love.*'

The interview room was silent.

'And where does the money come from?' I said.

For the first time, I saw her squirm.

'What money?' she said.

'Your beautiful home,' I said. 'Your daughter's wedding. The love nest in Hampstead. Your husband's women. The Bentley Bentayga with the nice polite driver. Are we meant to believe that recycling scrap metal pays the bills? Are we meant to buy the lie that dead cars pay for all that?'

Charlotte Flowers folded her arms across her chest.

And now she wanted a lawyer.

37

My boss was happy at last.

There was a lightness about DCI Pat Whitestone, and an easy smile, and she no longer seemed as though her attention was locked in some other, darker place. So when days were growing just a little shorter and the sun was shining on the last Sunday afternoon of true summer, we gathered in her small back garden for a party.

We were a motley collection of neighbours, her son's friends, and murder detectives from Homicide and Serious Crime at West End Central, all of us loaded with barbecued chicken on paper plates that sagged in the middle and most of us with something to celebrate.

Justin, Whitestone's teenage boy, was basking in the success of his final exams, and the tall, good-looking kid in dark glasses stood surrounded by his student buddies, all of them still young enough to be self-conscious about openly holding alcoholic drinks, all of them with the rest of their lives ahead of them.

Pat Whitestone stood grinning in the smoke of the barbecue. She looked more than happy. It was as if some weight had at last been lifted from her.

And I realised that I had not seen her looking like this since the death of Edie Wren.

The barbecue steamed up Whitestone's glasses and she took them off, blinking myopically as she cleaned them with the hem of an apron commemorating the Queen's diamond jubilee.

'So what happens with Justin now?' I said, indicating her son and his friends.

She handed me a cold Asahi Super Dry from a portable fridge.

'University,' she said. 'Which means moving out. And living in another town. And independence. And all-night parties.' She laughed. 'I don't want to think about the parties.'

I raised the Japanese beer in salute.

'Justin did so well,' I said. 'And so did you.'

'All him,' she said, sipping a small plastic bottle of mineral water.

We stood in the comfortable silence of people who have worked together for years, our dogs milling at our feet, Dasher the large yellow Lab and Stan the small ruby Cavalier both wild-eyed and salivating at the sweet scent of all that barbecued meat.

Stan suddenly spread his front paws and lowered his head, growling with menace at the far larger Labrador.

'An invitation to play,' Scout explained. 'Stan would never hurt anyone.'

The dogs chased each other to the end of the small garden and then back again. I took a sip of the cold Japanese beer. It felt good.

Because we were celebrating too. Everyone responsible for the abduction of Jessica Lyle was in custody or on the run or dead. Sightings of Derek Bumpus's great menacing bulk had been reported in Ibiza and Phuket, and he would eventually be run down, either days or months from now. Because nobody gets to run forever. Ruben Shavers was in his grave. And the two principal conspirators, Charlotte Flowers and Snezia Jones, the wife and mistress of Harry Flowers, were in Holloway prison, awaiting trial.

And in a quiet corner of the garden, Joy Adams and her girlfriend were eating from the same paper plate and flicking through the latest copy of *Grazia*. Jessica Lyle was on the cover. *The Woman Who Lived*, it said.

'So it's over,' I said.

'Not yet,' Whitestone said. 'But soon.'

She lifted the plastic bottle to her lips and took a brief sip. And in the scented air, so full of barbecued meat and mown grass and the summer city smell, I got a faint whiff of something else.

It was vodka not water in that plastic bottle.

'Ah, Pat,' I said.

'Don't worry about me,' she said. 'It's not the same. It's all under control.'

'Harry Flowers can't hurt you,' I said. 'He doesn't have that power.'

She nodded, humouring me. 'That's right,' she said.

A couple of Justin's friends appeared for a refill. White-stone loaded their plates with chicken and salad. I waited until they were gone.

'You're *safe*,' I said. 'You know that, don't you?'

She smiled at me through the smoke of the bar-becue.

'I know that I will be soon,' she said.

More guests were arriving. More of Justin's friends. Old colleagues of Whitestone from New Scotland Yard. She threw king prawns on the barbecue and ordered Justin and his friends to bring more wine and beer from the house. Some music began to play. Bob Marley and the Wailers, the eternal sound of summer in the city. And with Bob singing 'Lively Up Yourself' and with our host feeding the latest arrivals, I put down my Asahi Super Dry and my empty paper plate, and I went into the house.

I took the stairs two at a time.

It was a small house, an old terraced two-up, two-down that had somehow survived the Blitz and the property developers. I opened the door to the bathroom but quickly turned away. Not in here, I thought. I went to the next room, Justin's bedroom, impossibly neat for a teenage boy. Bed, desk, a poster of Steve Jobs on the wall.

I looked through his desk drawers, and felt at the back for a secret compartment. Nothing.

I looked under the bed mattress. I quickly rifled the bookcase looking for some hole in the wall beyond the books.

And it was not in here.

Strange kid, I thought, watched by Steve Jobs as I left the room, then going to his mother's bedroom next door.

I checked the wardrobes.

No safe.

A safe would have been the obvious place.

But there was no sign of a safe.

I took off my shoes, stood on the bed and rapped my knuckles against the ceiling. The ceiling would have been the next obvious place. But it felt solid.

Voices drifted up from the back garden. Smoke and laughter and Bob Marley singing about the joys that were waiting in his single bed. Someone came into the house and I froze but they did not go beyond the kitchen. I heard the fridge door open and close, the chink of cold beer bottles. Then I opened all the wardrobes and found nothing but clothes. I lifted the mattress of Whitestone's bed.

I paused at the top of the stairs, feeling a growing sense of relief.

Maybe I was wrong, I thought. There was nothing here.

I went into the small living room. The worn leather sofa, the new TV, a dining table for two. The dog's basket. And that was it.

I breathed out, feeling ready for a second beer. The back door was open and I could hear Bob Marley singing 'I Shot the Sheriff' and smell the king prawns sizzling. I had begun moving towards the sound of music and the smell of prawns, looking forward to the sunlight and the smoke and the laughter, when I suddenly stopped and turned around.

Dasher's basket.

Which was not really a basket at all but more of a bed. A deep, cushioned sleeping area with a high bolster around three sides, designed to enhance your dog's sense of security. Stan had one just like it, but in extra small rather than extra large. Designed for dogs who love to nuzzle and nest.

I felt under the velvet-soft mattress.

And that is where I found it.

I expected my hands to touch cold steel, but the firearm was made of high-strength nylon-based polymer.

Closer to plastic than steel.

Lightweight. Slimline. Fantastically user-friendly, sitting snugly in my hand as if we were made for each other.

The Glock that Jackson Rose had sourced for Pat Whitestone.

I felt my stomach lurch as I looked at the short, stubby block of death, precision engineered for all forms of personal protection.

I felt its weight.

Less than a kilo.

'I can't let you out of my sight, can I?' Whitestone said behind me.

Her face was ruddy from the sun and the heat of the barbecue. Her fair hair was pulled back in a plastic band. She wiped her hands, greasy from feeding so many, on her diamond jubilee apron. The lenses of her glasses were steamed up and smudged.

'You must know this is a mistake,' I said.

She shrugged.

'A single-stack magazine with a capacity of six rounds,' she said. 'I figure that should be plenty.'

'You know what I mean,' I said. 'Are you a hitman now?'

'I'm tired, Max. I'm tired of watching too many of them get away with it. Tired of clearing up their mess. I'm just so tired, Max.'

'What are you planning to do?'

'I haven't thought it through yet.'

'Then it's time you started thinking,' I said. I showed her the Glock. 'Listen to me, Pat. I can get rid of this for you. Let me walk out of here with it and I'll make it go away.'

'The gun is not the problem. Harry Flowers has his claws in me and he is never going to let go until one of us is done.' A beat. 'And what are you going to do? You going to rat me out, Max?'

'It's not going to come to that.'

'It might.'

'I don't want it to come to that.'

We stared at each other.

The sound of small trainers running down the hall.

'Daddy!'

I slipped the Glock back under the mattress. Scout stood breathlessly before us, Stan panting by her side.

'Justin and I made you dinner!' she said. She took my hand and began dragging me towards the garden. 'Come on, will you?'

Whitestone smiled at her. 'You hanging out with the big kids now, Scout?'

'Yes! They're my friends!'

'I'll be right there,' I promised. 'And get me a beer from the fridge would you, please, Scout?'

Her eyes were wide at the seriousness of this mission.

'Sure!' she said. 'But come soon!'

My daughter and our dog raced back to the garden.

Whitestone was waiting. 'I need you to support me on this,' she said.

'How can I, Pat? This is crazy.'

'No, it makes perfect sense. Did you hear what he said to me? *I own you now*. Do you think he means it?'

A pause.

'Yes,' I said. 'I think he means it.'

'There you go,' she said. 'So if Flowers gets found with one in the head and one in the heart, you going to rat me out, Max?'

'Please,' I said.

But she smiled as if it could not end any other way.

'He can't own me. I can't be his creature. He has poisoned so many cops. And he's not having me, Max.'

Dasher padded into the living room and curled up in his basket, as if something had been decided. For a moment we both watched him, full of wonder and envy at the dog's ability to fall asleep at will.

Then we went out to the garden where our children had carefully placed our dinner on two paper plates.

38

Sports day.

A big blue sky and the sweet feeling that another school year was done and dusted and the long summer holiday was coming soon. But Scout looked solemn as she shouldered her kit bag.

'Just try your best,' Mrs Murphy urged. 'That's all anyone can ever do.'

Scout nodded grimly. But what if trying your best was never quite good enough? What if trying your very best – really trying very hard – never got you among the gold, silver and bronze stickers that they handed out even for the heats – even for the heats! – so that children who did not have a sporty bone in their family tree came away with some sort of prize. What then?

We walked to school, the one day of the year that Stan did not accompany us, and I felt that we marched in the terrified silence of condemned men.

Because sports day was always a struggle for a summer baby.

With her birthday in late July, Scout was younger and smaller than all of her classmates. This only ever mattered on sports day, the one day of the year when I couldn't say to myself – ah yes, but Scout can read better than anyone else, and she is smarter, prettier and nicer than everyone else. None of that mattered a damn when the sun was beating down on the fifty-metre dash. On sports day Scout was expected to compete against giants and she always came home – my dry-eyed, uncomplaining, brave Scout – without a sticker.

But this year sports day was different. This sports day was special. This year – for the first time ever – I would not be cheering her on alone. Her mother was coming.

By the time Anne parked her car on a double-yellow line outside the school gates, the games had begun. You could hear the birdsong of the children, the bossy instructions from the tannoy, the cheers of the parents.

My ex-wife wore a little black dress, those serious high heels with the red soles and big round dark glasses. She looked as though she was going to a dinner party in Monaco rather than a primary school sports day in a quiet corner of North London.

'Thanks for coming,' I said.

I felt like hugging her. I felt like jumping for joy. I felt that Anne's presence would make a difference to this sun-drenched dark day. I honestly believed it might even inspire Scout to get among the stickers – not in the finals, but maybe a bronze sticker for coming third (out of four) in one of the heats? Was that too much to hope for?

'No problem,' said my glamorous ex-wife, frowning at my dopey grin. 'How are you, Max?'

There was a large phone in her right hand and she clutched it to her breast, as if to ward off evil spirits. We did not touch, of course, not even when she stepped on to the playing field and her spike heels sank into the soil.

I reached for her but held back when I saw her flinch.

'*Will parents please refrain from entering the sports field,*' ordered the voice on the tannoy. '*The year four 50-metre heats will begin at nine forty-five precisely.*'

'Jesus Christ,' Anne said, hobbling uncertainly, her long legs lifting like a baby giraffe as she sought to remove her spiked heels from the ground.

Her phone began to trill importantly.

'I'll call you in five minutes,' she told it.

She managed to work out a way of walking that involved stepping mostly on the balls of her Louboutin-shod feet.

It seemed to work, more or less.

'I know it will mean a lot to Scout that you're here,' I said.

She almost nodded.

We made our way to the track, Anne still trying to walk on the balls of her feet to prevent her heels from impaling her to the grass.

Several of the fathers had turned to look at her. And even more of the mothers. The fathers had been taught not to look at women and they had learned their lesson well, but the mothers gawped openly at this long-limbed vision in black.

It was nothing, I knew, to do with me arriving with her.

It was nothing to do with the single dad having a hot date. It was simpler than that. Anne turned heads. And even though I sometimes thought, *Well, you should have seen her ten years ago* – I knew that people – men, boys, women, all the women – would stare at her for decades to come yet. People looked, and they could not stop looking, as if she belonged to some newly discovered species. The life of Jessica Lyle would be the same. The people who are rated tens have this in common.

The kids were stacked up in ragged lines behind the starting line, moving up four at a time as their race was called. Scout was going through an elaborate series of warm-up exercises. Stretching her calves, touching her toes, running on the spot. She looked tiny next to her opponents. A tall girl. A fat girl. A girl who was both tall and large. They talked languidly among themselves as Scout prepared herself.

'Scout!' I called.

She waved excitedly when she saw us.

Anne waved back, smiling for the first time.

'Good luck!' she shouted, and I felt my throat choke with feeling.

Yes, I thought. Good luck, brave Scout.

A starting pistol fired. Four children began to hare down the straight, cheered on by their parents. Scout's race moved closer to the starting line. I gave her a thumb's-up as she ran on the spot, a big grin on her perfect face.

'I can't stay for all of it,' Anne said. 'I told you that, right?'

Children flew past us. We stood at the side of the track's freshly painted straight and now that she had stopped moving, Anne's heels began to sink into the playing field. She cursed like a sailor on shore leave, snapping around the heads of some disapproving mothers, and lightly placed a hand on my arm to steady herself.

We dreaded touching each other. We – this man and this woman who had once slept a deep contented sleep with our limbs entwined so that you could not tell where one began and the other ended – acted as if something catastrophic would happen if we dared physical contact. But Anne took my arm and it was no big deal. The sky did not fall down. We touched each other and it was nothing much. The days – years – when touching had meant anything were long dead.

'I have some news,' she said. 'Oliver and I are getting back together.'

Oliver? Her husband. The one after you, I thought. Do try to keep up, Max.

She grimaced.

'For the sake of the children,' she said, 'as the old cliché has it.'

'That's good, isn't it?'

She shrugged.

'Oliver has had a job offer,' Anne said. 'We have a chance if he's working again.'

'*Parents* MUST *refrain from entering the track area*,' said the bossy voice of the tannoy, as if wiping the snotty nose of some sobbing five-year-old after their calamitous egg-and-spoon race was the worst crime in the world.

'I was in one of those clinics,' I said, my mind veering away from it all – the sports day, Anne giving it another go with her husband for the sake of the children. Perhaps it was because she had taken my arm. Perhaps it was because we had dared to touch.

'The place you go for the twelve-week scan,' I said. 'You remember that day, Anne?'

She looked bored.

'Max,' she said. 'Don't get sentimental on me.'

377

Was it sentimental? I was just remembering something precious, something that was worth getting sentimental about. And trying to hold on to it before it slipped away forever.

She was talking on the phone again.

'Look, I'll be at the fucking restaurant on time, all right, Oliver? Now stop calling me.'

She hung up, glanced at her watch and then at me. My stomach fell away, because I knew what was coming, and I knew it had been a mistake to ask her here, and I knew I had been stupid to think it would mean something if she came.

She was dead right. Too sentimental, Max. And nothing good will come of it.

'Why are you here, Anne?'

She bridled. 'Because you *asked* me.'

'Because I just wanted us to be a normal divorced couple,' I told her.

'God, you and bloody normal, Max. Give me a break, will you?'

I was reaching for the words, but I was not sure I could even really explain it to myself.

'For you and me to get along,' I tried. 'For you and Scout to see each other in some kind of regular routine. Not all this other stuff getting in the way – as if we're planning the Normandy landings.' I stared at her. One of the 50-metre heats dashed by. 'That's all,' I said.

She snorted with derision.

'Listen, you never wanted *normal*, Max. You wanted wild. You wanted the woman that everyone else wanted.'

Even with the 50-metre heats in progress, there were still one or two fathers who were running their eyes up and down the view of Anne from behind. Her legs, her butt, her back. Even her back! I saw a mother elbow a father in the ribs and he looked no more upon the rear view of my ex-wife.

'You wanted different, Max. So don't complain that it worked out different from everybody else.'

'I just want Scout to be ...'

But, no, I could not find the words. They stuck in my heart and my throat. I wanted my daughter – our daughter – to be noticed and to count and to be loved. That's all. I wanted her to be more important than anything else. To both of us. And it was not like that, I saw now, no matter how much I wanted it. But that was the feeling that I could not put into words.

'I'll see Scout more often as soon as things settle down,' Anne said, one of those vague promises delivered in a tone that managed to be both defensive and resentful. 'Just get off my back about it, will you?'

And she sighed, an elaborate sigh, her punchline to all difficulties.

'*On your marks!*'

TONY PARSONS

And I looked in my heart and I could find no love for this woman. I could not even find the memory of love. We were going to be one of those banal couples that could not find a way to raise their child together after we came apart. That was the real cliché.

Whatever she said, there was nothing special about us, there was nothing different about us. There were millions of useless parents who brought a child into the world and then did not have the wit to raise it. And I saw with a sinking feeling in my gut that what was really special about today was that we were probably meeting for the last time.

Because it happens.

And most of those parents at that sports day – married or divorced or somewhere in between, and they covered the spectrum – would never have understood that you can bring a child into the world and then just wander away, and become too busy, and too preoccupied, and always have other demands on your time more important than the beautiful child that got left behind.

But I knew it was true. There are millions of children who never get the time they deserve. And that's what it is about – time. It is nothing as ephemeral as love. Children – all children – just want some of your time. Is that too much to ask? Yes, that's way too much, I thought.

And as the July sun hammered down on another sports day, my heart ached with envy for all those sheltered, civilised lives who would not have believed it possible.

I wished I was that innocent, and I wished I knew so little.

Anne's phone warbled again. She spoke urgently into it.

'Look, sorry and all that, but I have to go, Max,' she told me. 'Oliver has this *very* important lunch with his new boss ...'

'Yes,' I agreed. 'You go, Anne. It's OK. Really. It's fine. I've got it here.'

'*Get set!*'

She turned and hobbled from the field, the spike heels of her Christian Louboutins sinking into the junior school's playing field, as if it was pleading with her to stay for the prize-giving and sandwiches and sausage rolls. The mothers watched her rear as she left, and the fathers knew enough not to.

And I remembered that I used to say our marriage had not failed because it had produced our daughter.

But I could not lie to myself any more.

In ways that I did not understand – it had something to do with twisted priorities – we had both failed Scout.

I watched Anne walking to her car and the years with no contact, no contact at all, stretched ahead of us.

'*Go!*'

Then the starting pistol went and I turned away to watch my daughter run.

The other three girls were already far, far ahead. The tall girl. The fat girl. The girl who was both tall and large. First, second and third places would be divided between them, a nice sticker for all of them for doing well in their heat so they would not feel too bad when they were blown away by the natural-born athletic kids in the final.

Scout Wolfe, lagging way behind but running as if her life depended on it, with her stick-thin limbs and the face of an angel, the youngest in the year and small for her age anyway – she was coming home without a sticker to her name.

But I bent at the waist as she ran past, her head back, and I called her name.

And I laughed out loud, the tears streaming down my face, as she began to close the gap on the fat girl.

Scout sat up in bed, smelling of shampoo, smelling of the day – grass and lemonade, sweat and sugar and dirt and soap, teriyaki crisps and ice cream – and held out her hand for the book I was holding.

There was a bronze sticker on her pyjamas, curling at the edges like a sandwich that had been left too long in the sun.

'Listen, Scout,' I said, giving her the book.

382

'Dog Songs *by Mary Oliver*,' she read. '*Poems.* New York Times *bestseller. Winner of the ...*' She paused to consider the unfamiliar word. '... *Pulitzer Prize.*'

Damn good reader, my girl. Always. She flipped the book over.

'*Mary Oliver's* Dog Songs *is a celebration of the special bond between human and dog*,' she read.

'We are on our own, Scout,' I said, and I knew that there was no other way for me to say it.

She stared at the book, but she was listening to me. I could tell.

'I tried to pretend for a long time that we are not on our own,' I said. 'But I think we are, and I think we just have to get on with it. Even though your mum and I are not together, I thought that we might somehow still – I don't know – be a sort of unit.'

A sort of unit? This was rubbish. I made a failed marriage sound like faulty kitchen furniture. Why don't you say the word you are afraid to say, Max? The word that you really mean.

'That we would still be a *family*,' I said. 'But just a family that doesn't live together. And I see now that it is never going to be like that.'

I watched her face for a while, waiting for some reaction, stunned as always by the overwhelming and unconditional feeling of love that she stirred in me.

'Sorry,' I said, and I meant it. 'Sorry, kiddo.'

383

'*Oliver's poems begin in the small everyday moments familiar to all dog lovers*,' she read. Scout appreciated a good blurb.

'Scout,' I said. 'Your mum.'

'She's busy.'

In the years ahead, the way Scout said those words would change. She would not say those words at sixteen as she said them at eight. The years ahead would gild those words with mockery, and cynicism, and a hard-earned wisdom.

But she was eight years old now and she could still say the words – '*She's busy*' – with a childish acceptance that tore up my heart.

'Yes,' I said. 'She's really busy.' A pause. 'So – what that means – to you and me – we're alone, Scout.'

She put down the book.

Dry-eyed and calm.

She studied the sleeping dog on her bed for a moment and then she looked at me.

'No,' she said. 'We're not alone. We're never alone. Because we have each other. And Stan. And all of our friends. And Mrs Murphy. And Lara.'

'Who's Lara?'

'Lara is the slightly chubby girl that I beat in the race. She was crying after she didn't get a sticker and so I comforted her and told her she would probably do better next sports day and now we're friends. But mostly,

Daddy, we have each other and so we can't ever be alone. OK?'

'OK, Scout.'

She waited until she believed that I believed it, too.

Then she handed me the book.

'It looks good,' she said. 'But, Daddy?'

'Yes, Scout?'

'It doesn't always have to be a poem about dogs,' she said. 'There are all kinds of poems in the world.'

I stood at the window and I watched the meat market come to life.

Mrs Murphy was still here but going through the last rituals of the day, preparing to go home soon.

I watched a group of meat porters cross from one of the pubs to the market. One of them, a large white man with a shaven head, stopped and turned and looked up at our building, his eyes scanning the windows, as if he was not sure of what he was looking for.

And then we were staring at each other, me and the man in a bloody white coat, looking up at the lofts.

And I saw that it was Derek Bumpus.

'Mrs Murphy?'

'Yes, love?'

'I may need you to stay a bit later,' I said without turning around.

'No problem,' she said. 'Is everything all right?'

Bumpus was looking up.

His mouth was moving.

He was saying something.

He was asking me a question.

It was a question that he had asked me before.

It was the one question he knew would make me go after him.

'*How old is your kid?*' he said.

And I went out into the night.

39

He was waiting for me at the end of the street.

A bulky man in a bloody white coat, one hundred metres away, standing on the corner of Cowcross Street, with nothing left to lose.

Making sure I saw him before he ducked down the side street.

I started running down Charterhouse Street, speed-dialling Whitestone.

She answered immediately.

'I have him,' I said. 'Bumpus.'

I turned the corner of Cowcross Street. It was down those many narrow winding roads in Smithfield that herds of cattle were driven for five hundred years or so. What makes Cowcross Street different is that it has an underground station.

He glanced over his shoulder to make sure I was following before he ran inside.

'He's getting on the tube,' I said. 'He wants me to come after him.'

Silence at the other end of the line. I thought she was going to tell me to be careful, that it looked like a set-up, that he was going to step out of the shadows and stick a knife in my ribs.

But that was not what she was thinking.

'I know where he's going,' Whitestone said.

Then I was inside the tube station and Whitestone's voice was gone and so was the phone signal.

I stuck my phone in my pocket as I saw Bumpus heading down the escalator, running down the steps, shoving aside anyone who got in his way.

A train was coming in.

The westbound Circle line, the only tube line that never ends, the underground line that keeps looping the city forever.

When I got to the bottom of the escalator, the man in the bloody white coat was at the far end of the platform.

He got on the train. And so did I.

I started heading towards him as the train left the station, the carriages packed with late commuters.

We were coming into the next stop as I reached the last carriage.

There was a man in a bloody white coat with his back towards me.

I grabbed him by the shoulders and spun him around.

The man cowered with terror, one of the lost souls who spend their lives riding the Circle line, never bothering anyone, happy for the city to leave them alone.

'He told me I could have it!' he said.

I pushed him away as the doors opened and the King's Cross crowds began swarming into the carriage. And that's when I saw Bumpus, already on the platform after stepping out of the driverless carriage at the very front of the train, grinning back at me as I cursed him and forced my way through the crowds.

He turned towards the exit, harder to spot now without his meat porter's coat, but the great ugly melon of his shaven head still visible above the office workers and the tourists.

He paused at the top of the escalators, making sure I was still on his trail.

'Stop that man!' I shouted. 'Police!'

That gave Bumpus a laugh.

Nobody was going to stop anyone on the London Underground.

Down there, you are on your own.

I came out of the tube station and into the night, the great Gothic towers of St Pancras looming high above, like a castle in a fairy tale, and I saw him heading away from the station and north, beyond the shining towers of glass and steel to that older, unchanging part of the city.

And then he was gone and I had lost him.

I stopped and caught my breath.

And now, like Whitestone, I felt that I knew where he was going.

No, that was wrong.

I knew where he was leading me.

The area beyond the great railway stations of King's Cross and St Pancras is a wasteland that feels like it has been forgotten by the world.

Warier now, I walked down the road where I had found the dead boy with the scooter.

No sign of Bumpus. No sign of anyone. But I walked north, beyond the vast concrete wasteland to the yellow sodium glow of a light industrial estate. And I saw the skyline made of scrap metal, the jagged peaks of all those finished cars piled on top of each other.

I took the road that led to Auto Waste Solutions.

And I saw that it was all lit up.

The silence.

That was what I noticed.

I had never heard Harry Flowers' yard silent before. Usually there was the scrape of two tons of dead metal being dragged across the yard, and the shouts of the men, and the diesel rumble of the forklift truck and, above it all, the deafening pounding of the car compactor.

The gates were open but I moved away from them, skirting the car pound next door.

The metal fence was designed to stop you driving away with a car, not from getting inside. I scaled it with no problem, dropped into the car pound, and edged closer to the border that it shared with Auto Waste Solutions. And in the valley between two soaring mounds of scrapped cars, I could see into the yard.

Harry Flowers stood by the Bentley Bentayga, its engine idling, as he watched a lorry being unloaded by Mo Patel and his cousins.

I struggled to understand what I was seeing.

Cellophane-wrapped pallets.

Hundreds of them.

Industrial-sized pallets with what looked like thousands of small packets.

And I understood that Derek Bumpus never wanted me to find him.

He wanted me to witness this scene.

But I stared past them all because on the far side of the yard, beyond the great scarred car compactor, its giant maw as black as a cave in the night, I saw a slight, bespectacled woman with neat fair hair watching from the shadows.

Pat Whitestone.

Then the point of something sharp pressed into my neck just below my right ear.

I felt it pierce the skin with the passing pain of a vaccination, and then the dribble of blood on my neck, as warm as soup.

Junior Flowers stood there with a pair of gardening shears in his hand. There were a couple of Mo's cousins with him, both with cricket bats, looking as though they were about to open the batting at Lord's.

'Deep breath, piggy,' Junior advised me.

Junior led me down into the yard. Derek Bumpus was sitting on the back of the lorry with a shocked, sickened look on his face. His mouth was a mess. Someone had very recently knocked his front teeth out with a cricket bat.

'Big Del was leading the law here!' Junior told his father, gesturing at Bumpus with his gardening shears.

'Shut those gates,' Flowers growled.

Some of the cousins rushed off to do his bidding. There were more cousins than I had seen before, cousins who had never been at the house. They stared at me without interest or fear.

Flowers considered Bumpus with disappointment. He indicated the lorry. I could see more clearly now what was on the shrink-wrapped pallets.

Thousands of small blue-and-white packets. More white than blue.

'This is what he wanted you to see,' Flowers told me. 'My former employee. This skinhead Judas. This is what he wants you to find.'

He addressed the dazed man sitting on the back of the lorry. They had not bothered to restrain him in any way. Knocking his front teeth out seemed to have slowed him right down.

'Was that the plan, Del?' Flowers asked.

Bumpus gave no indication that he understood what was being said to him.

Mo and his cousins stood around waiting for instructions.

'Get the pigs in and save your own skin?' Flowers said 'Your last shot at revenge. Nice try, fat boy.'

I stared at the back of the lorries.

'Pills,' I said, understanding at last.

Pills.

Thousands of pills.

A lorryload of pills in blue-and-white packets sitting on cellophane-wrapped pallets.

Flowers winced with professional pride.

'Ah, they're far more than pills,' he said.

We stared at the back of the lorry.

He gave the nod and the unloading continued, Junior cutting off the cellophane with his gardening shears and the cousins breaking them down into neat, smaller stacks, and Mo watching the proceedings while tapping away at a calculator.

'This is prescription-only medication,' Flowers said. 'Factory made, FDA-approved. Your doctor and your local chemist are the drug dealers now.'

'Bent doctors,' I said. 'Crooked chemists.'

He ignored me.

'It's all changed since the days when friend Mahone and I were shipping MDMA, weed and white powders,' he said, studying the contents of the lorry. 'Big Pharma are the only drug dealers that matter these days. And who can compete with them? Nobody wants home-made drugs. Drugs as a cottage industry? That's all over. The future belongs to Big Pharma. Prescription drugs are a trillion-dollar industry – Mahone and I never dreamed of this kind of dough! There's never a bad batch! It's all perfectly legal! What's your problem? We have a pill for that! We can cure you! Anxiety? Stress? Depression? We have a pill for that – factory made, Government-approved, sure to keep your doctor happy. Oh, it may make you feel like slashing your wrists six months from now, but who cares? I'm just a middle man.' He shook his head. 'I hand it to these pharmaceutical companies – they know what people want and what they don't want. Nobody wants to dance all night! Nobody is expecting to have their mind expanded! Nobody even wants to get high any more! Nobody even wants a rush! That's all over. Big Pharma understands. *People just want oblivion.*'

'Downers,' I said, looking towards the lorry. 'Tranquillisers.' I looked back at Flowers. 'What's this – Xanax? So you got the doctors and the pharmacists working for you, Harry? Or are you working for them?'

Whitestone moved through the half-light between the piles of wrecked cars, edging towards the huge metal bulk of the car compactor, and I saw the Glock in her right hand.

I closed my eyes. Then I opened them.

I watched her aim the handgun at the back of Harry Flowers' head.

But he abruptly moved towards the dazed and battered man sitting on the back of the lorry.

'No more talk,' Flowers said. He turned to his son. 'Let's give Del and the detective some free samples, shall we?'

Junior grinned and began to cut the plastic off the nearest pallet with his gardening shears. 'How's your social anxiety disorder?' he asked me.

'Hold them down,' Flowers told the cousins.

A swarm of cousins put us on the ground.

Junior was laughing, slashing at the cellophane, then tearing open one of the individual packets, pressing his finger against the silver foil that contained the pills. Again and again and again.

Getting a fistful of Xanax.

'Open wide,' he told Bumpus. Two of the cousins pulled Bumpus's bloody mouth open. He howled with agony and I saw that his jaw was probably broken. Junior emptied the handful of Xanax into his mouth and then helped the cousins to clamp Bumpus's jaw closed.

Bumpus's huge body writhed and fought but eventually he choked them down.

'Now the pig,' Flowers said.

'Down the hatch,' Junior told me, taking a fistful of my hair and bending my neck backwards.

Fingers clawed at my face, pulling my mouth open. My lips, my teeth, my jaw.

I lashed out with my feet, trying to smash someone's knee, but there were too many of them.

It is not like the stories that they tell you about tough guys.

Multiple assailants can usually do what they like with you.

Hands and boots held me still as they recalibrated, some of them abandoning my mouth to concentrate on pinning me to the ground. Now there were fewer fingers on my tongue, inside my teeth, pulling my lips apart. But they were getting the job done.

Junior yanked my head back again.

Then the pills were poured into my mouth.

They slammed my jaw closed, and I felt my teeth bite on to the tip of my tongue.

I felt some of the pills sliding down my throat. Others were jammed behind my teeth, stuck to the roof of my mouth, the inside of my lips, caught in my throat.

I felt my stomach heave.

I retched, trying to sit up, my mouth still held shut.

And then I swallowed.

'Don't be sick now,' Junior said, patting my back.

They were already lifting Derek Bumpus from the ground.

They carried him to the car compactor, a cousin at each arm and leg, and heaved him inside a machine that is built to pound 2-ton cars made mostly of steel into flat-pack scrap, a piece of kit that sat on the back of a lorry looking like a small garage with one wall missing, a machine that is built to break things that were never meant to be easily broken.

They threw him on the metal slab of the car compactor and he did not struggle or fight or protest.

He lay there like the human sacrifice in some pagan ritual.

As if he was already dead.

I hung my head as the fog descended. And I felt what Flowers had been selling all these years.

Oblivion, he called it. A bottomless darkness.

I sank into it, nearly grateful.

Junior patted my back again, almost tender, and I felt the gardening shears in his hand, slapping lightly against my spine. He took my face in his hands and turned it towards the crushing machine where Bumpus lay.

'Don't look away,' he said. 'You're next.'

Harry Flowers was ranting at his comatose goon.

'Look what you made me do!' he was telling Bumpus. 'All those years we had together! You were a kid from a care home and you worked the doors and I took you in! I gave you everything! Look at you now!' Flowers shuddered, his features frowning with a terrible revelation. 'You are *exactly* what's wrong with the working man in this country, Del.' Shaking his head with disappointment. 'I'm sorry but it's true. Always expecting something for nothing! Always believing the world owes you a living! You fat, ungrateful bastard.'

But Derek Bumpus was not completely lost to the fog.

'Please, Harry …' he begged.

'No, no, no, no, no! Don't you *please Harry* me. It is a pleasure to work with people of faith.' He indicated Mo and his cousins. 'Yes – the Pakis, Del! I know you never liked them, but I have a lot of time for people who believe in something more than the next pint in their face and the next pound in their pocket.'

I looked for Whitestone but I could not see her. And then suddenly there she was, moving beyond a pile of junked metal and torn rubber and shattered glass, lifting her hand, again aiming at the back of Flowers' head, then lowering her aim, going for his broad-shoulder back. Jackson had coached her well.

Mo was moving towards the car compactor.

Bumpus lay there, still and silent, medicated to the void.

There was a button on the side of the machine, the white paint worn away to scratched silver metal.

Harry Flowers stopped him.

'You do it,' he told his son.

'What?' Junior said.

He sniggered with embarrassment. He tapped the gardening shears nervously against his thigh.

His father nodded.

'Press the button. Time to bust your cherry.'

The yard was silent. Junior looked around, his chin trembling.

And then Junior began to cry.

Mo and his cousins looked away.

'Gutless,' Harry Flowers said softly, not remotely surprised, as if that was the worst thing of all.

His son began to sob harder.

I wanted to throw myself at them. I wanted to run away. I wanted to call my gang and have them tear these people to pieces. But the pills had taken hold and I could feel myself slipping into the blackness.

My head felt so heavy.

When I lifted it, there seemed to be a mist in front of my eyes.

In the shadows I saw Pat Whitestone with the Glock in her hand, and I saw her finger curl tighter around the trigger and I closed my eyes waiting for the crack of a gun that seems to split the air.

And then there were the sirens. At first it seemed like a noise heard in a dream, or underwater. But the sound was real and it was getting closer.

Mo and his cousins stared at each other. And then they ran for the gates.

Junior froze, just as I had seen him freeze when Frank Lyle came around a corner with a hammer in his hand, paused somewhere between a paralysed rabbit and roadkill.

His father was in his face.

'Gutless,' he repeated, the saliva flying.

Junior wiped his snotty nose.

'Gutless?' he said. 'Who do you think knocked that teacher down? Who do you think knocked nice Lawrence off his fucking bicycle? Me! *I got you that girl!* I ran over that fiancé and then I reversed over his head! And you tell me to bust my cherry! You tell me I'm gutless!'

Harry Flowers stared at his son, too stunned to speak.

And then he snorted with contempt.

'I don't need you to get me a woman, you little cry baby,' he said.

Junior tried to turn away but his father grabbed a handful of his jacket, turning him around with one hand as he almost casually cuffed his face with the other.

'Be a man,' the father told his son. 'That's all I want. That's all I ask. Is that really too much for you?'

And the son stopped crying.

'Be a man for once in your pathetic little life,' Flowers told Junior, laughing at him, even as he lifted his hand to strike him again.

But Junior lashed back at his father, still with the gardening shears in his hand, and when the two men took half-a-step away from each other, the gardening shears were sticking out of Harry Flowers' neck, the blood pumping steadily from a severed artery.

You could smell it. Harry Flowers fell at the feet of his son.

I saw Whitestone step back into the shadows.

Or perhaps I just dreamed it in my Xanax fog.

Then there were blue lights everywhere and also a florist's van – *'Beautiful' Blooms of Barking*, it said on the side – and it opened up, as if by magic, to reveal soldiers – no, not soldiers, but Specialist Firearm Officers in grey body armour with short, lightweight assault rifles – Sig Sauer MCX, the Black Mambas – and their faces were covered to protect their identity and to provoke terror in the enemy.

'Armed police! Drop the weapon!'

Junior Flowers wiped the teary snot from his nose and yanked the gardening shears from his father's throat, his mouth twisting with the effort.

'Show me your hands! On the ground now!'

A couple of Mo's cousins were being dragged into the light by uniformed police officers and Junior considered them for a second before he charged at the shots, showing them his teeth and holding the gardening shears like a javelin.

One of them shot him twice. Or two of them shot him once. There was the yellow muzzle flash close to my head, the noise that assaults your eardrums and instinctively makes you duck, and Junior was thrown backwards as if by some angry god.

These shots are trained to hit the centre of mass, the largest part of the body, the middle of the chest.

And Junior Flowers was dead before he hit the ground.

I looked up and I saw Jackson Rose. He gave me that gap-toothed grin that I have been looking at all my life and helped me to my feet.

My legs did not work. I sank to the ground.

'We're still mopping them up,' he said. 'Can I leave you for a minute? I'll come back for you. You know I will, right?'

I nodded.

Jackson left me alone. They all left me alone. I sat on the ground of Auto Waste Solutions. Blue lights pierced the chemical-induced fog. There was running and fighting and orders and screams.

And then there was the voice.

'Please ...'

I got up and staggered on liquid legs to the car compactor.

Unnoticed in his drugged state, Bumpus lay on the car compactor as if he was on a slab in the morgue, or on an operating table, waiting to have some terminal sickness cut from him.

The blue lights swirled on his round, brutal face.

I leaned with my back against the car compactor, fighting the sickness, struggling in the mist, resisting the urge to sleep forever.

I spat out a Xanax that had been tucked behind my tongue. And then another. The taste of the pills was bitter as vinegar.

Then I pulled myself to my feet, leaning on the scarred machine for support.

'Help me,' he said.

'Her name is Scout Wolfe,' I said.

'What?' he said.

'She is eight years old,' I said.

I saw the light change in his eyes.

'Don't,' he said.

And with my legs finally giving up on me, I reached for the button.

40

Dogs live in the moment.

There were two packed suitcases by the front door, but Stan stretched his limbs and lifted his butt and did a spot of early morning grooming – languid licking, energetic scratching – as if we were going on just another walk around the neighbourhood.

It was a cloudless Sunday morning with everyone gone, the 500-year-old meat market all closed up and silent until the small hours of Monday morning. The office workers were out in the suburbs and the club kids were all tired out and tucked up in bed. Smithfield was shuttered for the weekend – the pubs, the shops, the cafés – and only the great cavernous restaurant Smiths of Smithfield was open for business and doing a roaring breakfast and brunch trade to hipster couples, many of them with pushchairs, who still made their lives in the city.

But it was all so quiet and still that as Scout, Stan and I walked under the meat market's ancient arch, past the line of old red telephone booths and the plaque on the spot where they had executed William Wallace, that it felt as if the city belonged to us. The strip of shops on the far side of the market were closed but music was pouring from the flat above one of them – Sinatra talking to a bartender about the woman who just went away, Frank confessing that he would be happy to tell the guy all about it, but a man has to be true to his own personal code. That's so true, Frank. There was a sign below the window that had been worn away by more than half a lifetime of weather and work.

MURPHY & SON
Domestic and Commercial Plumbing and Heating
'Trustworthy' and 'Reliable'

We went around the back of the shops and up a flight of stairs. Mrs Murphy opened the door, framed by growing grandchildren. They were all much bigger than I remembered and I expressed the dumbfounded adult sense of wonder that time had not stood still. Their pale freckled faces crowded around Mrs Murphy. Shavon, a year younger than Scout, and her kid brother Damon, and Baby Mikey, around four now, a toy toolkit including a plastic hammer and screwdriver fastened around his pot belly. Their bandy-legged mongrel pushed his way through the crowd and began the butt-sniffing circle dance with Stan.

'Biscuit! No! Stop! Leave him, Biscuit!'

Stan went off into the house with Biscuit without glancing back and I saw Scout wince with pain at our dog's total lack of regret about leaving us. She handed Mrs Murphy a bag containing Stan's supplements to aid his joints, digestion and itchy skin. He had quite an elaborate health regime. As he progressed further into the flat, Stan was greeted by the rest of the family. Mrs Murphy's husband Big Mikey – a suave, wafer-thin man with neat silver hair – and their son Little Mikey – a black-haired heavyweight – and Little Mikey's wife, Siobhan.

Stan was in good hands.

'It's only seven days,' Mrs Murphy said, touching Scout's hair. 'He'll be fine. And so will you, young lady. Here.'

She had made us sandwiches.

Scout was bewildered.

'Don't they have any food on the plane?'

'Ah,' Mrs Murphy said, 'but British Airways don't know how you like your sandwiches, do they?'

She had us there.

'I'll just go and say goodbye to him,' Scout said, handing me the sandwiches as she went into the flat.

Mrs Murphy looked me in the eye.

'I know you want – I don't know what you would call it – a joined-up life,' she said. 'A unified life. You want it for Scout and you want it for yourself and you feel that if you got that life then everything would work out. *But you have it already.* It doesn't matter if you don't look like every other family in the school – or the world. It doesn't matter if you love each other. That sounds corny.'

'No,' I said. 'It doesn't sound corny to me.'

'But you *are* complete,' she said. 'You and Scout. You already have that unified life. That joined-up life. That family. You just haven't quite realised it yet.' She felt like she had said too much. But sometimes people feel that way when what they have really said is everything. 'But I'm an old lady,' she said. 'What do I know?'

Scout was back.

'Quite a lot, probably,' Scout said, joining the conversation.

Mrs Murphy shooed us away.

'Go on, the pair of you,' she said. 'Off with you. See you in seven days.'

We carted our suitcases down to Charterhouse Street and looked for a cab. We only had to wait a few minutes before one appeared, and Scout bounced up and down on her junior Asics, excited by the sight of the greatest view in London, one of the greatest views in the world, up there with the Taj Mahal and the Hanging Gardens of Babylon – the sight of a black London cab with its yellow *For Hire* light on, shining like the sun on a late summer day.

'Yes!' Scout said, punching the air as she had when she came third in the heats of the 50-metre dash.

Because children live in the moment too.

When I awoke in the recovery room, my head as light as freshly spun candyfloss after having my stomach pumped, a couple of DIs from New Scotland Yard who I had never seen before were waiting to talk to me.

It was the hot debriefing, also known as the golden hour interview, aimed at obtaining as much detailed information as possible from those involved in an incident, especially the chronological breakdown of events.

'We know what happened,' one of them said, and I realised that they seemed very young to me.

'The cousins are keen to cooperate,' the other one said.

'They told us about the spat between father and son.'

'Families, eh?' said the other one, and they both had a smile.

'Bumpus?' I said.

'We found him lying on one of those – what's it? – car compactors. Everybody missed him. The uniforms. The shots. He was just lying there. You were having a little nap underneath.'

'Looks like they were planning to recycle him.'

'But they didn't get around to it. One of the paramedics finally spotted him.'

'So Bumpus is in custody?' I said.

They looked at each other.

'The morgue,' one of them said. 'Someone shot him. Point blank in the heart.'

'And what about the gun?' I said. 'Did you find the weapon? Do you have any prints?'

One of them yawned. The other looked at his watch. They were done with me. And they had had a long day.

'What gun?' they said.

Then they let me sleep.

'Going somewhere good?' the taxi driver asked us as we headed west to the airport.

'Sicily,' Scout said. 'The jewel in the Mediterranean.'

Our driver nodded, suitably impressed.

Scout and I smiled at each other and then we settled back, alone with our thoughts.

The black cab sped west to the airport and the tower blocks along the Westway loomed high above us as the Sunday streets of Notting Hill bustled with life below, and already I could see the planes heading to the airport, thin flashes of molten silver in the renewed blue of a perfect sky.

Scout was reading her book. *Dog Songs* by Mary Oliver.

She was right – there are all kinds of poems in the world. But there was no getting around the fact that some of the best ones are about dogs. And we missed our boy already.

Then I heard the bells of an ice cream van in those endless streets of the sprawling, eternal city and I saw that Scout had closed her eyes and was leaning back in the seat of that black cab, as if she was listening to the bells of a Sunday morning church service, or the bells of St Paul's Cathedral itself, rather than some Mr Whippy van getting the last of the summer trade.

Scout was making a wish.

And I turned my face away to watch the planes, because finally I had learned enough to not ask my daughter what she was wishing for.

Because then it could never come true, could it?

HIGHER ENGLISH
CLOSE READING
PREPARATION

Colin Eckford

SCOTTISH
EXAMINATION
MATERIALS

HODDER
GIBSON

The Publishers would like to thank the following for permission to reproduce copyright material:
Photo credits
Page 3 © Barbara Walton/epa/Corbis; page 9 ©Ellen Senisi/The Image Works/Topfoto; page 15 © Image Source/Rex Features; page 21 © D.C. Thomson & Co., Ltd.; page 26 © Mascarucci/Corbis; page 32 © Tim Hall/Getty Images; page 38 © Photos 12/Alamy; page 44 © Paul Healey Photography, photographersdirect.com; page 49 ©Dion Ogust/The Image Works/Topfoto; page 55 © Baker/L.A.Daily News/Corbis Sygma; page 61 © Jim Erickson/Corbis; page 67 © Fotex Medien Agentur GMBH/Rex Features; page 73 © Bettmann/Corbis; page 79 © Dalle/Rex Features; page 85 © Scotsman Publications Ltd; page 89 © Roger Bamber/Alamy; page 96 © Hulton-Deutsch Collection/Corbis; page 102 © Carl De Souza/AFP/Getty Images; page 108 © Mary Evans Picture Library; page 113 © Alex Segre/Alamy.
Acknowledgements
'Harry Potter and the Money-Making Machine' © Melanie Reid, published 9th February 2007 and reproduced with the permission of The Herald, Glasgow © 2007 Herald & Times Group; 'Change Our Schools, Not Our Children' by Johann Hari published by the Independent (15th March 2007) and reproduced with permission; 'Tipping the Scales' by Polly Toynbee. Copyright Guardian News & Media Ltd 2004; 'Desperate Dan' © Ben Macintyre. NI Syndication Limited 2004.; 'A Nation of TV Addicts' by Libby Purves published by the Times (9th September 2003) and reproduced with permission; 'A Jolly Way to Kill Time' reproduced by permission of Katie Grant; 'The Croc Hunter' by James Kirkup reproduced by permission of the Scotsman publications Ltd.; 'Friends Reunited' © Melanie Reid, published 14th January 2003 and reproduced with the permission of The Herald, Glasgow © 2007 Herald & Times Group; 'Fools, Damn Fools and Experts' © India Knight. NI Syndication Limited 2007.; 'The Celebrity Circus' © Joyce McMillan; 'What Homeschooling Taught Me' © Ben Macintyre. NI Syndication Limited 2005.; 'TV Soaps' © Richard Kilborn; 'A Hundred years of the Aeroplane' by George Monbiot (The Guardian, 16 December 2003) reproduced by permission of the author; 'Mothers and Fathers' © Natasha Walter, published by The Independent and reprinted by permission; 'Grumpy Old White Men' © Joyce McMillan; 'A Parable for Our Times' © Magnus Linklater. NI Syndication Limited 2007.; 'The Trial of Lady Chatterly' © Brian Masters, reprinted by permission of Lucas Alexander Whitley Ltd.; 'The Blue Rigi' © Ben Macintyre. NI Syndication Limited 2007.; 'The Explosive Device' © Christopher Small; 'The Casino Culture' by Simon Heffer reproduced by permission of the Telegraph Media Group.

Every effort has been made to trace all copyright holders, but if any have been inadvertently overlooked the Publishers will be pleased to make the necessary arrangements at the first opportunity.

Although every effort has been made to ensure that website addresses are correct at time of going to press, Hodder Gibson cannot be held responsible for the content of any website mentioned in this book. It is sometimes possible to find a relocated web page by typing in the address of the home page for a website in the URL window of your browser.

Hachette's policy is to use papers that are natural, renewable and recyclable products and made from wood grown in sustainable forests. The logging and manufacturing processes are expected to conform to the environmental regulations of the country of origin.

Orders: please contact Bookpoint Ltd, 130 Milton Park, Abingdon, Oxon OX14 4SB. Telephone: (44) 01235 827720. Fax: (44) 01235 400454. Lines are open 9.00–5.00, Monday to Saturday, with a 24-hour message answering service. Visit our website at www.hoddereducation.co.uk. Hodder Gibson can be contacted direct on: Tel: 0141 848 1609; Fax: 0141 889 6315; email: hoddergibson@hodder.co.uk

© Colin Eckford 2008
First published in 2008 by
Hodder Gibson, an imprint of Hodder Education,
An Hachette Livre UK Company,
2a Christie Street
Paisley PA1 1NB

ISBN-13: 978 0 340 94627 5

Impression number   5 4 3
Year   2012 2011

Cover photo (and page 1) © Brand X Pictures/Photolibrary
Typeset in 12pt ITC Garamond by Fakenham Photosetting Limited, Fakenham, Norfolk
Printed in India
A catalogue record for this title is available from the British Library

Contents